# FIRE AND ICE

A Hawk Tate Novel

DUSTIN STEVENS

*Fire and Ice*
Copyright © 2016, Dustin Stevens
Cover Art and Design: Paramita Bhattacharjee, www.creativeparamita.com

Warning: All rights reserved. The unauthorized reproduction or distribution of this copyrighted work, in whole or part, in any form by any electronic, mechanical, or other means, is illegal and forbidden, without the written permission of the author.

This is a work of fiction. Characters, settings, names, and occurrences are a product of the author's imagination and bear no resemblance to any actual person, living or dead, places or settings, and/or occurrences. Any incidences of resemblance are purely coincidental.

*For Austin.*
*He hoʻomaka houʻana.*

*Nature has no principles. She makes
no distinction between good and evil.*
Anatole France

# Part One

## Chapter One

Sam Cuddyer stood with the front of his thighs pressed flush against the kitchen counter. Leaning forward at the waist, he rested his right palm alongside the polished steel wash basin, his left hand holding a satellite phone tight with his cheek.

Under normal circumstances his regular cell phone would be just fine, the farmhouse sitting a mere four miles outside of town. The unexpected winter storm that had arrived early that morning had wiped out the traditional signal for the area though, dumping a wet and heavy blanket on everything, shrouding the world in a foot of white that showed no signs of slowing.

The lone exception to the ghostly pallor was a misshapen circle 50 feet in diameter behind the house, the snow stripped away, replaced by a blackened smudge. As Cuddyer stood with the phone mashed against his cheek, feeling his heart rate increase with each ring in his ear, he could see the telltale signs of what had happened laid out before him.

The remains of the free standing garage were precious few, the entire back end of it blown completely away, charred debris strewn out wide. Some of the smaller pieces still rested atop the snowpack, most having already made their way to the ground beneath, their heat pushing right through the fresh powder.

A few small flames still licked at the bottom of the structure, their orange tendrils rising like fingers against the darkened backdrop of the night sky. Beyond them the wreckage could just barely be made out. What remained resembled the charred corpse of a miniature roller coaster, copper tubing and piping blackened with soot.

"Who is this?"

There was no greeting of any sort on the other end of the line, no hint of recognition, nothing but the gruff response of someone who did not appreciate being called at such a peculiar hour.

"Cuddyer," Sam muttered, not wanting to say the word, but knowing there was no way around it. As he did, he shifted his focus from the carnage in the backyard to his own reflection in the glass before him.

His skin still wore the effects of the last hour, streaks of blood and wood char smeared across the leathered surface like some form of war paint. Both seemed to start high on his temples and traverse over his cheekbones, ending in the grizzled beard that covered the bottom half of his face.

At a glance, there was no mistaking the kind of man Sam Cuddyer was or the life he had lived, a look he had worked hard to cultivate, even harder to maintain. In his experience people tended to steer clear of what they didn't understand, made a point of staying even further away from that which they feared.

Now, more than ever, Sam Cuddyer looked like a man to be feared.

The cruel irony of it was at the moment, fear was the predominant feeling roiling through him.

"Hold on."

There was a loud sound as the phone was dropped, presumably onto a steel surface judging by the echo. The lines around Cuddyer's eyes tightened just a bit at the harsh clang of it in his ear, making no effort to pull the phone away as he waited, knowing the next voice would be no more welcoming than the first.

"What?" a second man asked, Cuddyer recognizing the voice as the one he was looking for.

"We've got a problem," Cuddyer said, bypassing any preamble, knowing better than to even attempt to soften the blow.

More than once he had heard the stories of people who attempted such an approach.

"How bad?" the man asked, his tone not changing one bit.

"Elias," Cuddyer said, keeping his answers short, following the instructions that had been laid out for him months before.

A long moment passed, Cuddyer able to hear the man on the other end breathing loudly, the first sign of anger seeping in.

"Pinched?"

"No," Cuddyer said, shaking his head just slightly. "Worse."

"Wor..." the man snapped, cutting himself off in the middle of the word and letting out a second angry sigh.

Another moment slid by, Cuddyer offering nothing as the man digested the information.

"Dumbass blew himself up, didn't he?"

Shifting his attention to the yard out back, Cuddyer looked past the remains of the garage still burning, completely ignored the scattered bits of wood and machinery scattered about. Instead, he honed in on the path cut through the snow connecting the garage and the rear door of the house, seeing the trenches that he and Jasper had cleaved while dragging Elias inside, the blood left in their wake already beginning to darken as it froze in place.

"Pretty much," Cuddyer said.

"What the hell kind of answer is that?" the man asked. "Either he did, or he didn't."

Cuddyer was aware of what the man was getting at the first time, though he still couldn't quite bring himself to say the words. He knew what reaction they would bring, that it would do little to change the predicament they now found themselves in.

"Most of the product is gone. He's alive, but just barely."

"How much is most?" the man asked. If he had any concern at all for the state of Elias, he did nothing to show it.

In the mad dash of the preceding hour Cuddyer hadn't stopped to take inventory yet, though a few cursory glances told him most of what they'd been working on for the previous week was gone, vaporized into the Montana night sky.

"Best guess, 80 percent," Cuddyer said, his eyes sliding shut as he delivered the news. Pushing himself upright from the counter, he raised his free hand to his brow and began to knead it, the leathered skin rough beneath his fingertips.

"*Eighty percent*," the man replied, spitting the words out, venom now obvious in his tone. "Are you shitting me?"

With every fiber of his being, Cuddyer wished he was. "Nope."

He could hear the phone being lowered as the man continued to drone on in the background, pushing out a rant of obscenities that covered every swear word in at least two different languages. More than once Cuddyer had been present for such an outburst, the explosion bordering on humorous to him as he watched the man bellow in a combination of English and Spanish.

The only difference was, now that hostility was aimed in his direction.

After the better part of two minutes he could hear the phone being raised back into position, the heavy breathing returning to his ear.

"Two days. You can have two extra days. That's it."

There was no way of knowing exactly what Cuddyer had expected upon making the call. His only thought was that he had to report it up the line, needed to make sure the higher-ups were apprised, aware that nothing shady was going on. Once the storm passed and Elias healed, they would start again, though how long that would take was anybody's guess.

Never, not once, had he expected this.

"I...um, what?" Cuddyer managed, his tongue feeling two sizes too large for his mouth, resembling sandpaper as it scraped against the roof. "Two days? For what?"

"*For what?*" the man asked, forced emphasis on both words, the sound letting Cuddyer know that he thought the question was a stupid one. "Before you better have the product ready to go, that's what."

The bottom fell out of Cuddyer's stomach, his mind seizing on the words as his body went rigid. "But, sir, there's no way."

"Then I suggest you find one. My boys will be there at noon on Saturday to collect."

No words came to Cuddyer as he leaned forward, letting the cracked Formica countertop hold him upright. His head spun as he tried to make sense of what he was hearing, the image of the destroyed lab out back at the front of his mind and refusing to move.

"And Cuddy?" the man said, the words pulling Cuddyer out of his fog. "Don't you even think about trying to skip out on us. You know what happened to the last guys that pulled that shit."

Cuddyer said nothing as the line went dead in his ear. He kept the phone pressed to his ear a moment longer before dropping it to his side. There he let it slip from his grasp, falling to the floor, the sound of plastic breaking as it hit the wooden planks.

"What did he say?"

The question seemed to float in from far afield, finding Cuddyer's ears but barely penetrating his consciousness. Not until it was asked a second, and then a third time, did it make enough headway to reach Cuddyer, his head turning to see Jasper standing in the open doorway connecting the kitchen to the living room.

"What did he say, Sammy?" Jasper asked, seizing on the movement as a sign of recognition. "Are they sending somebody to help Elias?"

## Chapter Two

"Do me a favor, will you?" Yvonne Endicott asked as she pulled the needle through the loop of the suture on the side of Mrs. Madeline Everson's face. In a move practiced 100, if not 1,000 times before, she tugged the needle gently, driving the knot down flush with the paper-thin skin of the woman. Once it was in place, she took up a pair of scissors from the stainless steel stand beside her and snipped the ends clean.

"What's that?" Everson asked, her voice coming out as little more than a wheeze, a combination of her age and the fact that she had barely breathed since Yvonne went to work on her.

"Please tell your husband that next time, there's no need for you to get cleaned up before coming into the emergency room," Yvonne said, dropping the remains of the suture onto the tray and taking up a small square packet. Folding one corner down, she tore it away and squeezed a small bit of the antibacterial ointment onto a cotton swab.

"Oh, now," Everson said, pursing her lips in the way that older folks tended to whenever they thought someone younger was just being foolish. To accentuate the point she waved a hand before her, just missing the swab in Yvonne's hand.

"You have to understand, he didn't mean anything by it, just that there is a certain dress code that applies when going out in public."

Reflexively, Yvonne smiled as she cast a look down the length of the open room, nothing but a row of empty beds staring back at her.

Not exactly what she would describe as *public*.

"Okay," Yvonne said, having had enough similar conversations in the preceding two months to know not to bother pressing it further, "but from now on, it's okay to leave a little blood on there. Washcloths can carry all sorts of bacteria, and scrubbing a wound with one is just asking for infection."

As she offered the gentle admonishment, Yvonne daubed the ointment into place before covering the area with an adhesive bandage, the center pad sufficient to protect the six stitches.

"Yes, Doctor," Everson replied, letting it be known that she was playing along but had little intention of changing her ways.

That too was something Yvonne had encountered too many times to count since arriving.

"Okay," Yvonne said, using her heels to roll the stool she sat on back a few inches and slapping at her thighs for effect. The sound carried through the empty room as she peeled off her latex gloves and tossed them onto the tray along with the other supplies from the procedure.

"That's it?" Everson asked, raising a gnarled hand to her brow and softly touching the bandage pressed flush with her hairline. "We're all done?"

"All done," Yvonne said, raising her voice a tiny bit, trying her best to put on a joyful demeanor for her patient.

"How's it look?" Everson asked.

"You'll barely even know it's there," Yvonne said, resting a hand on the woman's back as she stood and steered her toward the waiting area outside. "Come see us again in a week, and we'll take those out, you'll be good as new."

A small smile crossed the woman's features as she looked up at Yvonne. "Thank you, Doctor, I do appreciate it."

Yvonne walked alongside her as far as the door before stopping, the same smile still affixed to her face. "That's what we're here for. Just be careful out there, that ice is no joke."

Bowing slightly at the waist, Everson nodded in understanding, raising one hand in farewell as she disappeared into the hallway, the nurse sitting at the registration desk rising to intercept her.

Pausing to make sure there was nothing further, Yvonne turned back to the empty room. One hand she thrust deep into the pocket of her white coat, the other she brought to her face, using her thumb and forefinger to rub her eyes.

"I told you I could have done that," a familiar voice said from the opposite end of the room. "Would have given me something to do, after all."

"Which is exactly the reason I did it," Yvonne said, dropping her hand away and opening her eyes. After the pressure from her fingers, colors were distorted, small circles of red and green dancing across her vision.

Halfway down the room, emergency department nurse Meredith Shek already had the supplies from the short procedure bagged up. She held them in one hand as she steered the table back into position with the other, her movements methodical, underscoring the same boredom that Yvonne felt.

Standing right at 6' tall, the overhead lights made her skin appear even more pale than usual, her straw-blonde hair hanging lank behind her head.

"How long you been on now?" Shek asked.

"Since 6:00," Yvonne said, using the front pockets to pull her lab coat across her body, the soles of her running shoes squeaking slightly as she trudged over the tile floor.

"Five hours is all?" Shek asked. "How bad were the roads getting in here?"

"No," Yvonne said, shaking her head slightly, "6:00 this morning. And it was fine then. Heck, I walked here."

"Eesh," Shek said, drawing the word out as she turned to look at Yvonne.

"Yeah," Yvonne said, following Shek as she walked to the opposite end of the room and deposited the bag into a waste receptacle. "Seemed like a good idea at the time."

"Ha," Shek said, the top of her head rolling back just slightly with the effort. "Lot of things seem like a good idea at the time here in Montana. It's the sudden changes you have to be prepared for."

Turning back to the room, Yvonne looked over the row of empty beds. "Thanks, I'll try to remember that."

## Chapter Three

The large Cummins diesel engine spat out a plume of black smoke as it finally turned over, the result of more than five minutes of cranking on the ignition. Hunched low behind the steering wheel, Cuddyer could see it in the side view mirror as it rose from the tailpipe, completely engulfing Jasper as he circled around the back, a snow scraper in hand.

Under different circumstances the image might have been amusing, maybe even enough to cause a laugh. As things stood, the only emotion Cuddyer felt was relief, the engine finally churning to life alleviating one concern, bringing with it a host of others.

"You alright, Elias?" Cuddyer asked, his voice barely audible over the sound of the engine. He turned to glance over his shoulder into the rear bench seat of the cab, the body of his partner stretched from one side of the truck to the other.

Cocooned under a mountain of pillows and blankets, the only thing that was visible was his face. Even in the dim interior of the truck it was obvious how pale he was, the effect even more pronounced against his dark beard.

Cuddyer hadn't expected an answer to his question, was not surprised when none came his way. Instead, he sat and watched as

Elias pulled in short gasps of breath, stale air that was just beginning to warm blowing in around them.

What had transpired in the previous hour was nothing short of Hell itself, the kind of thing he and Elias and Jasper often joked about. Idiot yokels who didn't know what they were doing, blowing themselves up, sending their profits and their empire sky high, nothing left behind but a vapor trail.

How this had happened Cuddyer had no clue, and at the moment didn't much care. All that mattered was their operation was obliterated, and the best cook in the state was lying behind him, fighting for every breath.

Less than 50 miles away was a veritable army demanding that business continue, giving them only an extra 48 hours to ensure that happened.

Cuddyer's left leg bobbed beneath the steering wheel as he jammed a thumb into his mouth, the tastes of grease and wood smoke crossing his tongue. Ignoring them both he went to work on the nail, gnawing at it until the salty metallic flavor of blood found his taste buds.

Things were moving too fast. He had to slow down, to figure out his next move, but right now he just didn't have the time for that.

Beside him the passenger door wrenched open, a puff of arctic air filling the cab, a swirl of ice crystals arriving with it. Just as fast, Jasper swung himself up into the seat and closed the door, brushing clumps of snow from the arms of his canvas coat and the front of his jeans.

"You get everything?" Cuddyer asked, staring straight ahead.

"Just like you said," Jasper replied. "It's all loaded in the back."

A grunt was Cuddyer's only reply as he continued to work on the thumbnail in his mouth.

They couldn't stay at the house, at least not at the moment. Right now they had a head start because of the weather, but it was only a matter of time before somebody saw, or smelled, what had happened. Once they did, they would report it, bringing out the police and God knew who else.

First thing in the morning Cuddyer would call again to let them know they had relocated, that nobody was making a run for it, but for the time being he was content to let it ride. He had already made one unwanted phone call that evening, better to let things simmer down before doing it a second time.

Besides, at the moment, they had more pressing matters to tend to.

"We going to the barn?" Jasper asked, lowering his voice in an attempt to match the demeanor inside the truck.

Cuddyer made no effort to hide his disdain as he stared straight ahead, letting the defroster clear away the thin layer of ice that had formed beneath the heavy snowfall, before pulling his hand from his mouth and dropping the gearshift into drive. Outside, snow continued to fall in thick, heavy flakes, the total accumulation now more than a foot, white the only color visible beneath the glare of the headlights.

Even with chains on the tires, the next couple of hours would be treacherous, the only benefit of the storm being that it would wipe away any sign of them within minutes of their passing.

Given where their first stop was going to be, it was a benefit Cuddyer intended to take full advantage of.

## Chapter Four

This was not how things were supposed to have played out. Six months ago Yvonne was a rising star in the Atlanta medical scene. She was young for sure, too green to be considered a threat to the established players, but she had been earmarked by all the right people as an up-and-comer to watch. Taken as a whole, their blessing had been nothing short of gospel, the kind of thing nobody else in town would dare oppose.

The reasons for her assent were numerous, the most obvious on display each time Yvonne looked into the mirror. At 5'10", she was taller than most of the people she worked with, certainly more so than just about every female besides Meredith. The stature provided her with a presence that couldn't quite be described as towering, or even imposing, but it was difficult to miss her.

The effect was accentuated by the mop of hair that extended from her head in a lazy halo, the black curls a direct inheritance from her mother. Long ago she had stopped trying to tame the mess, allowing them to go where they may, content to let them bounce of their own free will.

In the rare instances she wasn't wearing scrubs and her white coat, the figure of a track star just a decade removed could be seen. A minimum three times a week since graduating from Georgia, she had made it a point to put in at least five miles, the exertion doing far more to rejuvenate her than any amount of sleep ever could.

Everything, though, from the rising star status to the steady running, had ended abruptly with a phone call three months prior. Her father, a man she knew only through stories her mother told her for the first part of her life, had taken sick.

Had the call come 15 years before, Yvonne would not have thought twice. She would have expressed condolences, hung up the phone, and not thought about the matter again.

Those days were gone though. Beginning with the passing of her mother, he had made a concerted effort to be an active part of her life, even moving to Atlanta for the last two years of high school so she could finish without having to transfer. Not until she was safely away at college, no longer in need of a full-time parent, did he retreat back to Montana.

If her doing the same now, allowing him to spend whatever time he had left in comfort, could somehow square the enormous debt she felt toward him, it was something she was glad to do.

It just didn't change the fact that some days were better than others.

"Just got a call from Baxter," Shek said, entering the break room just far enough to rest a shoulder against the open door frame. "Completely snowed in."

From her spot on the end of the single couch in the room, Yvonne turned her head to the sound of Shek's voice, the words only confirming what she had long since resigned herself to.

"I'm sorry," Shek said. "I know this is turning into one heck of a marathon session for you."

Yvonne blinked away the fuzz of her previous thoughts, pulling herself into the room to engage in the conversation. "It's okay, I just wish there was more to do."

"Late night TV not getting it done for you?" Shek asked, gesturing with her chin toward the box television sitting silent on a folding table along the far wall.

"Not much of a watcher," Yvonne said, forcing a thin smile, the best she could manage.

Despite Shek's referring to the long day as a marathon, it was only that insofar as the suffocating boredom that pressed in on Yvonne. Working in County General on the west side of Atlanta, her usual shift was 20 hours, her call time more than twice that.

Twenty-five hour stints were not uncommon, 30 popping up with surprising regularity. Getting around the newly imposed shift limitations was never a big issue, appeased by punching out and returning, a combination of the hospital needing her on-site and her not wanting to go home.

To look at a clock, or a timesheet, the work would appear hellish, but in truth Yvonne had found it surprisingly palatable. There was always something to do, some new patient to meet, a sea of people passing through, keeping things light and interesting. The hours sped by, so much so that she had to download an app to her phone just to remind her to take time to eat and hydrate.

Finding the job here at Valley County had been a stroke of luck, something that went from idea to plan to execution in less than two weeks. It was an opportunity that Yvonne was thankful for, the chance to pay back an old favor, but there wasn't a day that passed that she didn't wish for something a little more invigorating to pass through the front doors.

"You should sleep," Shek offered. "The call room is empty, I'll come get you if anything comes in."

Yvonne paused a moment, even tilting her head to the side a couple of inches as if considering the idea, before pressing her palms into the seat cushions on either side of her and rising to full height.

"Actually, I think I might step outside for a few minutes. We don't get much snow in Georgia. I'm new enough here to still find it pretty."

## Chapter Five

The noisy engine strained to push the elevated chassis of the truck through the thick snowpack, the tire chains biting into the wet mess, inching them forward no more than 10 miles an hour. Mounds lining the side of the road indicated that at one point plows had been through before giving up, fresh snowfall covering everything again.

Giving up any attempt at deciphering the lanes on the road, Cuddyer aimed the nose of the truck down what he guessed to be the center line, using the previous efforts of the plows to guide him. The whole time he sat leaning forward behind the wheel, gripping it tight in both hands.

There was no radio inside the cab of the truck, no sound except that of the tires chewing snow, the chains rattling as they rotated, and the 460 cubic inches of the diesel engine wailing angrily.

Cuddyer left the heat on high, the temperature inside the truck rising steadily. He could feel sweat beginning to form beneath his beard, could sense the trickles that were starting on his scalp and threatening to streak down his forehead.

"Cuddy?" Jasper asked, his voice still low, his fear obvious. He placed the question out there gently, as if asking permission to do so, and when no response came, he pressed onward. "Where are we headed?"

Another grunt was Cuddyer's only response, a short twist of the head driving home the point. Instead, he kept his full attention on the road, watching as the heavy flakes continued to drift down, the headlights catching them as they passed by.

"How's Elias?"

In his periphery he could see Jasper's jaw drop open as he stared motionless beside him.

"Jasper. Elias. Check him," Cuddyer snapped, pushing each phrase out quickly, his voice little more than a grumble.

Jasper brought his knees up onto the seat, flinging drops of melted snow across the dash as he went. Leaning over the seat, he extended a hand a few inches from Elias's mouth before retreating back into his original position.

"He's breathing," Jasper said. "Seems to still be sleeping."

"Hmm," Cuddyer grunted in response, the statement confirming what he already suspected.

It was not the first time he had seen such an explosion, though it had been a long time since his original trip down this path.

His only hope was that this one ended better than the last.

"Cuddy?" Jasper ventured again.

Cuddyer let out a loud breath, the intention to let it be known he wasn't much up for talking at the moment, though he knew Jasper well enough to know that no amount of subtle cues would ever be picked up.

Much like going through Hell, the best approach was to push through as fast as he could and hope to reach the other side unscathed.

"They said we have two days to get them their product," Cuddyer said, glancing over to Jasper before turning back to the road ahead. Not a single tire tread marred the snow, the truck settling into an even gait.

Most of the time, their living outside of town was a good idea, the extra distance helping to avoid suspicion of them or their enterprise.

Tonight was not such a time.

"Two days?" Jasper asked, a small sputter in his voice as he computed what he'd been told. "But that..."

"I know."

"And all our equipment," Jasper continued, going through everything Cuddyer had thought upon hanging up the phone.

"Yup."

"And, we can't do anything without Elias," Jasper finished, hooking a thumb over his shoulder to point at their comrade in the back seat.

This time Cuddyer didn't bother to reply. He nodded once in agreement, the conversation over. Staring straight ahead, his eyes narrowed as he focused on a small glow on the horizon, the light just barely visible over the white sheen of the snow enveloping the world.

They would have one shot at this, and one only. Without thinking about it he lowered his left hand from the steering wheel and tapped at the pocket of his jacket, feeling the hard bulge of the .38 Magnum, before again gripping the wheel with both hands.

The plan was thin, at best. It would involve surprise and no small amount of dumb luck, with the hope that the perverse nature of it would be enough for them to arrive and depart before anybody put up too much of a struggle.

After that, it would be the job of the storm to erase their tracks, hiding them until the time was right to emerge.

## Chapter Six

Yvonne felt the wind push through her hair twice in a span of less than 10 seconds, one each on opposite ends of the temperature spectrum. The first was courtesy of the overhead heaters blowing straight down in the Arctic zone between reception and the outer doors, the space designed to provide a protective barrier from the frigid climate for those inside. It pushed straight down, beginning the moment she passed through the inner door, designed to kick on whenever one side or the other opened.

The second blast of air was courtesy of the Montana elements, bringing with it a swirl of ice crystals and the faint scent of pine. It swept in the length of Yvonne's body, pushing up beneath the bottom hems of her scrubs and gripping her face in an icy clamp.

It had the intended effect.

Whatever grogginess Yvonne had felt evaporated as she took two steps out the door, hearing it slide closed with great effort along the frozen tracts. As the two sides pushed together, the sound of the heater kicked off as well, the world falling silent as Yvonne took one last step forward, rock salt crunching beneath her feet, her toes just inches away from snow piled more than three feet high on the edge of the parking lot.

Drifts gave the impression that at some point during the day, hospital maintenance workers had attempted to keep the front walk clear. It appeared that such an effort had long since fallen by the wayside, though, as the snow persisted, the battle having been given over to the rock salt on the ground to keep things clear.

Besides, it wasn't as if there was a great deal of foot traffic, Mrs. Everson having been the last patient Yvonne saw more than two hours before.

Letting her eyes slide shut, Yvonne raised her face to the sky, feeling the cold air on her skin. She took in a deep breath, letting it lift her chest toward the heavens, cooling her from within.

Right now in Atlanta the daytime highs were already reaching 80 degrees, accompanied by the omnipresent humidity that seemed to smother the southeast for most of the year. Just thinking about it Yvonne could almost feel the sweat on her skin, could sense her hair curling tighter into a frizzled mess that no amount of mousse could ever hope to control.

The mere idea of it brought a smile to her face, her body rising a few inches into a full stretch.

She had signed up for this, she just had to keep reminding herself. She knew when she pulled the trigger on making a move that Glasgow was small, that it was cold, that the hospital barely saw in a year what her previous employer saw in a week.

The only thing she hadn't been prepared for, though, was the silence. She never would have thought it would get to her the way it had, finding herself almost longing for the sounds of traffic, the background din of voices, the familiar noises that let her know humanity was nearby.

Dropping herself flat to her feet, Yvonne released the breath she was holding and opened her eyes. The first few moments of invigoration had already passed, moving quickly into a bone-numbing chill, threatening to pull the feeling from her fingers at any moment.

The odds of her needing her hands anytime soon weren't good, but she still had far too much invested in them to risk frostbite.

Yvonne moved back for the door. She rolled her shoulders up to her ears and curled her hands into fists, keeping them tucked away deep inside her pockets as she took a single step, the sliding door opening, the heater again kicking on above her.

It was then, standing just a few feet away from the warmth and safety of the reception area, that she noticed the glow rising from the east and made a decision that would change her life forever.

# Part Two

## Chapter Seven

I have never been one for deep sleep. Even as a young man, my subconscious tended to stay just below the surface. No matter how exhausted I might have been, it was rare that I would succumb to total darkness, my mind, my awareness, refusing to leave me.

Over time, the skill has served me well, playing a role during both my time in the navy and later the DEA, sleeping in strange locations, being involved in difficult investigations, resting within yards of a hostile enemy.

None were conditions for slipping into a coma-like trance. Not only would doing so make me an easy target, it would lengthen the time needed for my body to pull back from it, to shift from rest into an alerted state.

Because of that, when the pounding sounded against the door of the cheap hotel room I had rented for a few nights, my body reacted the same way it always did. There was no exorcism-style rise from the darkness that had to take place, no sudden jolt that caused me to sit upright beneath the thin covers of the bed, lights popping before my eyes, trying to gain my bearings.

Instead, only two things moved, both in tandem.

First, my eyes opened, staring straight up at the ceiling above me.

The pale color, despite the late hour, told me that the snow had most likely continued, the whiteout just beyond the window allowing an exaggerated light to seep in around the curtains.

The only other movement came from my right arm, extending straight out at the shoulder, my hand wrapped around the grip of a Smith & Wesson, my pulse remaining even as I sat and waited.

The knocks came in a burst of three. There was a short pause, my body remaining completely motionless, before a second trio began.

Not quite threatening, but definitely loud enough to be heard.

"Jeremiah Tate."

The voice was male. Despite the fact that it had been muffled by the closed door, it was obvious that the man was older, or at least older than my 35 years.

His use of my full name also told me that it was likely somebody in law enforcement, having run the plates on my truck and gotten back the legal name on the registration. Nobody else in the world, from my parents to my school teachers growing up to my friends now, ever called me Jeremiah.

To anybody I had known for longer than a minute, I was Hawk. It was even the name I had registered the room under, telling me further that the person wasn't merely a motel employee.

Besides, they would have used the phone for that.

How I knew all of this from just two words harkened back to skills earned in a different life, the kinds of things that don't just leave a man, no matter how hard he tries to forget them.

"Jeremiah, this is Sheriff Rake Ferris. Can we talk?"

This time there were nine words, giving me more information to work with. The first and most obvious was what he said, asking if we could speak. There was no demand that I open up, no trying to impose his position.

There was the possibility that it was all just a ruse, a simple trick to get my guard down, but it seemed unlikely. Not at this hour, not in the middle of a blizzard that had arisen from nowhere and seemed to be settling in for the long haul.

Second was the fact that he had used his full name. If this were somebody merely trying to pose as the sheriff, to get me to open the door blind, they wouldn't have bothered.

During the previous winter I had seen enough election signs around to know that Rake Ferris was the name of the sheriff in Valley County. It seemed even more unlikely somebody would use a real name and not be who they said they were, though not impossible.

No malice seemed apparent in his tone. The words were delivered just loud enough to be heard, enough to call out to me directly and nobody else.

Blinking twice, I sorted all this information as best I could. Doing so only seemed to bring about a host of questions, starting with how he had managed to track me down and ending with why he had bothered. In between there were dozens more.

Pushing the gun under the pillow, a third round of knocking started.

The weapon was registered, everything legal, but I still didn't want to go through the process of explaining why it was out, in a motel room in the middle of the night.

Again, the kind of knowledge one accumulates living the kind of life I have.

"Just a second," I called, folding the blankets down to my waist and sitting up. In quick order I did an inventory of the room around me, looking over what little gear I had, a sizeable percentage of everything I owned sitting in a duffel bag on the floor or hanging in the closet.

The aging carpet beneath me was cool to the touch as I stepped out and grabbed up my jeans from the armchair beside the bed. Without pausing to pull on socks, I shoved my toes down into a pair of hiking shoes and pulled a Henley on over my head, not bothering to remove the ribbed tank top I had been sleeping in.

Stepping over to the corner of the room, I braced my shoulder against the wall and peered through the narrow crack between it and the curtains covering the front window. The opening provided me just enough of an angle to see a few feet of the front walk and nothing more.

Standing right outside my door was a man who looked to be in his mid-50s, though it was difficult to be sure, most of his face obscured by the white cowboy hat on his head. A clear plastic cover was cinched into place around it, snowflakes and drops of water dotting the surface.

He was by no means a large man, looking to be several inches below 6' tall, wearing boots, jeans, and an enormous canvas coat that swallowed most of his upper body.

Most important, both hands hung empty by his sides, held out in plain view despite the cold.

Running a hand back over my scalp, I stepped across the room and unlatched the chain, pulling the door open to be greeted by a gust of Montana wind. It blew right through my clothes, sucking most of the heat from behind me.

"Jeremiah Tate?" the sheriff asked, making no attempt to step forward, his voice still non-threatening. "Can we talk?"

## Chapter Eight

Without his hat on I could get a good look at the sheriff, my original assessment pretty accurate. He still had the majority of his hair, though it carried a few swirls of gray in it, the same for his handlebar moustache.

The man wore a Montana life for all to see, heavy squint lines around his eyes displaying someone used to braving the elements. His skin had moved past what one would call tan and into a state that was permanently closer to leather.

Sheriff Rake Ferris was seated in the armchair that was previously serving as a clothes rack for my jeans, the hat turned crown side down on the table beside him. A small puddle had formed beneath it from the snow and water that had ran down from the protective covering.

He sat with both hands resting flat on his thighs, his left leg bobbing up and down in an urgent pace. The coat still covered the top half of his body, despite the warmth in the room.

"I'm sorry for showing up like this, waking you up in the middle of the night," he began, his voice carrying a touch of gravel, the result of a lifetime spent with cigars, whiskey, or both. He paused, waiting for some form of acknowledgement, and when I gave none, he added, "Believe me, I wouldn't be here unless it was important."

I had expected as much upon seeing him standing outside the door. For most of the preceding 24 hours I had been confined to the motel due to the weather, something that several people could vouch to. There was no way they could actually be interested in me for anything, the previous day being the first I had spent in Glasgow in more than a month.

My last time in the area had ended in a rather raucous manner, but that was well outside the town and had been vetted by the DEA office in Billings.

Ferris looked at me a moment as if waiting for me to say something. When nothing came back he pressed his lips together and nodded.

"Two hours ago a doctor was abducted from Valley Memorial Hospital," Ferris said, causing my eyebrows to rise.

"Abducted," I repeated, flicking my gaze to the window, toward the snow I knew was piled up outside.

Scattered thoughts passed through my head as I stared at him, trying to process what he'd just said and why he'd possibly come to see me about it. I knew, based on his demeanor and the conversation we were having, that he didn't consider me a suspect, though beyond that I didn't know much for certain.

"Meaning?" I prompted.

Ferris drew in a short breath, his leg continuing to move up and down like a sewing machine.

"An hour and a half ago we got a call from the front desk at the hospital. Yvonne Endicott was the doctor on duty today, and due to the storm she was forced to stay. Her replacement couldn't make it in."

I nodded, pulling my hands from my jeans and folding my arms over my chest. The name meant nothing to me, my mind doing a quick inventory before dismissing it as I continued to listen.

"I guess someone stumbled in from the bar down the street with half a beer glass jammed through his hand. The nurses thought Dr. Endicott had gone to lie down, but when they checked the call rooms, she was nowhere to be found."

It seemed that Ferris had practiced the speech a time or two on his way over, the sentences coming out in a rapid-fire cadence, matching his leg as it continued to move.

"There are a limited number of cameras on the grounds, so they had the security guard run a check back over the last half hour."

He paused there for a moment, so I asked, "And they saw her be abducted?"

"Mhm," Ferris said, "in a manner of speaking, anyway. The cameras are angled down to cover the entrances, but nothing out in the parking lot.

"All they saw was Endicott standing outside, just getting some air, when something caught her attention. She turned around and waited there as a pair of headlights swept over her."

Again, he took a moment, his eyes twitching slightly, as if he were watching the scene in his head without wanting to.

"As the lights got closer, she stepped off the sidewalk into the snow. Made it a step or two, right up to the edge of the camera's vision, before realizing she was in trouble."

There was a twinge of sorrow added to the last sentence that I didn't bother to comment on as I pressed ahead. "Did the camera see who grabbed her?"

"Two men, both dressed in dark colors, hoods pulled over their heads. Like I said, they were right on the edge of view, basically showing us just enough to see that she was taken against her will."

"Why didn't the guard see it when it happened?" I asked, feeling myself getting pulled into the story, even if I had no idea why I was being told.

"Said he was making rounds at the time," Ferris replied, his fingers curling up into his palms, forming a matching pair of fists. "I suspect he was actually asleep, but didn't press it."

At that the conversation fell away, Ferris seemingly recalling his prior interview, my own thoughts scattered. There were follow-up questions I could ask. They would have to wait.

For the time being I was more concerned with the man sitting in my room, pulling me from my slumber.

"How'd you find me?" I asked, ripping him from his thoughts and back to the present.

"This is a small town," he replied. "And these days we make a point of watching whoever passes through."

"Okay," I said, not pressing his explanation any further, "allow me to rephrase. *Why* did you find me?"

Ferris opened his mouth to respond before thinking better of it. He pressed his lips together tight, mulling over his response, before saying, "It's not exactly a secret around here what went down last month. We could all see the smoke for two days afterward."

I could feel my body tighten as I realized what he was alluding to, an encounter with a drug cartel from Los Angeles that had followed me up to my cabin outside of town. The entire incident had been cleared by the DEA, and I was even offered a job because of the ordeal, but none of that would have any effect at slowing the gossip mill from churning in the sleepy town.

"But I'm guessing by your tone and posture you don't actually think I had anything to do with this girl being taken," I said. "I only just arrived before the snow really started falling."

"I know that," Ferris said softly.

"Look," he said, his voice having fallen to just more than a whisper, "I know this is bad form. I don't want to be here, and I'm positive you don't want me here."

More than once I had heard talks begin in a similar way, ending up with me doing something I really didn't want to do, but ultimately having no choice.

"My entire staff is five people – myself, two deputies, a dispatcher and a janitor who is really just a retiree that likes hanging around the place. That's it."

I kept my reaction impassive as I listened to him speak, already knowing where this was going.

"In normal circumstances I could call the state police over in Billings, but they can barely make it to edge of the city with all this snow, let alone all the way out here," Ferris said.

More questions came to mind, though I remained silent, letting him go on.

"I even tried the feds, hoping maybe they could get a chopper or something in, but there's just no way, not until this lets up."

At that he turned his focus back to me. "And after speaking to every agency over there I could think of, that's when I remembered seeing your truck parked over here this morning."

I wasn't sure whether to be flattered that he thought of me or offended that I wasn't as invisible as I tried to be.

For five years my mailing address had been Glasgow, the cabin my home during the six months a year I wasn't working as a guide out of West Yellowstone, and not once had I gotten so much as a parking ticket. I kept to myself and didn't bother a soul.

"I was completely cleared in everything that happened here last month," I said.

"I know that," he said, raising both palms toward me and patting the air twice before lowering them. "But if half the story that made the rounds here is true, you're a hell of a resourceful man."

He watched me for a moment, waiting for a reaction, before adding, "Exactly the kind of man I could use to give a hand on this right now."

He was short staffed and facing a kidnapping case of a woman doctor I presumed to be a respected member of the community.

A blizzard prevented him from calling in the heavy hitters from the alphabet agencies, or even leaning on the state police to roll in anybody they could spare.

Still, the simple question of why me remained.

Seeming to sense my thought process, watching me remain rigid across the room, Ferris said, "I know how this looks and sounds. I do. I basically just told you we've been keeping tabs on you. I'm sure you're pissed about it, I would be too."

I offered a tiny grunt to let him know that was the case without making it so obvious as to derail the conversation.

"But right now I have a ticking clock. You've worked on this side of things before, you know how it goes. Every hour, every minute, that passes reduces our chances of finding that girl alive."

In this one instance he might have been overstating things just a bit, the snow piled up outside actually helping our cause. It would reduce the number of places the kidnappers could take her, narrow the search area significantly.

Still, I knew what he was trying to get at.

"This damn storm has cut off everybody but the people right downtown," Ferris continued. "I had a hell of a time just making it over here. That means anybody that has to come further than a few miles is out.

"You know how many people that leaves around here with any kind of law enforcement or military training? I don't have a lot of options."

A bit of the resolve bled from his face at the last statement. It truly wasn't anything personal. This was a man who had precious few choices, and he knew it.

He wasn't coming to find the man who had blown up his own cabin to take down some rogue drug runners, he was seeking out the former DEA agent who knew how to handle a gun.

He had no idea who I was, that's why he had called me Jeremiah when standing outside the door. I was a warm body, and that's all he was concerned with at the moment.

"Anyway," Ferris said, letting out a sigh as he stood, taking up his hat from the table beside him. "I'm meeting my deputies at the station in half an hour to brief them and start doling out assignments."

He paused, as if he were going to make one last plea for assistance, before thinking better of it.

With just a simple nod he turned for the door, disappearing into the cold without another word.

## Chapter Nine

Wood Arrasco heard her long before he saw her.

It started with a long, deep sigh, the same sound she made every time she woke up. Following just a moment later was the familiar groan of the springs on the old four poster bed, Maria going through the same ritualistic stretch that always came after the sound.

One, and then the other, without fail.

Under other circumstances the sounds would have brought a smile to his face, one of the few creature comforts he allowed himself.

As it were, it brought about a much different reaction, bordering on dread, knowing that a conversation he didn't particularly want to have would soon be coming.

Seated at the kitchen table, his legs propped up on a straight backed chair matching the one he was seated in, Wood raised the beer from the table beside him. He idly let a half-inch of the cold liquid slide down his throat.

A full minute passed after the creaking of the springs before bare feet could be heard touching the hardwood floor, shuffle steps growing closer before a silhouette stood in the bedroom door.

"Awful lonely in that bed in there," Maria said, grogginess obvious in her tone.

Wood shrugged, saying nothing as he continued to stare into the darkness. He loved Maria, always had, but he didn't have time for this right now.

"Whatcha doing out here in the dark?" Maria asked, not picking up on his cues, walking around the table and stopping beside him.

She stood there, neither saying anything, before Wood conceded that the conversation was in fact going to happen. He lowered his feet from the chair and used his heel to push it out a couple of inches.

"Thinking."

Maria looked at the chair for just an instant before bypassing it and taking another step forward, lowering herself onto his lap, nestling the top of her head beneath his chin.

"What about?" she asked.

The warmth of bed still clung to her skin as she settled against him. It passed through the front of the long sleeve thermal he wore and through the jeans into his thighs. Her long dark hair just inches away smelled like lavender, the combined effect putting his earlier agitation at bay.

She was the only person in the world capable of evoking such a response, a fact they were both very much aware of.

"That call earlier," Wood said, "from Cuddy."

"Hmm," Maria said, her voice seeming to already be retreating back toward slumber. "Remind me, which one is he?"

"One of our biggest suppliers," Wood said.

"Oh, right," Maria said. "The scary guy."

The right corner of Wood's mouth pulled up just a bit as he tilted his head back to look down at her. "Oh, really?"

Her eyes were already pressed closed as she made no effort to look up at him, a small smile the only reaction to his response. "Well, I just mean, between the hair and the dirty clothes and that God-awful smell..."

Wood couldn't help but agree. Sam Cuddyer was long past needing a bath and a haircut, his clothes could probably be used as fire starter logs, they were so contaminated with chemicals.

Still, at no point in his life would Wood have ever thought to use the word *scary* to describe him.

"What did he want?" Maria asked.

The mirth bled from Wood's features.

"They've had a problem."

"You don't do problems," Maria responded, shaking her head just slightly against him.

"Nope."

"How bad?"

Truth was, Wood didn't know how bad. From the sound of things, Cuddy's reliance on his partner had finally caught up with him, Elias the living proof of the mantra to never trust a cook who took too much pleasure from his own product.

If there was anything left of the man or the operation, was anybody's guess.

For the first hour after getting the call, that was Wood's chief concern. They had worked long and hard to become the preeminent supplier for the new Bakken oil fields. They now had a firm grip on the operation and a captive audience growing larger by the week. They could not afford to be without product for any length of time, because if they couldn't supply, there were more than enough vultures around just waiting to move in.

After those concerns, a second, even larger one occurred to him.

It had been some time since he'd been over to inspect the operation Cuddy ran, but it was by no means a small affair. The equipment alone was enough to fill a four car garage. If an explosion had taken place, the likes of which Cuddy seemed to describe, or that Wood envisioned in his mind, it would be noticed.

From miles away.

Right now they had the benefit of the storm dumping snow over everything from Bozeman to the Black Hills, but that wouldn't last forever. Once it stopped, somebody was bound to investigate a fire ball just a few miles outside of town and would almost certainly smell ethyl ether in the air.

He had no idea who the sheriff was over there, or even if there was one, only that nobody had found it necessary to make any payments as far away as Glasgow.

There was no trace of his organization over there, nothing to connect him to Cuddyer and his crew. Still, if somebody was determined enough to go snooping into things, it wouldn't be terribly difficult to see the relationship between the two.

It wasn't as if a lab that large could be exclusively for personal use.

"Bad," Wood whispered.

A small, barely audible sound passed Maria's lips, sleep not far away. Once more she pressed her shoulder against him, snuggling tight.

"So what are you going to do about it?"

## Chapter Ten

For three hours Sam Cuddyer's only movement was one short sprint from the truck to the front door of Valley Memorial Hospital and back again. It had been a short run, no more than a minute, but had filled him with enough adrenaline to redline his heart rate even now, long after.

His left knee, long a bane to him, was beginning to ache, and he could feel his tailbone rubbing against the seat beneath him. The bottom half of his jeans, soaked with snow as he tromped through it, were still damp.

Combined with the moisture from Jasper's and the girl's clothes, the interior of the cab was beginning to feel like a sauna. Condensation continued to bead on the windows, causing him to have to reach out every so often and wipe it away, thick wet swirls visible on the glass.

"Where we going now, Cuddy?" Jasper whispered, his body pressed tight beside him.

"You know," Cuddyer replied, leaning forward to see past Jasper to the girl on the opposite end of the seat.

She was tall – taller than Jasper and almost as tall as he was. Her hair was big and windblown, giving her an extra inch or two, providing a natural pillow for her head as it rested against the passenger window. From that angle Cuddyer could see that her face was angular with wide cheekbones.

If he was into black girls, even light-skinned ones like her, he might have found her pretty. As it were, his attention skipped right past her features to the brown and purple bruise along her right cheek, a small scrape revealing just a hint of blood.

He hadn't planned on hitting her, even less on using the butt of the gun to do it, but her yelling and struggling was something they could ill afford, standing out in the parking lot of the hospital. It had taken everything he and Jasper had just to drag her a few feet, her legs splayed out, burrowing into the snow, her backside anchoring her to the ground. Even the sight of the weapon had not had the intended effect, only causing her to scream with everything she had instead of frightening her into complicity as he had hoped.

Luckily for him, he had resisted the urge to just pull the trigger, instead wielding it as a club, her body going limp beneath its impact, bringing a thin smile to his face.

"She sure was strong, wasn't she?" Jasper asked, following Cuddyer's gaze and glancing over at her as well.

For a moment Cuddyer considered agreeing before turning to face forward again.

Still unconscious, her wrists and ankles both bound in wide swaths of duct tape, she appeared anything but.

"I've fought stronger," he whispered.

"Yeah," Jasper conceded, "but *women?*"

Again, Cuddyer fell silent, considering the statement. For as daft as Jasper could be, and often was, this time he wasn't necessarily wrong. The girl had clearly been in a scrap or two before, maybe even had some sort of training. Given her shape and skin tone, he wouldn't be surprised if she was an athlete of some sort, perhaps one of those crazy UFC types he saw on television.

She'd also obviously been around a gun before. Nobody seeing one for the first time would ever think to fight harder or yell louder, most falling into submission at the mere sight of it.

Every minute since loading her inside and driving away, Cuddyer had spent with both hands squeezing the steering wheel, his gaze alternating between the rearview mirror and the path ahead. The combination of the tension inside the truck and trying to stay on the road had his nerves pulled taut, every sense heightened, adrenaline causing his pulse to surge. Sweat coated his face beneath his beard, causing his skin to itch.

"How's Elias?" Cuddyer asked.

For a moment there was no response, Jasper simply sitting quietly and staring out the windshield. Renewed anger passed through Cuddyer as he glanced to his side, waiting for any sign of movement.

"Jasper, check Elias."

At the mention of his name, Jasper turned away from him, pressing his back flat against Cuddyer's shoulder. He looped a hand back, just as he had every half hour since leaving the house, returning with the same report he did each time.

"He's breathing, but it's still fast and shallow," he said. A low huff escaped his lips as he moved back to face forward, settling himself against the seat.

"How much further?" he asked. "I didn't think we'd be driving so long, and I had all that water before we left."

He had first met Jasper Maxx when they were just kids, he, the older boy down the street and Jasper, the younger one who never took a hint to leave him alone. The combination of time and relative isolation had eventually caused his stance to soften a bit, finding out many times over that there was always some use for a kid with unflinching loyalty.

Only on the occasional odd moment such as this did having him around ever present a problem, not because he had to fear him mentioning what they had done to the doctor, but because his friend's diminished intellectual capacity meant he had to be extra careful with every step he took.

"We've only gone 10 miles," Cuddyer said, painfully aware of how little progress they had made. Between the depth of snow and the lack of visibility, they had been forced to go no more than a few miles an hour, the diesel engine moaning as it powered through the growing mounds of powder.

"Oh," Jasper said, settling himself back against the seat and folding his arms across his chest. "And where are we going again?"

Cuddyer hadn't told him the first time, though it shouldn't have been hard to figure out. There was only one place that was even a possibility at a time such as this, something they had put in place months before in case this very thing ever occurred.

The fact that Jasper didn't know, hadn't already pieced things together, only served as a reminder to Cuddyer of what he was working with. The younger man could recite random comments Cuddyer had made years before, but asking him to use the smallest amount of deductive reasoning was simply not possible.

"Fallback," Cuddyer said, offering no further explanation, hoping it would be enough to end the conversation. They only had a little bit further to go, and there would be a massive amount of work to do when they arrived. He needed the next few minutes to think, to plan things out in his mind.

"Oh," Jasper whispered, raising his head as if he understood completely. "Fallback."

It was obvious from his tone that he had no idea what that meant, but Cuddyer made no effort to enlighten him.

He would find out soon enough.

## Chapter Eleven

"Shit."

The wind pulled the word away from my mouth the moment I said it, carrying it away into the Montana night. Along with it went a healthy spattering of snowflakes, wet and thick, clinging to everything they touched.

There was no earthly reason for me to be standing outside the front door of the Valley County Sheriff's Department. That is, aside from the moral implications, the notion that a woman was out there in this godforsaken blizzard, had been taken against her will by someone with intentions I didn't want to guess at.

The odds are she's a very nice lady. People with the God complex that afflicted many physicians rarely settled in places like Glasgow. Instead, hospitals like the one on the edge of town were where you found doctors who genuinely just wanted to help people and would work for schoolteacher wages.

I didn't know a single thing about Yvonne Endicott. What her motivations were, or what had caused her to be practicing in this place. She might have been a local who came back, the proverbial prodigal daughter returning. She may have agreed to work in a backwoods area for relief on her student loans.

She might have just needed a job.

As much as I'd tried to tell myself that these things mattered, none of them really did. It wasn't an issue of how old she was or what she looked like or where she went to school.

At the end of the day, she was a person who needed help.

Years before, I had made my young daughter a promise that I would always do what I could to help people in need. A month before, I had blown my cabin to bits and nearly lost my life making good on that promise.

Before that I had spent the better part of a decade as a member of the best unit the DEA had, running through some of the worst places on earth to ensure that bad men and their products didn't end up infecting American cities.

And as many times as I told myself this wasn't my fight, that I didn't know Rake Ferris or Yvonne Endicott or anybody else in Glasgow, there was no way I could walk away without at least trying to help.

No matter how much I wanted to.

A small bell hung from the ceiling, the top of the glass-paneled door slapping against it as I pushed inside, the ringing announcing my presence. I stomped my feet twice on the thick black rug beside the door, the bell sounding a second time as the door swung closed on a plume of snow crystals following me in.

The room was stifling after fighting my way through the snow and wind on my way over. Sweat was already beading up on my forehead and starting to run down my back beneath the heavy clothes.

I stood, surveying what looked to be an average small-town Sheriff's Department, my apprehension rising again as I heard the sound of boots against tile, culminating with Ferris appearing at the far end of the hall. He gave no reaction to seeing me there beyond raising a hand and motioning for me to follow him back into the room he had appeared from.

"Come on back, we're just getting started."

Once more I stomped my feet to knock any excess snow from my legs and shoes and pulled off the heavy coat and gloves before following him, the rubber treads of my hiking boots squeaking against the tile. I kept my gaze locked straight ahead, following the scent of coffee to the end of the hall.

I entered what appeared to be a makeshift conference room, a round folding table in the center and an odd assortment of chairs around it. On the far wall was a dry erase board, beside it a television perched on a metal cart. A black and white image was frozen across the screen, no doubt the footage taken from the hospital security camera.

To my left was a reclaimed end table with a coffee pot and stacks of Styrofoam cups, a microwave sat on an old refrigerator humming away in the corner.

A far cry from the facilities I had worked out of with the DEA, though nowhere near the worst I had encountered.

Ferris stood at the table, his tan Sheriff's shirt tucked tight into his jeans. The same tense look he wore when arriving at my room was still in place, his thumbs hooked into the front of his pants.

"Thanks for coming," he said, nodding slightly for emphasis. He gestured to his right and said, "This is Deputy Mavis Azbell."

I followed his lead and nodded to a woman with auburn hair pulled back into a ponytail. Her pale skin and light blue eyes both gave the impression she'd been asleep not long before. Much of her body was covered in a puffy down jacket as she leaned forward over the table, a mug of coffee between her hands.

"And that's Coop Baker," Ferris added, motioning to the man on the opposite side.

Like Azbell, his skin was pale, almost translucent, a harsh contrast to the weathered outdoorsman look of Ferris. Not much larger than his counterpart, he was older and completely bald.

"Guys, this is Jeremiah Tate," Ferris said. "Formerly of the navy and the DEA, he's agreed to give us a hand here."

"Good to meet you both," I managed, already sensing that the decision to ask me in was one that either nobody else knew about, or they did and openly disapproved.

Not that it really mattered, one way or another.

Each continued to study me, certainly superimposing the stories they'd heard onto the man who stood in front of them, before Azbell nodded slightly.

"You too."

Baker said nothing, merely turning his attention back to Ferris.

"I just showed them the footage from the scene," Ferris said, motioning over his shoulder to the television. "We can cue it up again so you can take a look in a few minutes."

It was clear from the statement and that no offer had been made for me to take a seat that right now Ferris was running interference, getting through what he had to as fast as possible and divvying up tasks so as to avoid any internal conflict.

At least, that's how I read it, because it's exactly how I would have handled things as well.

I nodded in agreement, folding my arms over my chest, letting him know I was good where I stood.

"Okay," Ferris said, "you both just saw the tape, which is all we know at this point. My preliminary interview at the hospital was only to establish that a kidnapping had taken place and to obtain a copy of the security footage.

"As soon as we're done here, Mr. Tate and I will be heading back to Valley Memorial to interview everybody present at the time of the abduction, see what we can find out."

At the mention of my name Azbell cast a glance in my direction, Baker remaining rigid beside her, making it a point not to acknowledge my presence.

Already, I could tell working with him was going to be a problem, making a mental note to never put myself in a position where I had to rely him to watch my back.

"In the meantime, I want you guys to start working the streets. They couldn't have gotten far in this storm, so start eliminating anywhere that hasn't been disturbed by tire tracks, try to narrow our search parameters as much as possible.

"Take your time, be careful, be thorough."

Baker grunted softly as Azbell nodded, neither making any attempt to rise from their seats.

"We'll all rendezvous back here later to share information."

Once more there were tacit gestures of agreement, though nobody said anything.

"That okay for you?" Ferris asked, looking up to address me directly. "Anything I'm missing right now?"

There was still far too much I didn't know about the case, having not even seen the video, much less having talked to anybody, to even begin to answer his question.

Instead, I said the only thing I could.

"Just one thing. Call me Hawk."

## Chapter Twelve

I had wondered earlier how the Sheriff had made it to the motel, but the thought didn't occur to me until after he'd left. For sure there was some snow on his hat and boots, but nowhere near enough to have made the three-block trek on foot.

The answer was parked out behind the station, a black Dodge Ram with a modified chassis sitting up on 32" tires. Around each one were silver chains, their links locked into place, ready to chew up the wet snow covering the streets.

A low, shrill whistle slid between my lips as I pushed my way through the calf-deep snow and came around on the passenger side, the frozen metal of the door squealing in protest as I wrenched it open. Ferris and I both piled inside, a healthy puddle of snow covering the floorboards beneath our feet.

The interior of the truck was just as spacious as it appeared from the outside, a pair of bucket seats with a console between them up front and a bench seat stretched along the back. The faint warmth of his previous trip still lingered, providing just enough heat to fog the windows.

"Nice cruiser," I said. "County budget must be better than I thought."

"Right," Ferris snorted, picking up on the bit of levity in my voice. "Damn county won't even reimburse me for gas when I have to use this thing."

I let the statement pass without comment, not particularly wanting to get into a long-winded discussion about the shortcomings of government agencies. More than once I had been a part of such tirades at nearly every level, the only thing that ever came from them being increased bitterness toward the people we worked for, and that accomplished nothing.

Besides, at this point we had just had our first conversation that was not short and stilted, an attempt at becoming colleagues for the very immediate future.

It was a start, which was why I was willing to bypass asking about my frosty reception inside just yet, focusing instead on the task at hand.

My own viewing of the video had revealed precious little, basically providing a visual for the original story Ferris had told me but adding no additional details. Shortly after midnight Dr. Yvonne Endicott had stepped outside. She wasn't taking a smoke break, didn't try to make a phone call, merely stood in the cold air for a few minutes, stretched, and was about to head inside when something caught her attention. She stayed where she was as lights, presumably from a vehicle, grew closer, drawing her off the edge of the front sidewalk.

It was an understandable action given the circumstances. There was no way anybody would be out joyriding, certainly not taking chances coming to the hospital unless they had an extreme emergency on their hands. When she saw headlights, she most likely assumed the latter, stepped out to try and help, and immediately regretted her decision.

By the time she realized something was wrong, it was too late, the pair of abductors on her, dragging her from view.

The cab of the truck was silent as Ferris nudged it out onto Main Street, the big vehicle bouncing around as it dug fresh trenches in the snow. The engine moaned in protest as the RPMs mounted to keep us moving. At no point did our speed exceed 10 miles an hour, the headlights illuminating a world that was blindingly white outside.

As with the start of any investigation, there were so many questions, it was difficult to know even where to begin. This time was worse than most, as at least with the DEA I had a file to work from, a list of transgressions or suspects to serve as a starting point.

In this instance I knew absolutely nothing.

"So how do you want to play this?" I asked. I left the question open-ended, meaning not only our first stop at the hospital but the investigation as a whole.

My showing up at his office had let him know I was willing to help, but beyond that not much more had been said.

Ferris let out a long breath, reaching to turn down the defroster fan.

"Most of the people living around here are lifers, know everybody in town and have long memories of local lore. They'll almost all know who Jeremiah Tate is and about the incident last month he was involved in. Almost certainly have opinions about it, too."

I had expected as much, saying nothing, content to let him continue.

"So, for the time being we'll tell them you're with the state, just happened to be in town and I asked you to lend a hand." He glanced over my way and said, "You understand if we avoid saying you're with the federal government, right?"

This being Montana, I understood perfectly well.

"I doubt anybody will know you as Hawk, so we'll just use that as a first or last name, depending on the situation, if that works."

It was flimsy, and wouldn't take much to punch holes through, but I got where he was coming from. As it should be, his thoughts were most likely on the case. The cover story was something he'd thrown together in a hurry, certainly sufficient for the purposes of covering some interviews of hospital employees who were scared or angry or both.

"That works," I said. "You want to divide and conquer or for me to fade into the background?"

His answer to this question would tell me a lot about how the next day or two would play out, about whether his coming to me was about help or sheer manpower.

Ferris chewed over the question for a moment, the muscles around his right eyes twitching once as he rolled through an intersection without bothering to stop or even slow down.

"Time," he finally said. "Right now, that is the most important thing. Let's divvy folks up and get everything we can. We know the hospital is the one place she isn't, so let's shoot to be in and out in less than an hour."

## Chapter Thirteen

The world came back to Yvonne Endicott one painful sense at a time. The first thing she noticed was the hard feel of the concrete beneath her. Splayed flat on the ground, a deep bone-chilling cold radiated up from it, easily passing through her light scrubs, wracking her body with shivers.

A moment later came the taste of blood. Gritty and metallic, it was dried along the roof of her mouth, crusted between her teeth. Time and again she ran her tongue over it, trying to moisten it enough to peel it free before pushing it out in a thin plume of spittle.

Next was the smell, something harsh like ammonia, only much stronger. It filled her nose, passing straight to her brain, intensifying the pain she was in.

The last sense to hit her was when she opened her eyes, bright light pulsating through the slits, sending a searing ache up her body. Just as fast, she pressed them closed before trying again, opening them just a little in an attempt to get her bearings.

A slight groan passed her lips as she raised a hand to her face, feeling the throbbing ache on her cheek, knowing every time her heart beat, sending a new jolt of blood through the area.

Bit by bit the events from earlier returned to her, each coming back in short snippets, like individual scenes spliced together in a rough cut.

Standing outside the hospital. Seeing the lights approach. Trying to help whoever was coming. Seeing the two men come toward her. Attempting to fight them off.

The gun.

With each of the memories came a renewed sense of fear, of urgency, as she recalled the events. There was no way to know where she was, what was happening. The truck was not at all familiar to her as it pulled up, just one more in the unending line of oversized vehicles she'd seen since moving to Glasgow.

No details about the men had stood out beyond that they both had beards and hooded sweatshirts, again just two more everyday occurrences in her new town.

Keeping her vision narrowed to just slits, Yvonne fought against the roiling agony in her brain. She knew it was her body's way of trying to protect her, to fend off whatever had occurred, though at the moment she needed to get past it, to inventory what she knew and how she could act on it.

The last thing she remembered was the taller of the men swinging the gun at her, gripping the barrel. That meant he had probably used it like a hammer to knock her unconscious before they picked her up and took her away. Coupled with the extreme light sensitivity, it was likely she had a concussion, though how much more, she had no way of knowing.

Otherwise her body was stiff, sore, frigid, but didn't appear to have any real damage. There didn't seem to be anything indicating she was raped or abused further, but again she wouldn't know for sure until she could examine herself.

Whenever that might be.

Nearby she could hear the sound of metal scraping against metal. Interspersed was a pair of voices, one deeper, seeming to give orders, the other concerned with little more than compliance.

For a moment Yvonne lay where she was, trying to determine if she knew them, to figure out what they were saying. She pressed her eyelids tight and focused as much as she could before giving up, the effort bringing too much agony, the reward nothing at all.

If she was going to discover anything, whether it be where she was or who had taken her, she was going to have to risk being seen awake.

Drawing in two deep breaths, Yvonne rolled over onto a shoulder, facing the sounds. There she stayed a moment before popping open her eyes as wide as she could, gritting her teeth as the light around her poured in, causing her head to feel like it might explode.

The room she was in was cavernous in its dimensions. Nothing more than one open space, it appeared to be a barn of some sort, the roof above rising almost two stories in height, the walls made of corrugated metal, the brown paper backing of insulation visible. The floor was bare concrete, the light provided by a series of fluorescent tubes hanging in fixtures overhead.

She was on the floor next to a wall, a pair of men working no more than 20 feet away near two long rows of roughhewn wooden tables that covered most of the length of the room.

In unison the men moved with purpose, setting up some sort of contraption on the tables, buckets and coils and pieces of copper piping strewn about.

It took a moment for Yvonne to process what she was seeing, glancing to the white plastic barrels stacked high along the back wall, noticing the canisters of fuel piled nearby.

Only then did the answer she was seeking come to her, causing her stomach to seize.

Drugs.

Methamphetamines, to be more exact.

The men were building a meth lab.

Yvonne had never been in the presence of the substance, though she'd treated enough patients hooked on it to know the effects it could have, had seen enough television shows to have an idea of what the production consisted of.

Staring at the men before her, seeing the vastness of the operation she'd been pulled into, an involuntary gasp slid from Yvonne's lips.

That tiny mistake was all it took. It drew stares from both men, each standing rigid before the smaller turned to his partner.

"Looks like she's awake, Cuddy."

## Chapter Fourteen

Without surprise, the graveyard shift was manned as thinly as possible. And because of the storm, all non-essential personnel had been sent home hours earlier, the hospital reduced to a bare bones crew, just enough to keep it running in case somebody could get there.

Judging by the look of things as Ferris and I had walked in that was highly unlikely, the waiting rooms all empty, more than two-thirds of the lights turned off. The resulting effect was a lot of shadows and silence, the things bad horror movies were made from, the place seeming closer to abandoned than the only hospital within more than 100 miles.

That meant there were few people for Ferris and me to talk to, all of them gathered in a small break room deep within the bowels of the facility. Nobody had been waiting for us at the door as we arrived, Ferris needing no direction as he took us straight to them, giving the impression it was not his first time making the trek.

They looked up as we appeared in the doorway, a man in a bad security guard uniform and three women, two of them in scrubs, a fourth in jeans and a double knit sweater. All four had puffy eyes and matted hair, wearing the events of the evening plainly, their faces betraying just the slightest bit of hope as they glanced in our direction.

From the outside looking in, the room was tiny, containing only a sofa and a card table with plastic chairs surrounding it. Along one wall was a small stand with a television on it, the usual assortment of vending machines on the back wall.

"Thank you all for being here," Ferris said, getting right to it. "Mr. Hawk, from the state, will be assisting me with the interviews."

The story was close enough to pass, especially with a group like this that was bordering on exhaustion.

"Mr. Breckman," he said, nodding to the man seated in an orange plastic chair beside the card table, "if you wouldn't mind, I'd like to speak to you first. Mr. Hawk..."

He let his voice fall away, allowing me to choose whomever I wished to open with.

"Who was the last person to speak with Dr. Endicott?" I asked, filling in the gap instantly, not wanting to give the impression that this was a disjointed operation in any way.

Right now the people in the room still bore some semblance of hope. We needed to do everything we could to cultivate that, to use it to our advantage before they became scared or bitter.

After that, they wouldn't be of much use to anybody.

A moment passed as the three women exchanged glances, none saying much of anything.

"Ladies," I said, leaning forward and bracing a shoulder against the door frame to stare in at them. "I apologize if I seem brusque, but the clock is ticking. The sooner we get past this, the sooner we can get on the road and find Yvonne."

The technique was one I had learned years before when speaking with witnesses in the DEA. In the immediate aftermath of a crime, most fell into one of two distinct categories, succumbing either to anger or fear. The only way to deal with it was to push them past it, to jolt their senses, to give them something to focus on instead of the situation at hand.

If that something had to be a dislike for me and my methods, so be it.

The use of her first name was a trick I'd developed on my own, making sure to personalize the victim, to ensure the witnesses understood the gravity of the situation.

Fortunately, most of the time, it worked.

On the far end of the couch a young woman stood, rising to a surprising height. Stopping just a couple inches below my own 6'3", she was dressed in light green scrubs and had her hair pulled back, her pale complexion splashed with deep red splotches across the cheeks.

"I think that would be me," she said, glancing to her cohorts before taking a step forward.

"You have somewhere we can speak in private?" Ferris asked, ignoring the girl and focusing on the woman in jeans still seated on the couch.

The woman's jaw dropped open a fraction of an inch, surprised at being addressed directly. "Down the hall on your left. One of you can use my office, the other our CFO's right beside it. Both are unlocked."

Extending a hand to the guard, Ferris motioned down the hall before turning and walking toward the offices. I remained where I was by the door, allowing the guard and the young woman to pass before bringing up the rear, the makeshift convoy moving in silence through the dim hallway.

Ferris opened a door and flipped on the light switch, motioning for the young lady to step inside. Without being prompted, the guard went into the office next door, Ferris pausing just briefly in the hallway. For a moment it looked as if he might try to give me pointers on how to proceed, before thinking better of it and disappearing into the second office and closing the door behind him.

In another life, I had conducted dozens of interviews, if not more. Some were done as part of a team, others solo. At times they were angry drug lords or frightened mules or any of a number of types in between, but I had never addressed a situation like this.

As terrible as the abduction of Yvonne Endicott was, it just wasn't the type of thing that landed on the DEA's plate.

The young girl's back was turned to me as I entered, having already lowered herself into the lone visitor chair in the office. Her posture appeared rigid as she sat and waited, not bothering to look my way as I circled the desk and pulled out the chair behind it.

"Good evening," I said, lowering my voice just a little, not wanting to seem too imposing. Earlier I had raised it to get their attention, though now I had to be careful not to push too far, to cause her to recede entirely into herself.

"My name is Hawk. I'm helping out the sheriff on this investigation."

I paused there, long enough for her to get the hint that it was her turn to speak, wanting to make her an equal participant in the conversation, instead of someone I had to pull information from.

"Meredith Shek," she whispered after nearly a full minute had passed. "I was the floor nurse with Yvie tonight."

I nodded, noting her use of a nickname, before asking, "Do you guys normally share the same shift?"

The right side of her face scrunched just slightly. "I guess? This is a pretty small place and we're usually understaffed, so we all overlap quite a bit."

"Hmm," I said, nodding again. It was exactly as I had figured before entering, but wanted to give her the impression it was a vital piece of information, the hope being that at some point she would add something that was. "How long have you and Yvonne worked together?"

"Couple months now," Shek said. "She just started this winter, moved up here from somewhere down south. Atlanta, I think it was."

I kept my features impassive, not wanting her to see any emotion on my face or guess at the myriad questions springing up in my mind.

"Was she from here?" I asked. "Just moving back?"

Shek thought for a moment, her gaze rising to me and then on up to the ceiling.

"I know she's not from here," she said, "but I actually don't know where home is originally."

That too sent off warnings in my mind, such information being the kind of basic small talk that was usually ticked off in the first couple of days of encountering a new coworker.

"You don't know?" I asked, my eyes narrowing slightly. "Even after a couple of months?"

"Well, no, not exactly anyway," Shek said. "She always just said Atlanta, so we took it at face value. Now that I think about it though, I'm not sure if she meant that was her home or just where she'd been before coming here."

The explanation made sense, though it still seemed a bit odd that nobody thought to press it.

"Any idea what brought her up here?" I asked. "This is a long way from Atlanta, not the kind of place someone just ends up if they have no connection to it."

Again, Shek's gaze settled high above me, the look on her face relaying that these were questions she'd never previously thought to ask. She remained that way a long time before finally whispering, "I don't know," no small amount of guilt present in her voice.

As much as I wanted to keep pushing on this line of thought, to determine where Yvonne Endicott had come from, what had brought her to the backwoods of Montana, I needed to move on. While there might be legitimate answers for what had happened to her lying somewhere in her backstory, it did me no good to keep digging at something that the woman before me clearly had no knowledge of.

"Okay," I said, "tell me about this evening."

I stopped there, adding no clarifying comments or questions, not wanting to limit her scope in any way. I wanted whatever she recollected to be unfiltered.

"Um," Shek said, leaning back in the chair and folding her hands together in her lap. "I came on around 8:00 this evening, didn't see Yvie until a couple hours later. An older woman – Mrs. Everson – had slipped on the ice and hit her head and come in for a couple of stitches."

A quick flash of a smile crossed her face, disappearing just as fast. "Normally it would have been something I would have handled, but I think Yvie was so bored she took her back and did it without even letting me know the case had come in."

"Is that usual, to not see each other for a couple of hours at the start of a shift?" I asked.

"It's not unusual," Shek replied. "Besides, I came on at 8:00, and Yvie'd been here since 6:00 this morning. During that time she was probably in the break room or grabbing a quick nap or something, and I was making rounds."

I nodded, superimposing the information with what I'd seen on the way in. The hospital was dead, there was no denying that. If someone, especially coming from Atlanta where things were probably nothing short of chaotic, was to have spent 18 hours in this place, they would be crawling the walls.

"Did Yvonne seem agitated, nervous, anxious, when you did see her?"

"No," Shek replied, shaking her head, the bottom of her ponytail visible as it swung from side to side. "Like I said, she just seemed sort of resigned, bored, looking to pass the time."

"Is that why she went outside?" I asked, watching as she again went rigid, her shoulders rising up toward her ears, her fingers locking together in her lap.

"I didn't even know she had," she whispered. "Not until after the alarm went up and everybody started trying to find her."

As much as I was hoping that some easy answer, that a magic piece of information, was going to pop out from our interview, I knew well enough that that was not how these things went. I could keep leaning on the girl, ask about the search of the hospital once they realized she was gone, but there wasn't anything of value I was going to get from it.

The reactions of every person in that break room made it clear at a glance that they were stunned by what had happened, had been trying in vain to put some reasoning to it, but were coming up empty.

All too often that's how such things tended to go - especially early in an investigation.

"Is there anything else at all you can think of?" I asked. "Any patients or coworkers Yvonne might have had friction with? Any reason, no matter how slight, you can think of for something like this happening?"

Shek's eyes went glassy for a moment as she receded into thought, trying to put an answer to my question. I watched as she chewed on it before again shaking her head.

"No, nothing like that. I mean, she always kept somewhat to herself, was kind of quiet, but she was very nice to everybody, employees and patients alike."

I expected that very response, and asked, "And when you say she kept somewhat to herself?"

"Oh, I don't know," Shek said. "It wasn't bad or anything, just, like, she was very *aware* of herself at all times."

I had no idea what she was trying to tell me, choosing to remain silent, letting her fill in the gaps for me.

"But, I mean, I think if I moved to a place where I was the only black person in town, I probably would be too."

## Chapter Fifteen

Sheriff Rake Ferris waited until he heard the door to the neighboring office close. He knew that Hawk had come of his own volition, had set off no negative vibes, but couldn't quite shake the feeling that he needed to keep his attention at least quasi-split for the time being.

The stories that had floated into town just over a month earlier bordered on mythical, ranging from Hawk being a recluse who just wanted his privacy, to a man who was up to something and got called on it, to his being a coldblooded killer who had lured his prey out into the wilderness and disposed of them.

Whether any of that was true Ferris had no idea, had accepted the fact that he probably never would. As with most things, the truth probably rested somewhere in between, known only to Hawk, God, and maybe a handful of others at best.

Multiple times he had tried to press on his contacts in Billings for information, once even making the trip over and buying a couple of rounds of beer, only to find out they were just as mystified as he was. The story Hawk had told them seemed to play out with the evidence at hand, but the sheer audacity of one man taking out five others in the middle of a Montana night seemed nothing short of a tall tale.

Going to ask him for help wasn't especially high on the list of things Rake wanted to do, the move in no small part predicated on wanting to eliminate the man as a suspect, to keep him close so he could study him.

Thus far, nothing Hawk did or said seemed to indicate anything was wrong, his willingness to take part in the investigation bearing just the right amount of trepidation for someone in his position with nothing to hide.

Still, for as much as Ferris would take advantage of his presence and his skillset, he would be careful about giving him too much leeway just yet.

Shifting his thoughts away from the man in the office next door, Ferris removed his hat and stepped away from the door. It was his second time inside the office that evening, his second time meeting with Myles Breckman. Both appeared to be exactly as they were the last time he had encountered them, the office a Spartan affair with a large L-shaped desk that ran halfway along the back wall before jutting straight out at him. A single chair sat on either side of it, various pictures and knickknacks strewn across it.

Not exactly the kind of thing he would envision for a hospital CEO, more functional than aesthetic, but pretty standard for someplace like Glasgow.

Breckman was seated in the guest chair, his left leg crossed over his right, his fingers laced together around his knee. His top row of teeth was jutted out over his bottom lip, gnawing softly on it, his gaze fixed on the painting directly across from him.

Ferris knew the man from a lifetime of living in Glasgow, Breckman just a few years behind him in school. Despite that, he appeared much older than the sheriff, his thinning hair completely white, loose skin hanging from the underside of his jaw.

He was dressed in faded slacks and a white guard's shirt, a thin jacket over it, the outfit doing nothing to hide the fact that he couldn't have weighed more than 150 pounds.

Who or what he was supposed to be able to guard against, Ferris could only guess.

"Rough night, huh?" Ferris opened, walking over to the padded black leather chair behind the desk and lowering himself into it. He left his hat in his lap, not wanting to drip water on the desk, and stared across at Breckman, waiting for a response.

There was none, save a slight nod.

"I know we spoke earlier," Ferris said, "but I want you to walk me through everything again. Now that a little time has passed, you've been able to think about things a bit more, I want to know if there's anything you might have overlooked before. Anything at all."

The only things to move on Breckman were his eyes, watery blue as they shifted from the painting to Ferris, his chin still angled away.

"No," he said softly. "It happened just like I told you."

"Really?" Ferris said, raising his eyebrows a touch, letting it be known that he didn't appreciate being lied to.

It had only taken a moment during their previous encounter to know that the man had been sleeping when the abduction took place, no doubt a habit he'd picked up years before and never thought to change, especially during times as slow as tonight.

"Really," Breckman said, his face still turned away from Ferris.

Silence passed slowly, Ferris openly staring at him before opting to change directions and come at things from a different angle.

"Why don't you walk me through the whole day," Ferris said. "What time did you come on?"

The question seemed to surprise Breckman, his head turning to face Ferris, a quizzical look on his features as if trying to determine where the sheriff was going with things.

"Noon. Roy, the other guard, lives outside of town. He called and asked if I would come in early so he could make it home before the snow got too bad."

"And he thought you'd be better able to handle it?" Ferris asked.

"Yeah. I have snow tires on my rig, only live a few blocks away, so I told him I'd come in early."

"And it's just the two of you?" Ferris asked.

"Four," Breckman corrected. "Three of us rotate through on eight hour shifts while one is off. Sometimes they have the extra man run double coverage during the day, but that's not too often."

"Hmm," Ferris said, nodding slightly. "And you were next in line on the rotation for today, after Roy?"

"I was," Breckman said, his eyes narrowing just slightly. "Besides, I'm usually the guy they call anyway. The others all have wives or kids. I live close by and don't do much, told them I'd be happy to cover."

Ferris's mouth turned up just slightly, as if buying into the story completely. "And I'm sure the overtime pay doesn't hurt."

"Sure doesn't," Breckman said, seeming to agree before realizing it, the look on his face indicating almost immediately that he regretted it.

Ferris let the smile grow on his face at the admission, the information and the reaction fitting with what he'd already pieced together hours before.

Breckman was a longtime fixture in Glasgow, the kind of guy who took on odd jobs such as security guard at the hospital, stayed until he'd worn out his welcome, then moved on to the next one. He'd never been accused of anything malicious, seen more as a lethargic sort who never did a single thing that wasn't explicitly requested and routinely followed up on.

Still, Ferris had to press just to be sure.

"So things are tight?" Ferris asked.

The look on Breckman's face clenched as he stared at Ferris. "No tighter than anybody else. I do alright."

"Yeah?" Ferris asked. "Not starting to get up in years a little? Tired of living in an apartment in town? Beginning to think about getting your own place, maybe head toward retirement?"

Breckman's features grew even more strained as he remained stiff, his look just short of incredulous.

"I mean, hey, I know how it can go," Ferris said, lifting his hands from his lap and spreading them before him. "We're not 25 anymore. The winters are longer and colder than they used to be."

Silence passed between them for a moment, a cord in Breckman's neck jumping slightly. "What are you getting at, Sheriff?"

Ferris made no effort to answer just yet, lowering his hands to his lap, allowing Breckman to see his own face harden.

"I'm saying I know you weren't making rounds when things went down. What I don't know is if you were just sleeping, or eating, or jerking off in the bathroom, or doing something else you shouldn't have been, or if you actually had a role in all this."

Going after someone he had known for decades like this wasn't how Ferris would have liked to approach things, but he was brutally aware of the ticking clock hanging over the investigation, the short timeframe meaning that he had no other choice. Under better conditions he would have filled Hawk in, let him play the bad cop role, having no qualms in letting every person in town hate the outsider.

In this instance, though, Ferris knew he couldn't do that. He had to be the one to ask, to look across at Breckman and see his response, to know for certain if he was lying or not.

For a variety of reasons.

"So tell me, Myles, is that how it went? Somebody called the old security guard, asked him to look away for a few minutes?"

Disbelief seemed to spread on Breckman's features as he stared back at Ferris, his upper body trembling slightly.

"Or maybe they went even further than that," Ferris pressed. "Slid you a neat little stack of cash, all wrapped up with a band around it, and you fed them the schedules of everybody here tonight? Maybe even called and let them know that the coast was clear? That a young female doctor was standing right outside, all they had to do was pull up and grab her?"

At that Ferris stopped, content that he had made his point. There was more he could have added, more character assassination quips he could have tossed in, but there was no point.

He had drawn blood, the shock on the man's face confirming it before he lowered his head.

"How long have we known each other, Rake?" Breckman whispered, the question just barely audible.

Ferris noted the use of his first name, the quiver that seemed to pass through his voice.

"Long time," Ferris conceded, "which is why this conversation is taking place here instead of down at the station."

He let the comment settle for a moment before adding, "I'm going to ask you once more, and that's it, did you have anything to do with this?"

Another long pause, Ferris allowing the words to hang in the air, before adding, "Because your story doesn't make sense. It just doesn't add up."

Across from him Breckman's head rose slowly, tears pooling in the corners of his eyes.

"Sleeping," he whispered, his voice detached, low, as he looked away, a flush of blood coloring his cheeks. "I was asleep in the call room."

He kept his gaze averted, turning to look at the floor, and added, "We all do it from time to time when things are especially slow. Hell, the last time anything bad happened here was over a decade ago. Aside from your office, this is the safest place in town."

He glanced up once, his features twisting slightly, as if he were in pain and may begin to cry at any moment.

"The place was dead quiet. One old couple had come in at 9:00, nobody else since. There wasn't but a handful of employees, all of them just kind of puttering around."

He drew in a short gasp, fighting for air, the emotions, the reality of the situation he was in, that he had caused, crashing in around him.

On the opposite side of the desk, Ferris did nothing to ease his guilt. Instead, he leveled his gaze on the man, already content with his response, but needing to hear him say the words just the same.

"But I didn't have anything to do with what happened. I swear to God I didn't."

## Chapter Sixteen

Cuddyer had no intentions of hurting the girl. If everything went as planned, and she did what she was supposed to, he would have no qualms with taking her back to the hospital, or dropping her off at home, or driving her any-damned-where else she wanted to go once the storm let up and the roads cleared.

Despite what his appearance seemed to indicate, what the few people around town he interacted with seemed to think, he was not an evil man. He derived no pleasure from causing pain, did not spend his weekends kicking dogs or punching small children.

His appearance was more apathy than anything, the beard something that had started years before to combat the Montana cold, had stayed because he didn't feel like going through the hassle of shaving all the time. His clothes and the smell were a byproduct of the way he made a living, something he had tried to combat in the past, but had finally accepted as inevitable.

Even the scars on his face, the many more that traced his arms and torso, were a result of the harsh chemicals he spent so much time working with, not some form of sadistic self-mutilation.

He knew the rumors about all those things bothered Jasper, had even heard the man go as far as to try and defend him before, but to Cuddyer the stories provided a cover far better than anything he could have ever concocted for himself. They kept people at arm's reach, kept their attention focused anywhere but at him, which fit his purposes perfectly.

Hiding in plain sight, or some such cliché he had heard before.

While he had no deep-seated need to harm the girl, he needed her to believe that he would like nothing more. For their purposes he needed her compliant, which could be achieved only if she was on the verge of being petrified at all times.

Kidnapping her had been a solid first step, smacking her with the gun a necessary act that had turned out to be an excellent follow-up.

"Keep working," Cuddyer said to Jasper, the younger man nodding in response, his mouth hanging open, just as it always did whenever he was scared or uncertain or both. It was a look Cuddyer had seen far more times than he would have liked over the years, though he had long since stopped commenting on it.

Some things just were the way they were.

All things considered, putting up with such a tiny quirk was a small price for unfettered loyalty.

Taking up the hammer on the floor beside him, Cuddyer looped around the table and walked toward the girl, allowing the head of the tool to slide from his grasp, gravity pulling it toward the floor before he tightened his grip around the handle. The simple act seemed to have the desired effect, the girl's eyes opening wide as she pressed herself back against the wall, athletic shoes sliding across the dusty concrete floor in an effort to gain purchase.

A small smile crossed Cuddyer's face as he moved closer, stopping just a couple of feet away from her. He stood with his weight balanced, silhouetted by the overhead lights, staring down at her.

Twice the girl opened her mouth, unbridled fear obvious on her face. Cuddyer could tell she wanted to ask questions, but no words passed her lips, her throat gripped tight, unable to produce a sound.

"You're going to do something for us," Cuddyer said, the look on his face growing more pronounced. Flicking his wrist just slightly, he tapped the head of the hammer against his leg, watching as her eyes traveled from it to him and back again.

"And if you don't, my friend here and I are going to have some fun with you and then take you for a drive in this blizzard."

The threat was something Cuddyer had come up with on the drive out, the sort of thing he knew would get her attention, would conform with whatever she already thought she knew about them.

"Do you understand?"

It took a moment for the girl to understand that it was a direct question and that a response was required. Cuddyer could see her mental faculties begin to work, her head nodding up and down, her hair bouncing around her head.

A few hours earlier the girl had not been afraid as he pulled the gun, still fighting with everything she had, even trying to scream at the sight of the weapon. Now, taken far from her element, stripped of anything resembling equal footing, she had regressed into exactly the position he had hoped she would - frightened and compliant.

"Get up."

There was no movement of any kind, the girl remaining curled tight at the foot of the wall, one shoulder pushed in front of the other as if cringing for an attack she knew was coming.

Taking a half step back, Cuddyer tapped the hammer again along the outside of his thigh. "Get up."

The words came out just shy of a growl, a command that could only be construed as such. He kept the scowl in place, waiting as she slowly drew her feet up under her and rose, using the wall as a brace.

The uneven sway of her upper body, the grimace on her face as she reached full height, told him she was still feeling the effects of the earlier blow, which was a good thing. The less able she was, the less likely she was to try anything.

Jutting his head toward the corner of the building, Cuddyer grunted softly, motioning with the hammer for her to move.

Using the wall as a guide, the girl kept one hand extended, her fingertips never more than a few inches away, as she inched along.

Glancing to his left, Cuddyer noted Jasper standing in the exact position he had been five minutes before, openly gawking at everything taking place, the same look on his face. Fighting the urge to gesture, or yell, or make any acknowledgement at all, Cuddyer turned his focus back to the girl, keeping equal pace behind her as they steadily moved forward.

Ahead of them a makeshift wall extended out from the side of the barn. Constructed from sheets of plywood, it was just eight feet tall, the wood unpainted, nailed together in a hasty fashion months before. The previous blonde hue of the boards had started to fade, the corners beginning to grey, the crude structure just barely visible in the corner of the huge room, beyond the reach of the overhead lights.

"Door, on the side," Cuddyer said, keeping his voice clipped, his sentences short, as he directed her around the corner. He could sense her body tense up as she pushed out away from the wall, her body seeming to teeter as she walked an uneven line to the front corner and again tapped a hand against the wood, using it for support.

Circling out wider, Cuddyer watched as she moved a bit further, finally making her way to a faded white door, a brass knob the only fixture of any kind. Taken from an old mobile home at the time the structure was built, it stopped a full foot shorter than the plywood walls.

"Open it," Cuddyer said, watching as the girl stopped just outside the door and took a deep breath, her shoulders rising and falling. "Now!"

The word jolted her. He could see her hand tremble as she reached out, turned the knob, and shoved the door open.

"Go on in," Cuddyer said, waiting for her to enter before following her, stopping just outside.

The space was a simple square, measuring a dozen feet in either direction. Along the side wall was a folding table, whatever supplies he and Jasper had been able to wrangle from the house tossed on it in a heap. On the opposite wall was an old wooden rocker with the varnish rubbed away by years of someone's backside pressing against it.

Most of the room was taken up by the bed directly across from the door, the frame made of chipped green metal, the mattress a throwaway from one of the motels in town.

Elias lay motionless, still buried beneath the pillows and blankets, not having moved since they deposited him there upon arrival.

"I'll be back in an hour," Cuddyer said, reaching into the room and grasping the door by the handle. "Fix him."

## Chapter Seventeen

Ferris's original projection turned out prophetic. Almost an hour to the minute after walking into the hospital we left, me with at least one new piece of data, hoping he had even more.

After releasing Shek from our discussion, my next interview was with Sandy Watson, a middle-aged mother of two who served as Chief of Medicine for the hospital. She had even less information than Shek, having arrived only a short time before the abduction, calling 911 when it was discovered that Yvonne had been taken.

Like Shek, she had displayed the correct amount of trauma to the incident, asking more questions than she answered. Most of them were inquiring how or why such a thing could happen, the most common responses from someone who had lived a pretty ordinary, if not somewhat sheltered, life.

To most people, things like abductions were something they saw on television or read about in the newspaper. They occurred in exotic, far-flung locales such as Miami or Los Angeles, not in their own hometown.

Certainly not on a snowy night in April, when most people should be home, either in front of a fire or already curled up in bed.

If only.

I finished my pair of interviews before Ferris, releasing Watson back to the break room and taking the opportunity to step outside and look things over for myself. I had already read the original statement from the guard, had seen the overhead video, but wanted to take a glance to see what I could determine.

The storm showed no signs of letting up as I stepped out the front door of the hospital, taking two small paces away from the entry. Behind me the glass doors slid shut, the squeaking of their frozen metal tracts adding to the sound of the overhead heater pushing hot air down from above.

Once the doors were closed, the world became silent, snow continuing to blow at a diagonal in the strong wind. Every so often a gust would whip up the icy crystals from the ground, pelting the exposed skin of my face and neck.

I raised my head, spotting the camera that had taken the video of the incident. Tucked high beneath the soffit overhead, a small red light indicated it was recording.

Stepping around a squat trash can, I pressed myself against the building, a snow embankment tight against my calf, and stared out at the scene, superimposing the video onto the view before me.

The actual expanse of the area was larger than it had appeared on screen, the breadth of the camera's angle being close to 20 feet. Closing my eyes, I imagined Yvonne standing where I had been a moment before.

Judging by the way things were situated, the car had come from the north. It would have turned into the parking lot, causing the flash of light that caught her attention.

Over the last few years I had spent precious little time in Glasgow, but I knew that most everything in the town limits lay to the south of the hospital. Whoever had approached Yvonne had not been coming from town and had access to a vehicle powerful enough to handle country roads despite the weather.

Neither point would narrow the field a great deal, but it was a start.

Stepping away from the building, I walked to the edge of the sidewalk, peering down at the path Yvonne had taken. In the hours since

# Fire and Ice

the incident several fresh inches of wet snow had fallen, filling in the bottom part of her tracks, rounding out the edges.

It would be impossible to see any shoe or tire treads, get a clear read on sizes either.

Placing my feet in the same spots as Yvonne, I moved out from beneath the awning, snow hitting my exposed scalp, stinging slightly as it touched my warm skin. Away from the protection of the building the wind struck me head-on, sucking the breath from my chest.

The tracks seemed to bear out what the video had shown, as it moved away from the sidewalk. It went in a straight line for about 20 feet to the parking lot before the trail became a bit muddled from lots of foot activity.

The tire tracks told me that the abductors had come in at the northern corner of the lot and moved through in one sweep. Their only stop had been to grab Yvonne, before exiting the opposite corner of the lot.

Whether they turned back north or went on into town, I didn't know, though I would make a point to check as we drove away.

Again, not much, but something.

Tracking was a skill I had been taught in the navy, but had honed to an art working in Yellowstone. Following someone or something across the forest floor had become second-nature to me. More than once I had managed a successful hunt based on nothing more than a few disturbed pine needles or the outer edge of a print in the soft earth.

This was different though, the snow a temporary trail that changed with the temperature, the wind and the continuing deluge constantly shifting things.

Shoving my hands into the front pockets of my coat, I held it closed in front of me, my gaze dancing over the scene.

A young woman had been standing in front of the hospital. She spotted an approaching vehicle, presumably a large truck or SUV, and stepped out to help, realizing too late that it wasn't help they were after.

The video proved she had resisted, meaning that they must have subdued her in some way. The fact that Shek said nobody had even known she was gone meant it must have been fairly quick and quiet.

Behind me I could hear the metallic wail of the doors opening, followed by the heaters blowing hot air.

"You find anything?" Ferris called, his voice sounding far away, carried by the wind.

Holding a hand up to give him pause, I kept my attention turned to the crime scene. Zeroing in on Yvonne's tracks, a few long trenches showed where she had tried to retreat, had been pulled back by the attackers.

I tried to envision everything, picking out the individual trails of the converging parties, seeing the indentations where the three came together, the snow mashed flat.

Numbness began to creep into my toes as I raised my feet high out of the drift and crept forward to stand in the center of the packed snow. There it was no more than a few inches deep, much of it having been kicked aside or trampled, the struggle short and furious.

I lowered myself into a crouch. Extending my hand out, I brushed away the fresh snowfall, leaving only the hard surface beneath.

There, I found exactly what I feared I might.

No more than the size of a silver dollar, already frozen solid, crusted almost black, was a circle of blood.

## Chapter Eighteen

Maria's question had resonated in Wood Arrasco's mind for the better part of an hour.

*What are you going to do about it?*

His initial reaction, his very first instinct the moment the call had come in, was to get in his truck and drive straight to Glasgow. There he would survey for himself how extensive the damage was, both to the lab and to Elias. If either or both was beyond repair he would simply wipe away the entire mess and move on.

The only thing that had stopped him was the snow piled high outside, knowing that there was no way he would make it there, not during the dead of night, most likely not for a couple of days.

This was no time for him to be impulsive. As annoying as the call had been, as bad as it could be for his enterprise, there was no need to cut his losses just yet. First, he must step back, assess, see how bad things were and if anything could be salvaged.

Too much time, money, and resources had been expended gaining the foothold that he had. It had been a long and arduous road for him to rise to the head of The Prairie Dogs, the only Latino to ever ride with them, let alone lead them.

Just as difficult had been his struggle to take over as the chief supplier for the burgeoning oil fields, his crystal meth keeping the workers cranked long beyond what the normal human body could withstand, making both the workers and their employers a lot of money in the process.

There were three different subcontractors supplying the drug to him, Wood knowing better than to do it in-house, but none were as good or as prolific as Cuddy. What role the old man had in it he could only guess, everybody knowing that the real talent was Elias, a meth-making idiot savant who could barely read but somehow produce the best product in the western half of the country.

It was that product that had helped seal the deal for Wood, keeping the employers and workers coming back and asking for greater quantities each month.

Leaving Maria curled against his chest, Wood slid his right hand across the table and tapped out a single text message. He knew despite the hour that it would be read and the directive acted upon, something he made a point not to do unless the situation called for it, as it now did.

After sending the message he remained seated for another 20 minutes or so before rising and carrying her into the bedroom, returning her to her side of the bed and pulling the blankets up to her chin.

Not once did she wake, her face serene, her long dark hair splashed across the pillow.

For a moment Wood stood over the bed, staring down at her, before reaching out and grasping a tendril of hair. He rolled the end of it between his fingers, feeling the soft strands against his skin, before dropping it and retreating from the room, pulling the door closed behind him.

He returned to the kitchen to see a flash of headlights appear through the front window, knowing already who it was. Crossing to the refrigerator, he pulled out two Cold Smoke's and placed them on the table, remaining standing as a light knock tapped at the door, followed by it cracking open just an inch.

"Prez?"

The voice was familiar, barely above a whisper, following the standard protocol for any late night meetings. There were only two people allowed to visit Wood after hours, both of them knowing not to disturb Maria's sleep or to tell another soul about his deference to her.

"Come on in, Trick."

On cue the door swung open, bringing with it a twirl of icy air, a couple of snowflakes making their way in as well. Along with them came a man who stood a half foot shorter than Wood, snow clinging to his legs.

Stopping just inside the door, he acted as if he might stomp his feet to knock the snow off before thinking better and bending over, using his hands to wipe it away. Once the black denim was again exposed, he stood, shrugging out of a down parka to reveal a long-sleeve flannel with a black leather vest over it.

"Everything alright?" he asked.

Trick Reynolds was Wood's second-in-command, someone who had made his way up through the ranks at the same time. As recently as six years before both had been nothing more than foot soldiers, muscle for whatever the men in charge wanted done, but a solid half-decade of upheaval had changed things dramatically, creating a void they were both glad to fill.

So far, the arrangement had worked out well for everybody involved, the organization for the first time proving to have some solid business acumen, the enrollment numbers on the rise.

"I got a call earlier tonight," Wood said, gesturing toward the table. As he did, he circled around and settled himself back into the same chair, reaching out and wrapping a hand around his beer, signaling Trick to do the same.

"From?" Trick asked. He reached out and grabbed the other beer, tilting it to his boss before taking a long pull.

In the dim light of the kitchen, Wood could see his friend for the first time, his face red and puffy from the cold, a faint crease down the side of it indicating he had been asleep when the text came in.

The rest of his head was hidden beneath a black watch cap and a goatee, the tuft of hair extended several inches from his chin.

"Cuddy," Wood replied, lifting his beer and taking a drink.

"Oh, shit," Trick said, the words sounding like a groan as he rolled his head to the side. "How bad?"

If there was any concern about being summoned at such an odd hour, any animosity about the intrusion, he did nothing to show it. Instead he cut straight to business, just as Wood knew he would, just as he always did.

One of many reasons he had been chosen for the post.

"Dumbasses almost blew themselves up," Wood said.

"Jesus Christ," Trick replied, spitting out the words. His entire body rocked back as he said them, packing as much force as he could into his lowered voice, shaking his head from side to side.

"Yeah," Wood said. "I guess it took most of the operation up with it."

Trick continued to shake his head before leaning forward and resting his elbows on the table. There he remained, contemplating the information.

"They still have the backup place, right? The one we paid for in case something like this happened?"

"Yeah," Wood said, nodding, having already considered that as well. At the time of construction it had seemed like an unnecessary expenditure, decided on against his better judgment, a pre-requisite from one of their buyers before agreeing to do business.

Apparently, they had had experience with meth, and the men who made it, before.

"The problem is Elias," Wood said.

The skin around Trick's eyes tightened as he winced, lifting his beer to take another swig. "Dead?"

"No, but Cuddy seemed to think it was bad. Like, not-being-able-to-cook-for-awhile bad."

"Shit," Trick replied, verbalizing the exact thought Wood had been having most of the evening. "I mean, it was only a matter of time, that boy can barely tie his own shoes."

"I know," Wood said, "and that other one Cuddy has is even worse, but I'll be damned if they don't make some sweet selling stuff."

Raising his eyebrows slightly, Trick nodded in agreement, remaining silent as he continued to work on his beer.

"What did you tell him?"

"Told him he had two days," Wood said, raising one shoulder in a shrug, "though to be honest, at the time I was just pissed off."

"Right," Trick agreed.

"It's going to take them at least half that long to get the new lab up and going, and that's assuming they can get him on his feet and working."

"Right," Trick said again. "I'm assuming the buyers don't know?"

Wood flicked his gaze over to him, shaking his head. "You're the first person I've told."

He didn't bother adding that he had already shared it with Maria, knowing that it would be assumed.

Another moment passed as Trick considered things. He placed his Cold Smoke on the table beside him and folded his arms across his chest, using one hand to stroke his goatee.

"Well, right now we have enough put back to last a week or more, and with the weather like it is, they won't be pumping a lot, so they won't have as much need."

Wood grunted in agreement. "But after that, we could be hurting."

"And we already know they won't wait," Trick said. "If we're not ready, they'll find someone who is."

That one statement was what had kept Wood up most of the night, an inevitable truth that they could not avoid, no matter how badly he wanted to.

There was only one choice, something he wasn't terribly excited to do, but had no way around.

"First light, I want you to peel off two men and go check on them. I know it's a blizzard, but we can't take the chance."

The kitchen fell into silence, Trick's attention focused on the floor as he thought about it. Wood had seen the pose enough to know he was working through the logistics in his head, would not speak until either a question or solution presented itself to him.

"Snowmobiles?"

"If you want," Wood said, "or the coaches. I'll leave that to you, whatever you think is the best way to get there."

"Hmm," Trick said, nodding slightly, continuing to chew on things. "And when we get there?"

"Assess and report," Wood said. "From there we'll figure out how close they are to being operational, if we should help them get up and running, or just cut our losses and figure something else out."

## Chapter Nineteen

The pressure in Yvonne Endicott's head was explosive. Just the act of waking up, of opening her eyes and letting light in, had been brutal. Following it up with a surge of fear-based adrenaline and being forced to walk across the barn had her entire body quaking.

The moment the door closed behind her, pinning her into the makeshift room, she sank down into the ancient rocking chair, the wood groaning in protest beneath her. Despite the small ceramic space heater whirring on the table across the room, the chair was cold, passing through her scrub pants and causing goose pimples to rise on her skin.

Pressing her eyes closed tight, Yvonne cupped a hand around either elbow and bent forward at the waist, drawing her body in as tight as she could. There she remained for several minutes, willing herself not to cry, trying to push aside the enormous fear that gripped her, threatening to suffocate her.

There was no way to know what time it was or how much had passed. The last thing she remembered was standing outside the hospital, but how long she had been unconscious was anybody's guess.

Yvonne raised her left hand to her face, using her fingers to gently probe her cheek. The surface was warm to the touch, the area puffy. A quick glance confirmed there were no mirrors in the room, though if she had to guess, she had a lump the size of a quarter protruding from her face. At least a few hours had passed, allowing the body to begin the healing process, nutrient-rich blood rushing to the area.

A few hours.

The thought brought a shudder as she again leaned forward, pulling herself in tight, trying to generate some body warmth, to shake the chills brought on by lying prone on the concrete floor.

Even in a snowstorm, the distance they could have traveled in that amount of time would leave a large search radius for the authorities to cover. And in this weather the odds of someone just passing by and noticing them were low. A quick glance around the room confirmed that the door was the only way in or out.

In short, she was a prisoner, trapped to do their bidding. Beyond that, she could only guess what would become of her.

Another quiver passed through her body, thinking of the two men standing outside, of the things they could do to her here, without anybody around to stop them.

A sheen of hot tears surfaced in her eyes as she thought of her situation. Two months before she had been in Atlanta, where it was warm, where things like abductions from the hospital sidewalk and blizzards didn't occur. Perhaps the occasional brush with a shady character, almost always the unwanted advances of leering men, but never anything like this.

A single tear slid down her face as she thought about it, considering if this was to be her fate, her reward for packing up everything and moving to Montana. She made no effort to wipe it away, to stifle the single sob that slid from her throat, her mind wandering, landing on the reason she was there in the first place.

Her father.

Nearly as fast as they had arrived, the tears receded, replaced by a steely resolve.

She was not alone. There were people who would notice her absence – her father, her coworkers – they would have almost certainly reported it by now. They would be looking for her, they would send others to look for her.

Yvonne's eyes slid open, her head rising a few inches, looking up from the ice crusted on her shoelaces and taking in the room around her, seeing it again for the first time.

She had been given a directive. There was a purpose for her being there. As much as she hated the notion of doing anything for these men, she knew she must.

Whatever it was, whatever task they presented her, she had to perform. Doing it meant staying alive, buying the precious time she needed for somebody, anybody, to come find her.

## Chapter Twenty

It felt like thousands of tiny needles were jabbing into my feet and ankles, the capillaries in my lower extremities begrudgingly opening up, allowing blood to rush back in. After tromping through the snow for the better part of 20 minutes, all of it dense and wet, my shoes and jeans were both soaked, making the journey back to feeling normal difficult, despite the heater in the truck on high, all of it aimed straight down at the floorboards.

Beside me I could see Ferris was enduring his own kind of pain, squeezing the steering wheel in both hands so tight the veins bulged along the backs of them. He sat with his bottom pressed back into the seat, his back arched forward, as if he might launch himself out through the windshield at any moment.

"How much we talking?" he asked, his teeth gritted, his voice low.

It was the third time already he'd asked the question, each time his animosity rising a little closer to the surface.

"Hard to tell," I said, keeping my tone clear, careful not to let him think I was getting annoyed. "Maybe an inch, a little more, in diameter. Hardly ideal conditions for forensics though."

I could see him wince slightly at the word *forensics*.

Deciding to push past his line of inquiry, to open things up a little wider, I asked, "Anything new from the guard? From the hospital CEO?"

In my periphery I could see him glance my way before going back to the street, the snow continuing to fall, the engine strain a bit louder than it had been earlier.

"The CEO was a wash. She'd been called in when things went down, didn't know anything."

"Any ideas on motive?" I asked, knowing that even someone who had not witnessed the crime could be of value, just as Meredith Shek had been.

"Naw," he said, shaking his head. "Both had nothing but nice things to say about her, said everybody felt the same way."

"Hmm," I said, bending forward. Starting mid-calf I wrapped both hands around my legs and began to rub, kneading the cold material and my skin beneath it, trying to help along the warming process. "Any chance this could have been racial?"

I had purposely moved into that position before asking the question, both so we could each clearly see the other and so he would know it wasn't meant as an adversarial question.

"No," Ferris said, turning to glare in my direction, his jaw set, before looking back out the front window. "This isn't that kind of place."

"Every place is that kind of place," I countered. "It only takes one bigot to take it there, and in my experience no town is the world is immune to those."

"Well, we are."

He made the statement with a hint of finality that seemed to coincide with a handful of other peculiarities I had noticed since his arrival at my door hours before.

While it made sense that he needed manpower and was willing to lean on anybody available with proper training, it didn't add up for him to do so that fast. There was a video that had showed what happened, and in a town the size of Glasgow he should have had a list of usual suspects and locations to check into before calling for outside help.

Especially in a blizzard, where the search area was much smaller than usual.

The fact that he had come straight to me, would have grabbed others if they were available, was a red flag. Coupled with a fuse that was getting shorter by the moment and his outright hostility at the mention of blood at the scene, warning sirens were beginning to go off for me.

There were two ways I could handle it. The first was choosing to remain quiet, to continue observing and try to ferret things out for myself.

Of course, being that subtle had never been my style, which left only option two.

"What's your angle in all this?"

The question seemed to catch him unaware, his mouth opening and closing before he turned to stare in my direction. His grip slackened slightly on the steering wheel, the truck slowing.

"What?"

"Your angle," I asked. "This means much more to you than just a kidnapping."

Instantly, the hardened demeanor came back into place, Ferris waving a hand in my direction, dismissing the notion. "I'm the sheriff here. Something like this happens in my town, it's on me."

I let a moment pass, sufficient enough that he could see I was considering his response, though in reality I was only waiting a reasonable amount of time before responding.

"Yeah, I get that," I said, "but there's more to it. Something tells me if Myles Breckman had been the one snatched instead of Yvonne Endicott, things might be a little different."

Once more Ferris turned to look at me, shock on his face. "Are you trying to insinuate that I pick and choose..."

"I'm insinuating nothing," I said, cutting him off, raising my voice to stop him before his moral tirade really got off the ground. "I'm merely stating this is personal to you. It's obvious as hell, and I'm wondering why."

"Why? Does your being here hinge on it?" Ferris asked, going back on the offensive, ducking my question in the process.

"No," I countered, "but it might go a hell of a long way in helping us solve this thing."

Ferris's right hand came up off the wheel, a finger outstretched as if he was about to give me a stern talking to, a principal on the verge of scolding an unruly child, before stopping. Slowly his hand returned to the wheel, his body relaxing as he again glanced over to me, some of the fire having drained from his features.

In its place was a twinge of weariness, the lines on his face the clearest they had been since he first arrived at my door.

"Yvonne Endicott is my niece."

Of everything in the world Sheriff Rake Ferris could have said, perhaps short of telling me she was his lover, I don't think anything would have surprised me more. I made no effort to hide that fact as my eyebrows tracked up my forehead, whatever adrenaline I had bleeding away as well.

"Your niece?"

"My niece," he said, pushing himself back against the seat behind him. The engine bucked slightly as he pressed the pedal down a bit harder, moving past a stop sign and making a right, the name on the sign along the side of the road obscured by a sheet of snow clinging to it.

While the explanation certainly explained his actions, and his reactions, to everything that was going on around us, it also managed to open up other questions.

It was obvious that the revelation was one he had hoped could be kept hidden until after this was over, the girl found and unharmed. With just one sentence his entire demeanor had shifted, changing to one now much more befitting a man of his stature.

"Where are we headed now?" I asked, signaling that it was time to move on.

A moment passed, the heater still working hard to blow out hot air, before Ferris said, "I have to give the deputies an update, and there's someone you should probably meet."

## Chapter Twenty-One

The resemblance was uncanny, once I was able to get past all the distractions and actually see the man sitting across from me. If I had to guess I would peg him as somewhere in his mid-to-late 50s, though he easily could pass for a decade older.

Again, whether that was what my eyes were seeing or my mind was computing based on everything else, I couldn't be sure.

If the man had been surprised at all for us to be calling at such an odd hour, there was no indication of it. He didn't seem to mind that Ferris knocked only once before pushing the front door open, very much awake, as if expecting us.

Seated in an overstuffed chair on the far side of the living room, he had the same watery blue eyes as the sheriff, even the same shaped face.

Beyond that, though, the resemblance was lost.

Any muscle mass the man had once had was gone, withered away, hidden beneath an enormous velour robe that gapped over a thin white t-shirt and pajama pants. Most of the hair was gone from his head, what was left snow white, like wisps of cotton.

Clear tubing ran down from both nostrils, connecting to a green oxygen canister on the floor beside him. On an adjacent night stand were a bevy of medication bottles, all lined up neatly, an empty water glass beside them.

"Hey, Mike," Ferris said, settling himself onto one end of a leather sofa. "How you feeling? You need anything?"

The man in the chair raised a hand to wave him off, making it no more than a couple inches from his lap before giving up and lowering it.

"Who's the new guy?"

The voice came out much stronger than I expected, certainly not befitting a man in his physical condition, my mind again making assumptions based on appearances and nothing more.

"This is Mr. Hawk," Ferris said, motioning for me to take a seat on the opposite end of the couch. "He's helping out in the investigation."

The man sat and stared at me, his lips moving just slightly, no sound escaping as he put things together in his mind. "Hawk? As in..."

"Yeah, that was me," I said, glancing over to Ferris, seeing him tense just slightly.

There was no point in avoiding it, the man having clearly heard about the prior incident, if not from Ferris himself, then most certainly from the townspeople. At the time I had not given much thought to how the event might be construed, having never really spent any time in town, my residing nearby more of a self-imposed exile than an effort to become a part of bucolic Americana.

What had transpired was bad, no doubt, but it paled in comparison to what would have happened had I not come back to Montana.

"My name is Mike Ferris," he said, openly appraising me. "Rake's older brother, Yvonne's father."

Neither the last name nor the skin tone matched up with what I knew about the victim, though I let it go without comment.

In my experience, it would come up soon enough anyway.

"Sergeant, U.S. Army, retired" Mike said, as if reading my thoughts. "Spent two years at Fort Benning, Georgia, enjoyed some

# Fire and Ice

time with a young lady I met there. Wasn't until after I put in my service and returned home that I even discovered I had a daughter."

The words of Meredith Shek echoed somewhere deep in my mind, reminding me that Yvonne had come from Atlanta.

Still, I remained silent, allowing him to continue. Now that an explanation was being given, I wasn't about to cut it off.

"We gave it an honest effort, but you know how things go. I had been back up here more than 15 years before we even spoke again, her calling out of the blue to tell me she was dying and that I had a teenager who would soon need a caretaker."

He stopped there, shifting his gaze from me to his lap, his head hanging as if the story had sapped most of his energy. I could see his chest rising and falling in short, rapid breaths, hear just the slightest of wheezes through the quiet living room.

"My brother has Stage 4 carcinoma," Ferris said, cutting off the story, his gaze locked on Mike. "When Yvonne found out, she offered to come up and help take care of him."

I nodded just slightly in understanding.

"Everybody we've talked to speaks of her in glowing terms," I offered. "You should be quite proud."

A single sound escaped his lips as he attempted to respond before falling into a fit of coughing, his entire body shaking from the exertion. A string of spittle hung from his lip as he hacked, his right hand rising to cover his mouth, the other attempting to brace himself in the chair.

Beside me, Ferris rose a few inches from his seat, walking hunched over toward the end table and taking up a handkerchief, passing it over to his brother.

I watched the interaction for a moment before averting my gaze, focusing on the brick fireplace directly across from the couch, a four-by-five elk mounted on the wall above it.

The coughing lasted three full minutes before he could breathe normally. As it subsided, Ferris returned to his seat, Mike resuming his position, wiping the bottom half of his face with the handkerchief.

"I am proud," he managed, his voice a fraction of what it was just a few moments before, "and damn worried. Some assholes have my daughter out there, doing God-knows-what to her."

It was obvious from his tone that he felt the same guilt I had sensed from Ferris earlier, both of them claiming responsibility for her being in Montana, for getting her home safe.

Five years before I had lost a daughter, and a wife, both taken as a direct result of my job as a DEA agent. If there was a soul on the planet who understood a parent's guilt, and the need not to have others dwell on it, it was me.

"Is there anybody up here who would have reason to do something like this?" I asked, ignoring Ferris as he turned to stare at me, a flash of something behind his eyes. "Any encounters she might have had since arriving? Someone with a long standing grudge against you?"

Another quick burst of coughing erupted, this one hidden behind the handkerchief, before Mike shook his head. "Like you said, everybody loves Yvonne. She's been a peach since she got here.

"As for me," he continued, motioning toward his lap, "if anybody had any problems, they'd just come finish me off themselves. Not like I could do anything to stop them."

He paused, his eyes glassing over a bit, before adding, "Hell, they'd be doing me a favor at this point anyway."

It was clear that Ferris had no intention of conducting any kind of interview, content to let me do it.

I was reasonably certain that if in his position, I would probably do the same. Family is meant to be a source of comfort, of support, not someone who steps in and starts poking holes into lives.

"What about her race?" I asked, putting the question out there in a voice that surprised even me. "I know there are a lot of stories about folks in Montana..."

"Supremacists, militias. Yeah, we've heard them too," Mike said. "And believe me, I've thought about that, even worried about it before she arrived."

He stared at the floor, contemplating the notion, before raising his gaze to look at me.

"I'm not saying those things – or at the very least, racial intolerance – don't exist here. Hell, you've only got to look as far as the tribes nearby to see that they do.

"I just honestly don't believe that happened here. Not with Yvonne."

## Chapter Twenty-Two

The small space heater had gone a little way to raising Yvonne's core temperature, helping her to fend off the cold. The surge of adrenaline that passed through her system once the initial shock and accompanying fear wore off had done the rest, not yet bringing her to the point of sweating, but managing to pump enough blood through her system to stave off numbness.

Once she had collected herself, rising from the rocking chair, the first thing she had to do was inventory the meager supplies that were laid out for her. Looking more like the scattered contents of an old medicine cabinet or first aid kit, what she had at her disposal was nothing more than a couple of bottles of rubbing alcohol, some gauze bandages, elastic tape, Vaseline, a nearly empty tube of Neosporin, and a small handful of individual packets of expired pain relievers, minus four Advil tablets that she had dry swallowed herself.

The effects of the Advil managed to take the harsh edge off the pounding in her head. The overhead light in the room was still too strong to even glance at, but at least she could open her eyes without succumbing to piercing pain.

In addition to the first aid supplies there were also things that would not do her or her newest patient any good, including Rolaids, throat lozenges, Nyquil, and even a couple of glycerin suppositories.

Yvonne moved them to the side with her hand, placing them along the back of the table.

Armed with the knowledge that she had precious little of even the most basic medical supplies, Yvonne turned her attention to the bed. Taking a deep breath, she allowed her shoulders to rise and fall, examining the man before her.

Buried beneath a mound of old and faded blankets, it was impossible to get a read on his height or weight, the only thing visible his face. From what she could tell he was a middle-aged man of Caucasian descent, his skin tan, a patchy beard and mustache around his mouth.

That was it.

Since she had been in the room, he had made no sound, his body lying completely still, cocooned within the blankets. She herself had taken a direct shot to the cheek with the butt of a pistol, the blow knocking her unconscious for hours. Whatever had put this man down had presumably occurred well before they came for her and showed no signs of relinquishing its grip on him any time soon.

The sound of metal slamming against metal sounded from the barn, drifting in through the opening above the door, reminding her of her deadline. She didn't know what would happen in an hour when the man returned, but didn't especially want to find out.

He had hit her once with the butt of his gun. Something told her on the next visit he might be inclined to use the opposite end.

Yvonne extended her hands toward the man, her fingertips making it almost to his chin before pulling back slightly. There they remained before again moving forward, taking the top cover and folding it down to his waist.

Beneath the wool blanket was another one just like it, stains of an indeterminate origin spread across it. Not wanting to consider the source, Yvonne moved on, finding a third and then a fourth blanket encasing the man.

As she gradually unwrapped her patient, any previous trepidation she had faded away, replaced with a growing agitation aimed at both the man before her and the situation in general. Disregarding the possibility of him waking, she stripped back the final few layers, ripping them away, leaving them piled on his thighs.

The sight she found buried beneath the covers stopped her cold, her mouth gaping open, her eyes bulging.

The man was dressed in a long-sleeved shirt that had previously been white, his torso and most of his upper arms stained with blood. The overwhelming odor of something potent, even more so than what she had smelled out in the barn, burned her nostrils, bringing tears to her eyes.

"Jesus," she whispered, staring down at the man, seeing the garment stuck to his skin in several places, the material still damp, indicating that the wounds were open.

Releasing her grip on the blankets, she took up the hem of his shirt and lifted it away from his stomach, the shirt clinging to him in places before coming free. As she did so a second, stronger smell hit her, the familiar scent of blood and decay, of singed skin.

"Chemical burns," Yvonne whispered, peeling back the fabric and staring down at what she saw.

Lesions dotted the man's chest, ranging from an inch to more than three times that in diameter. Dark body hair had been burned away, the rest matted together by blood and fluids, stuck flat against his skin.

Yvonne turned and again surveyed the supplies she'd been allotted, dismissing most of them immediately. If there was going to be any chance for her to help this man, to even begin treating the burns covering most of his body, the pain so great it had apparently shut down his nervous system, sent him into a coma for his own good, then she was going to need more than the meager pile on the table.

Even if meant doing something she really, really didn't want to do.

## Chapter Twenty-Three

The clock on the dash of Ferris's truck showed that it was a quarter past 3:00, the green glow shining brightly, almost mockingly. Time was passing, the number of things that could be happening to Yvonne almost infinite, all of them unthinkable.

Compounding that feeling was the scene outside, the headlights illuminating snow that continued piling up, wiping away any hope of tracking her abductors, slowing our own progress to a painful degree.

"Sorry about that," Ferris said, flicking his gaze over to me. "Before Yvonne came here, a lot of his care was on me."

I hadn't been exactly sure what the trip to Mike's was meant to do, the visit seeming only to slow us down rather than aid the investigation in any way. My assumption was that it was out of deference to his older brother, but with that one sentence he managed to clear things up for me.

He had gone to check on him, to make sure he was okay there unsupervised.

"Where to next?" I asked, pushing right past the statement, having known enough men like him to know that the topic wasn't one he would want to linger on.

Ferris pulled in a deep breath, holding it several seconds before letting it out.

"You know, I've been sheriff here for the better part of two decades. Seen a lot of burglary, auto theft, even a murder-suicide once, but this is my first kidnapping."

I nodded at the information, waiting for him to continue, eventually turning to glance his way as nothing more came out, before realizing what he was trying to say.

He was asking for my input, seeking advice, tacitly admitting that he wasn't entirely certain how to proceed.

In my time with the DEA I had covered only a couple of abduction cases, both instances involving key witnesses who had disappeared before they could be brought under protection. In both cases we did eventually find them, though the shape they were in precluded them from ever giving testimony, a clear message being sent by some angry cartel leader.

Still, it was a start, a basis to know the general steps for handling this situation.

"Makes sense," I said, "especially in a place like Glasgow. You'll always have the occasional assault or burglary or any number of petty crimes.

"Kidnapping though, that takes an entirely different criminal."

Ferris offered a low grunt in agreement, the sound barely heard above the groan of the engine. "Meaning?"

"Meaning, aside from crimes of passion, stealing someone's car or a television or even something off their front porch is nameless, faceless. They don't have to look someone in the eye, don't have to stare at the consequences of their actions.

"They don't see a human being, they see an object, something they want, nothing more."

Again Ferris grunted, letting me know he was following, allowing me to continue.

"But to drive up and snatch a person?" I asked. "That means it's either extremely personal, or not at all. No middle ground."

We came back up on the main drag of Glasgow, turning left without pausing at the stop sign, retracing our path from just a short time before. Already the bulk of our tracks were filled in, the edges rounded over with fresh snow.

Snowflakes continued to fly at our headlights at an angle, illuminated for just a moment before disappearing, replaced by hundreds more just like them.

Any hope we had of the snow stopping by morning appeared to be waning fast, the weather having no interest in aiding our investigation.

"Either personal or not at all," Ferris said, his tone letting me know that he wasn't quite sure what I was getting at, though he was trying.

"Right," I said, picking up on the unspoken question. "Someone either knew, and wanted, Yvonne, or they wanted something in particular, and she just happened to fit the bill."

I could almost see the light bulb going off above Ferris's head as it rocked back a few inches, parting his lips, processing the new information.

"And since we've already heard that the likelihood of someone having any ill will toward her was low..."

My eyebrows tracked a bit higher as I considered the point. "Could be the complete opposite. Maybe someone had an eye on the new girl in town, thought this was the only way to get her attention."

It was thin as hell, and extremely unlikely, but more than once I had made the mistake of jumping at conclusions. As the youngest member of my team, the guys around me had even turned it into a running joke my first year, always reigning me in, making sure I fit theories to facts instead of the other way around.

At first I had bristled at the treatment, needing a couple of embarrassing situations to play out before seeing the error of my ways.

"In a blizzard, though?" Ferris said, his face scrunched up slightly, bearing the disbelief that was apparent in his voice.

"The other side," I said, not bothering to respond to his question, letting him know that I was in agreement with his assessment, "is the non-personal.

"Something happened, meaning maybe these people needed a

doctor. They probably drove up, planning some sort of elaborate scheme for gaining entry, and found it was their lucky day."

Ferris's head dipped so low, his forehead nearly kissed the steering wheel as he turned to glance at me.

"She was standing right outside waiting for them, even stepped out into the snow to try and help."

I met his gaze, nodding once in agreement. "And there are few things in the world more recognizable than someone in a white coat and scrubs."

Ferris maintained his stance, hunched over the steering wheel, before thrusting himself back against the seat. Releasing his grip, he smashed his right hand down against the wheel, letting the sound echo through the truck for a moment before doing the same thing again and again.

"Damn it," he muttered. "Damn it, damn it, damn it!"

I remained silent, keeping my eyes aimed forward. Long ago I had discovered that it was impossible to tell someone how to react in certain situations, even less so when family was involved.

If anger, guilt, some unknown emotion that he had not yet let surface, was his natural response to things, then I was certainly in no position to tell him he was wrong.

More than a full minute passed after the outburst, Ferris steaming, his breathing much louder, easy to hear over the rumble of the truck.

"Who?" he finally whispered. "Who would be in need of a doctor, at that time of night, and be willing to go out into this to get one?"

As he asked the question, he waved a hand toward the windshield at the storm going on around us.

"And more importantly, who wouldn't just call and ask for help?" I added. "Or just bring the sick or injured person into the hospital, since they were already there?"

Again Ferris fell into silence, processing my questions, fitting them with what precious little we did know.

"None of the townsfolk," Ferris said. "If this was a local, you're right, they would have called the hospital or my office and asked for help."

"Mhm," I agreed, "but you said it yourself, the oil rigs have brought a lot of new faces into town. That narrows it somewhat, still leaves a lot of possibilities to consider."

"Yeah," Ferris sighed. "It also begs the question, what happened that they needed a doctor but couldn't risk stepping inside the hospital?"

He let the truck idle to a stop, the deep snow bringing us to a halt within seconds of his taking his foot off the gas. He left the big truck in the middle of the street and pulled his hands free from the wheel, clenching his fingers, a couple of the knuckles popping.

"Thoughts?" he asked.

"Just one," I replied, glancing over to him before motioning to the far end of the street with my chin. "Where's the most likely place for the kind of people were talking about to be during a storm like this?"

## Chapter Twenty-Four

There was no telling how long the sound had been going on before Cuddyer was made aware of it, his attention aimed down at the two pieces of copper piping he was working with, their ends coming together to form a right angle. Both were clamped in a bench vise, an acetylene torch in his hand, melding them into a solid corner piece.

Not until he felt Jasper swat at his arm, jerking his attention up, almost sending the blue flame across his skin, did he know that anything was going on.

"What?!" he snapped, his eyes flashing behind the clear plastic safety glasses he wore.

He rarely raised his voice at Jasper, knowing his sensitivity and penchant for pouting, yet another of the costs for the sake of unshakeable loyalty.

"Um, well," Jasper stammered, shrinking back a few feet. No further words crossed his lips as he motioned toward the room in the corner.

Raising the torch, Cuddyer turned off the gas feed at the base, extinguishing the flame. He held it a moment, continuing to glare at Jasper, before the reason for his intrusion became obvious.

The sound was muffled by the enormity of the room and the heavy blanket of snow outside acting as insulation.

It was persistent though.

It took a moment for Cuddyer to place it, a solid object hitting the door, loud enough to be heard but not enough to try to break free.

She was trying to signal him.

Tossing the torch down on the bench, Cuddyer shifted his gaze from the door to Jasper, nodding slightly.

"You did good," he said, watching the simple statement pull Jasper forward, leaving him beaming with pride, just as it always did.

The pounding grew louder as he walked across the floor, wondering what had happened, what she could possibly want.

The most obvious answer was that Elias was dead, his injuries too severe, whatever vegetative state he had been in eventually claiming him. The thought caused Cuddyer's stomach to tighten, bringing a whole slew of concerns, the largest being what to do with the girl.

Not especially wanting to deal with that at the moment, Cuddy pushed the notion aside, trying to call to mind any other reasons she could be summoning him. The last time he had seen her she was just short of unresponsive, wobbly on her feet, her eyes wide with fear.

For her to actually be reaching out meant she must need something, but what that would be he had no way of knowing until he opened the door to check.

Digging the keys from his pocket, Cuddyer stopped just outside the door and pounded on it twice with the side of his fist. He paused as the girl fell silent, raising his face toward the opening above.

"I'm going to open the door now. If you try anything, my associate and I will kill you. That means if you throw something at me, try to hit me, make a run for it, anything, we will kill you. Do you understand?"

"Yes."

The answer came back faster, stronger, than Cuddyer anticipated, his eyebrows rising a bit as he opened the pad lock on the door and slid it free, clasping it in the palm of his hand, ready to slap her with it if need be.

The hinges on the door whined just slightly as he pushed it open

## Fire and Ice

to reveal the girl standing in the middle of the floor, both hands shoved into the front pockets of her coat. Gone was the fearful gaze from a short time earlier, taking with it the foggy look of someone still getting her bearings.

In its place was a stare just short of resolute, making him tighten his grip on the lock in his hand.

"Show me your hands."

One at a time the girl slid them free from her coat, spreading her fingers wide for him to see.

"Keep them out," he said, taking a step into the room and glancing about.

The table along the side wall had been pulled forward into the space, the heater positioned so it was aimed the length of the bed. The supplies sitting on top had been divided into two piles.

Elias's body was visible on the bed, the blankets peeled back, the hem of his shirt pulled up to his neck. It did not appear that he had moved since they had placed him there, his eyes still closed.

"What do you want?" Cuddyer asked, adding a bit of a growl to his voice for effect.

The girl stared at him, her nostrils flaring ever so slightly, before stating, "I need some things."

"And you have them," Cuddyer said, nodding toward the table. "Use those."

"They aren't enough," the girl replied. "This man is suffering from chemical burns, he's in shock."

Cuddyer said nothing, processing what she was saying, glancing between her and Elias.

They probably should have left him at the hospital. If not for the fact that they were under a deadline, with some truly ruthless people watching the clock, he would have. It would have been hell concocting something to explain the burns, but they would have gotten through it.

That option was gone though. He needed Elias up and moving. Work was coming along outside. He and Jasper could build the rig, but they needed Elias to actually run it, to use whatever knowledge he seemed to have to produce the best stuff around.

"I told you to fix him."

"And I'm telling you I can't," the girl said, lowering her voice to match his tone. "Not with this sad little pile of crap you gave me."

Cuddyer cast his gaze to it, the scowl deepening on his features.

"I'm a doctor. I need supplies."

Again, shifting his eyes past her, Cuddyer focused on the exposed torso of Elias, at the gaping wounds covering his body, the slick sheen of raw skin shining under the overhead light.

"Make a list."

## Chapter Twenty-Five

"Bar's closed."

The man behind the battered wooden bar that ran most of the length of the room delivered the message without looking our way, his back turned as he counted out the evening's take from the cash register beside him.

Ignoring the statement, Ferris and I walked straight in, snow and water dripping from us, the wooden floor beneath us echoing with every step.

"I said. . ." the man began again, looking up into the mirror lining the back wall, stopping short as he recognized Ferris. "Sorry Rake, didn't know it was you."

"That's alright, Ned," Ferris said, coming to a stop and resting his hands against the edge of the bar.

The place reminded me of a dozen others just like it I'd been in, none within the last five or six years. Consisting of a single room, it was stretched out nearly three times as long as it was wide, the bar being the most dominant feature. Much of the remaining space was filled with small square tables, two or three chairs around each one. The far wall had doors in either corner for men's and women's restrooms, an upright jukebox sitting between them, a small area for people to dance before it.

"Heard you had some trouble in here tonight," Ferris said, "guy ended up over at the hospital."

A moment passed as the man finished his count, stacking the bills up in front of him before turning. "Naw. I mean, yeah, he went to the hospital, but there wasn't any trouble. Guy was fooling around and busted a glass, cut his hand up pretty good."

Beside me Ferris remained silent, staring at the man. In the reflection behind the bar I could see his expression relaying that he didn't quite believe the story, my own saying much the same.

"Seriously," the man said, raising his hands to either side, "half a dozen folks in here saw it. Guy even paid for the glass before going to get his hand looked at."

The man stood somewhere between Ferris and me in height, his head shaved clean. A circle beard encased his mouth, a mix of salt and pepper that was trending hard toward the former. He still wore a plain white apron around his waist, obscuring his lower body.

"Besides, how'd you hear about it?" he asked. "Things that slow in the storm you're getting calls like that?"

From the way he asked the question, the expression on his face, it was clear he had not yet heard about Yvonne Endicott. Given the time of night, and the few people who did know, it wasn't terribly surprising, though it did present an interesting situation for Ferris on how to proceed.

Play it vague and hope to gain something useful, or make it public knowledge and rely on shock value for information.

It seemed Ferris was having the same internal debate beside me, casting a look my way before turning back to the bartender. He extended a hand out to his side and said, "Ned, this is Mr. Hawk, a liaison from state law enforcement. Hawk, this is Ned Stanson, owner of the bar."

"Owner, operator, bartender, bouncer, you name it," Ned said, one corner of his mouth turning upward as he reached across and shook my hand, his grip firm and calloused.

# Fire and Ice

"Good to meet you," I said, choosing to say nothing more, allowing Ferris to steer the conversation whichever way he saw fit.

"Hawk is helping me look into the abduction of Dr. Yvonne Endicott from the hospital this evening," Ferris said, not even waiting for us to release the handshake before jumping right in, dropping the news from nowhere.

At the sound of it Ned froze, his hand locked onto mine, before blinking himself alert and releasing the grip. For a moment he stared at the sheriff, his eyes a touch wider than they'd been before, his lips parting slightly.

It was something I'd seen many times, the man trying to digest what he'd just been told, not quite believing it.

"Abducted?" Ned finally managed. "You mean, as in..."

"Kidnapped," Ferris said, "taken right off the front step of the hospital."

"Well...I..." Ned stammered, leaning forward and resting both palms against the back of the bar. "That's awful. Damn."

"Did you know her?" I asked, jumping in for the first time.

"No," Ned said, casting a glance my way before moving back to Ferris, "but I knew *of* her. Everybody in town did."

"Anybody seem to have taken a special interest in her?" Ferris asked.

"Good or bad," I added, moving a bit closer so Ned could see us both without having to ping-pong his attention back and forth.

Another moment passed as Ned remained completely still, only his eyes moving as he glanced from Ferris to me and back again.

"What? You don't think..."

"We don't know what to think," Ferris said. "But we know there are only a handful of people who would be out in something like this, even fewer places they would go."

"And we know that some of the people who would seem the most obvious for this kind of thing..." I added, my voice trailing away, allowing the insinuation to speak for itself.

The gap between Ned's lips opened a little further as he leaned back, again raising his hands, this time to extend his palms toward both of us.

"Hey, I know what you're trying to say, and believe me, you're not wrong, but I don't know anything about this," Ned said. "Like I said, I know of the girl, but I've never seen her in here, never even met her."

"We're not saying you have," Ferris said.

"We're just saying you've probably had a good look at some of the people we should be talking to," I finished.

Again Ned glanced between us, the look of shock falling away.

"I mean, I can give you some names, but the only people in here tonight were regulars," Ned said. "I can vouch for pretty much every one of them. There wasn't but a handful that came in, all of us sitting around watching hockey, shooting the breeze.

"Trust me, if somebody was planning something like that, one of us would have noticed."

Ferris's face tightened a little more as he glanced at me, the combination of lack of sleep and strain beginning to show.

"Okay," I said, "maybe the person didn't come in tonight, but the odds are still good they've been in here. I imagine you get quite a bit of business from the oil hands in town."

Ned folded his arms over his chest, the right side of his mouth twisting up as he began to work at the inside of his cheek.

"I do."

"So maybe you could make a few introductions for us," I said. "Give us some people to talk to."

"Yeah," Ferris said, seeing where I was going and jumping in. "There's no way somebody just happened to show up tonight, in a blizzard, and pulled this off. It would have had to be someone in town, meaning they've crossed paths with somebody around here before."

A palpable tension passed between the two sides of the bar, the previous shock of the situation having faded from Ned, replaced by a deep-seated loyalty to his establishment and his patrons.

Standing where I was, it was almost quaint, in a misguided sort of way.

"We open in the morning at 10:00," Ned finally said, clearly hating the words coming from his mouth, even as he said them. "Come back then, I'll introduce you to everybody in the house. Maybe somebody will be able to help you, but I wouldn't count on it."

## Chapter Twenty-Six

Mavis Azbell and Coop Baker were both sitting in the front room of the sheriff's station as we entered. They hadn't been waiting long, both still wearing their outdoor parkas despite the unnatural warmth of the office. Red blotches dotted their cheeks, giving the impression that blood was just starting to recirculate.

The two of them had pulled their chairs out from desks so they could face each other. Upon our entry Azbell looked as if she might stand, Baker making a point of keeping his feet crossed at the ankles and extended before him.

His attitude and the sneer on his face gave me the urge to backhand him out of the chair. He didn't like me, that was apparent from the moment I walked into the station hours before. In truth, the feeling was mutual.

That was far from the most important thing to focus on at the moment.

"How'd it go?" Ferris asked, leaving his coat on and walking across the floor to the desk beside Azbell. He perched himself on the edge of it, one leg raised from the floor, slush dripping from his boot.

Azbell looked up and gave a tired sigh, shaking her head in response.

"It didn't," Baker said, his voice mirroring the posture he'd assumed on the chair. "We started by going around and knocking on any door that still had lights on inside. After that we moved on to trying to tail the tracks we saw in the snow throughout town."

Rolling his head toward me, he added, "Once we figured out we were just following you guys around, though, we decided to call it a night, start fresh in the morning."

"And we were almost out of gas," Azbell added, again looking up to Ferris, the line coming out as more of an apology.

Remaining just inside the door, I leaned my back against the outer wall and folded my arms over my coat, doing my best to ignore the tone and the accusatory glare of Baker, zoning in on what he said.

"How many houses? Anybody see anything at all?"

"Don't you think I would have said something if they did?" he responded, this time choosing not to look my way, as if that would better drive home his point.

"Deputy Azbell?" I asked, not acknowledging his comment in any way, moving straight past the man intent on turning an abduction investigation into a low-stakes pissing match.

Her mouth opened just slightly as she looked quickly to Ferris before turning her attention to me. Again she shook her head, her ponytail swinging just slightly behind her.

"No," she said. "Two of the houses, the people inside had fallen asleep watching television with the lights still on. They hadn't seen anything, looked like they hadn't moved in days.

"Couple of the others, people were awake watching the storm or just sitting around. Said they'd seen headlights pass by a few times but hadn't thought anything of it, didn't even think to get a look at the vehicles."

I nodded at her explanation, being very much in line with what I would have expected.

Major storms of any variety – snow, ice, rain, even wind – always drew out a few curious onlookers, those who stood in awe of nature's power and wanted to get a firsthand look.

Under the best of circumstances, the kidnappers would have grabbed Yvonne Endicott and been gone before an alarm could have

# Fire and Ice

gone up. It would have been a long shot for anybody to see something useful, having no reason to believe they should be watching for anything.

"Anything else?" Ferris asked, glancing between the two of them, leaving the floor open for either to jump in.

"No," Azbell whispered, delivering the word as if she felt guilty that they weren't able to offer more.

"Nope," Baker said, "just a whole lot of cold."

Opposite me I could see Ferris tense just slightly, Baker's attitude beginning to rub on him as well.

"Imagine being out in it in only a pair of scrubs and a lab coat," I said.

I didn't bother to go any further, hoping the sentence would be enough to let Baker know he could stop trying so hard to be a dick.

The words seemed to resonate, again pulling his attention over toward me. He uncrossed his ankles, drawing his feet up, giving the impression that he might stand.

I felt my hands ball into fists, a slight burst of adrenaline flooding into my system, bringing with it the first real warmth I'd felt all evening.

"Why don't you guys go on home for a while?" Ferris said, raising his voice just slightly. "Get some rest, be back here first thing in the morning."

The words seemed to stop whatever it was Baker had been thinking as he turned to the sheriff and gave a short nod.

"Yeah, that's a good idea," Azbell said, pushing herself up, the sound of her down coat rustling audible across the room. "Give me a ride home, Coop?"

Still perched on the edge of his chair, Baker cast one more glance my way before turning back to Azbell, a bit of the previous fire fleeing from his expression. "Sure, Mavis."

At that he stood, both of them ignoring Ferris and me as they departed, exiting through the front door, disappearing into the night.

Once they were gone the room fell into complete silence, Ferris and I standing on opposite sides of it, the two chairs pulled into the center of the room the only signs that the other two had ever been there.

"You planning on going home, too?" I asked, my chin aimed toward the floor, my eyes lifted just a bit to glance over at the sheriff.

"Hell no. You?"

"Not a chance."

# Part Three

## Chapter Twenty-Seven

Somewhere beyond the snow, Wood Arrasco assumed, the sun was just beginning its ascent for the day. Given the time of year, daybreak should be occurring just shy of 7:00, providing the first pale glow over the countryside.

Sliding his cellphone from his back pocket, Wood thumbed the screen to life, seeing the digital readout at the top telling him it was now 20 minutes past the hour. There was still no sign of light breaking through, nothing but the continuous curtain of white blowing at a slight angle.

After his conversation with Trick the night before, Wood had remained awake for more than another hour, thinking everything through. As much as he hated the idea of sending his best man and two others out into such a frigid Hell, there was no other choice.

Cuddyer and his crew were in the unique position of being both vital to, and knowing far too much about, the operation to just let things go and hope for the best. They either needed to be assisted, making sure everything continued moving as it should, or they needed to be eliminated.

It was no secret that the FBI had been poking around The Dogs for a number of years, predating his own involvement in the organization. Over time ATF and INS had also taken a run at them, both times finding just enough to confirm suspicions but not enough to make anything stick.

This was different though. It was only recently that his group had grown from dabbling in the drug game into a full-blown player, turning an opportunity in a remote location into a lucrative business. Until now they had been fortunate to stay off the radar of the DEA, but if they were to ever come close enough to get a good look at what was going on, there would be no way to avoid a trip to prison, compliments of the federal government.

The entire organization would go down, and it would be ugly.

He hadn't bothered to share those thoughts with Maria when he finally made it to bed, nor with Trick that morning. He had an inkling that both would already understand anyway with their uncanny ability to read him.

"It letting up at all?" a voice asked, pulling Wood from his thoughts.

Trick walked up beside him, already dressed in puffy arctic gear. Thick boots covered his feet, pulled high over the bottoms of his snowsuit, the black material reflective under the overhead lights. It stopped just short of his chin, a knit balaclava covering his face.

Perched on top was a pair of orange ski goggles, ensuring not one inch of him would be exposed to the cold.

Turning to look past Trick, Wood glanced into the cavernous barn behind them, one of several The Dogs kept throughout the area. This one in particular was used simply as storage most of the year, several black Arctic Cat snowmobiles and a pair of modified vans converted to snow coaches always ready for their use.

Four men worked quickly as Wood paused to watch, loading a small trailer hitched to the back of one of the coaches with a pair of snowmobiles.

The plan, as Trick had explained that morning, was to take the snow coach as far as they could, hoping the treads on it would be sufficient to get them to Glasgow.

If not, they would disembark, leaving one man behind with the vehicle while he and the other man took the snowmobiles.

Using the coach meant sacrificing a bit of time, traveling just half the speed of the smaller machines, but it offered the benefits of warmth for the men and space for needed supplies.

While effective at covering distances quickly, the snowmobiles were limited in hauling material that might be needed to get the operation back up and running – if that was even a possibility.

If not, the coaches provided ample room for those supplies as well.

"Weather report this morning said things might break sometime late today," Wood said.

He knew that Trick was overdressed for the larger vehicle, but would be able to move quickly if the time came for them to switch modes of transportation. Whatever discomfort he might endure would be worth it in potential saved time later.

There was no way of knowing what state they might find Cuddyer and his crew in, or even if they would find them at all, but Wood needed answers, fast.

"You good on directions?" Wood asked, already knowing the answer but needing to run through the list in his mind just the same.

"Yeah," Trick said. "GPS in the van, Mac riding shotgun just in case."

Grunting softly, Wood nodded. "Who else you taking?"

"Barnham," Trick replied, keeping his explanation to just a single word.

Again, Wood nodded, glancing over his shoulder to pick Barnham out of the crowd, easily distinguishable as he stood several inches taller than the others.

The two selections had been made with care, both filling specific purposes. Mac was brilliant with navigation, had directed the crew more than once when they found themselves isolated, far from base and in need of supplies. Barnham was one of the only members who had any real experience with the meth making process, a quasi-chemist nowhere near the level of Elias, but who would be able to give a hand in the short term to ensure demand was met.

Once more a litany of things Wood could say came to mind, each one getting pushed aside. He was not a parent seeing a young child off on a road trip, did not need to remind Trick to call and check in or to be careful crossing through the heavy snow bogs.

To be sure to pack enough firepower should Cuddyer decide to get any ideas.

The man by his side was someone who had been through just about everything with him, was chosen for this assignment for that very reason.

He would succeed, just as he always had, and then he would return. There was no need to insult him now.

"I'm going over to see Chance right after I leave here," Wood said. "Ask him to up the order in the short term, just in case."

He could see Trick arch an eyebrow in his direction, saying nothing.

"I know he's not as good as Elias, but most of those guys can't tell anyway. We can't run the risk of coming up short, you know that."

Trick nodded, reaching out and patting Wood on the arm.

"We'll find him, get this thing squared away soon enough."

## Chapter Twenty-Eight

Sam Cuddyer had decisions to make, none of which he was especially keen on making. The first was how to handle the request from the doctor who made it clear that if they were ever going to get Elias back on his feet, she was going to need more than some old bandages and whatever creams and ointments Jasper had been able to find around the house.

Once the original surprise at her change in demeanor and the anger at her audacity had passed, Cuddyer realized she was right. Living in a farmhouse with two other men, any medical supplies they did have on hand were limited.

If two of the three bathed on any given day it was a miracle, let alone stopping to apply antiseptic or a Band-Aid to every knick and scratch that occurred.

That meant the first major decision facing him was who was going to make a supply run. The thought of leaving his truck in Jasper's hands, asking the man to take the treacherous route they'd traveled the night before, now with even more snowfall piled on it, made his stomach clench.

Trusting him to enter a store and get the specific list of items the doctor was requesting without arousing suspicion caused that clenching to increase.

For all of Jasper's abilities, most of them stemming from his unfailing loyalty and intense eagerness to please, being smart was not one of them.

On the flip side, asking him to stay behind and finish setting up the equipment was also too much to ask. They were behind schedule, the reservoirs complete and ready to go, but the burners were still not working correctly, the piping needed to connect them all not quite assembled.

Trusting Jasper to stay behind and handle the torch, or do much else without his supervision, could lead to a disaster worse than what Elias had caused the day before.

As much as he hated the notion of being stranded there without a means of escape, The Dogs knowing full well where it was, having paid for the thing and stocked it themselves, he had no other choice.

Jasper would have to make the trip.

That instantly led to the second decision of when was the best time to go. While it was true that every minute that passed without the medical supplies was another one that Elias was not getting the help he needed, making it that much longer until he was up on his feet, they had to be careful how they approached town.

The night before had been a stroke of luck they could not hope to duplicate, finding the doctor standing outside, even believing they were in need of aid and stepping out to them. That ensured they didn't have to enter the hospital, meant that nobody saw them or the truck.

That bit of good fortune had worked only because the hospital was open. Anywhere else that would have the supplies they needed would be closed in the middle of the night under normal circumstances, definitely with the late season blizzard howling outside.

Waiting until morning was the only option.

The decisions gnawed at Cuddyer through most of the night, chewing at his thoughts, continuing to pull his attention away from what he was doing. Twice he had been forced to cut away a botched

# Fire and Ice

weld, starting over, his impatience rising, the pressure of the situation beginning to assert itself.

Minute by excruciating minute the night had worn on, Cuddyer doing his best not to lash out at Jasper, or storm over to the room and smash Elias for putting them in this situation. One piece at a time, he discarded the heavy clothing he wore, sweat dotting his exposed skin, dripping from the end of his nose.

Forcing his attention on the task at hand, he made it just past 7:00, the faintest light starting to show through the skylights above, before turning off his torch and tossing it aside. Pulling the thick welder's gloves from his hands, he dropped them to the floor, motioning with a finger for Jasper to follow him.

Digging the list the doctor had made from his pocket, Cuddyer stopped just short of the truck.

"You know the Albertson's on the edge of town?" Cuddyer asked, watching as Jasper approached, his uncertainty obvious.

"Yeah?"

"I need you to go there and get these things," Cuddyer said, shaking the paper once, motioning for Jasper to take it.

"Cuddy, if you're hungry, we've got canned goods in the back," Jasper said, hooking a thumb over his shoulder.

Feeling the venom within him rise, Cuddyer's eyes slid closed, a loud sigh escaping.

Of course he knew there was food stacked up in the back. He and Jasper had gone to Billings to buy it months before, had sweated their asses off piling it inside the metal building that was like an oven in the August sun.

Still, he pushed past that, not wanting to put Jasper on his heels again, needing him at his best to have any hope of making this work.

"I know," Cuddyer said. "This isn't for food. These are things for Elias."

"Oh," Jasper said, his eyes and mouth all three forming into perfect circles as he looked at the list and back up to Cuddyer. "And you want me to go?"

"Yes," Cuddyer replied, his molars clamping together, veins beginning to bulge in his neck. Every bit of him wanted, needed, the conversation to end quickly, to get back to work before his anger grew into something he could no longer contain. "I need you to take the truck into town and get these things while I finish up here."

The same look remained on Jasper's face as he stood rooted in place, his fingers fidgeting without stopping.

"You know the way, right?" Cuddyer asked.

Jasper remained rigid, his head finally rocking forward just slightly. "Well, yeah, but..."

"So I need you to take this and go," Cuddyer said, again pushing the list toward Jasper. "The keys are in the ignition, there's cash in the glove box. Don't talk to anybody you don't have to, be sure to keep an eye out for cops."

Still there was no movement from Jasper, seeming much more a small child than a man in his 40s, his entire demeanor displaying he would rather do anything else in the world than the errand he was being tasked with.

"Can you do that for me?" Cuddyer asked, walking forward a step and pressing the list flat against Jasper's chest. "Can you do it for Elias?"

## Chapter Twenty-Nine

The previous six hours were spent in a haze of internet searches and taking turns brewing coffee, neither Ferris nor I saying much of anything. The tension that had started with Baker had only grown in the time since, both of us feeling the pressure of time, not particularly adept at sitting still and waiting for things to happen.

After much debate it was decided that the only logical thing for us to do was wait for Ned's to reopen, to go back and lean on everybody we could and hope something shook loose. Already, we'd spent half the night driving around town, discovering nothing, the snow limiting visibility and wiping away any trace of someone passing through.

Continuing to circle around would be futile, only asking for us to get stuck and end up stranded, unable to help should something new arise.

Sitting and waiting had never been my strong suit, a feeling I sensed was matched by Ferris. Always erring on the side of action, to be the aggressor in any given situation, were maxims that I believed in wholeheartedly when conducting an investigation, knowing it was always easier to redirect on the fly than to try and get moving from a standstill.

Never before, though, had I found myself in an investigation like this, with zero leads existing in a suspect pool that was microscopic to begin with and confined by the elements intent on keeping us grounded.

Resigned to our situation, Ferris had taken a desk on one side of the office, me on the other, each of us going to work on the internet, seeing what we could find. As a member of law enforcement, he opted to begin with trying to pull any kind of record on Yvonne, the search coming back negative, just as we knew it would.

From there he moved on to NCIC, the National Crime Information Center, and ViCAP, the Violent Criminal Apprehension Program, both national repositories supported by the FBI, to determine if any individuals with criminal pasts had relocated to the Glasgow area.

While he did that, I went to work on the web, going through every possible permutation I could for Yvonne Endicott, just to make sure we hadn't overlooked anything or jumped to the wrong conclusion. I found some bio information but not a great deal more.

It wasn't uncommon for witnesses to speak highly of a victim, especially just minutes after something as traumatic as a kidnapping, but in this instance the online evidence really did play out much the same way. From what I could piece together, she was 31-years-old, had been a lifetime resident of Georgia. She had attended the University of Georgia on a track scholarship and stuck around for med school, graduating summa as an undergraduate and magna in the MD program.

Upon completion she had moved on to Cobb County General, working as an emergency medicine resident before leaving abruptly to head to Montana to care for her sick father.

She had no Facebook account that I could find, no Twitter, the only sniff of a social media presence being something called LinkedIn, which looked to be some sort of online resume service.

Nowhere did anything resembling a threat or an enemy of any kind surface, though that didn't necessarily mean they didn't exist, maybe even being the reason for such a small online footprint.

Despite that longshot existing, I couldn't help but think I was wasting my time.

Rising from my chair, I walked back toward the same small conference room that I had first entered earlier, the smell of coffee and cleaning solution fighting for supremacy in the air. The combination made for a curious scent that tickled my nostrils as I filled a white Styrofoam cup, took a long pull of the standard law enforcement swill, and stared at the darkened screen of the television.

One frame at a time I played the clip back through my mind, having already seen it a handful of times, knowing there was nothing more to be gleaned from it.

"Believe me," Ferris said, entering the room behind me, "I've stared at that thing three times tonight. If it knows anything, it's not talking."

The statement pulled the right corner of my mouth up as I turned to face him while retreating toward the table and leaning against it. A few feet away he refilled a camouflage mug and took a drink, seemingly unaware of the taste.

"If that damn camera had only been angled a few inches to the left," I said, letting my thoughts play out loud, "we'd have a look at a license plate..."

"I know it," Ferris said, nodding in agreement. "Or if she hadn't been standing outside, what then? Would they have come in looking for someone? Would Breckman have woken his ass up long enough to notice something was going on?"

Like him, I nodded, having considered the alternatives a dozen times myself, knowing that every last one was nothing more than wishful thinking.

"Okay," I said, placing my cup down beside me and folding my arms over my chest, "we need to find someone who needed a doctor, wherever they are."

In the front of the office we heard the door open, a bevy of footsteps entering, wet rubber soles stomping against the floor.

"Hello?" Azbell called out. "Anybody home?"

"God, I hope not," Baker said a moment later, his voice loud enough to be heard but pretending to be in a whisper.

Feeling the same hostility I'd had hours before, I glanced to Ferris and asked, "What would you say to splitting up for a little while? Letting me have a run at Ned's, off the record?"

## Chapter Thirty

It was still well before 10:00 when I entered the bar, but already there were a handful of patrons spread evenly around the room, confirming the impression I'd gotten the night before that the place was the kind of neighborhood hangout that didn't really have set hours. So long as the owner was around, people were free to come and go, a real life *Cheers* without the witty one-liners and overused laugh track.

Every person in the room turned and openly stared as I walked in, leaving the snow caked along the outside of my jeans and covering the tops of my shoes as I walked across the floor to the bar, Ned spotting me halfway across, meeting me there.

"Morning," he said, adding just a bit of false bravado to his voice, raising it for the benefit of the onlookers in the room, "your sandwiches will be up in just a minute. You want to come on back while you wait?"

He fixed his gaze on me as he asked the question, the entire thing clearly a scam, a bit of showmanship for the crowd.

A moment later he flicked his eyes to the side without saying another word.

"Yeah, that works," I said. "Appreciate it."

He led the way through a swinging door I had not noticed the night before, the smell of fried food hitting me in the face as I passed through.

The galley kitchen was narrow but ran the entire length of the building. It felt at least 20 degrees warmer than the bar we'd just left.

Walking straight ahead, Ned moved past a man standing over the stainless steel flattop, an array of sausage patties, bacon, and eggs in various states of doneness before him.

Standing an inch or two taller than me, the man was about the same age as Ned, wearing jeans and a plain gray t-shirt. A bush of frizzled hair stuck up a couple of inches from his scalp, matched by a beard that was just a little bit shorter.

Switching the metal spatula he was holding to his left hand, he thrust his right my way and said, "Rigby Myers."

"Hawk Tate," I said, matching the grasp, grease and sweat brushing against my palm.

"Rigby here is my cook four days a week," Ned said, having perched himself on a stool at the far end of the room. He sat with his arms folded and one foot raised onto the bottom rung of the seat, clearly not happy with what was taking place.

"Been doing it for a few years now," Rigby added, flipping a pair of sausage patties over, sending a few drops of grease to the floor.

On cue my stomach rumbled slightly, reminding me that I was running on nothing but bad coffee.

"Ever since I mustered out," he added without looking my way.

"Army?" I asked.

"Coast Guard," he said.

"Really?" I asked, my eyebrows giving away my surprise at the statement. "Coming from Montana?"

At that he paused, staring at the wall for a moment, before shrugging and offering me a lopsided grin. "Too tall for the Air Force. You serve?"

"Navy," I replied, leaning over to Ned, questioning where this was all going without saying as much.

I mean, Rigby seemed like a fine guy, perhaps even Ned too, his clear distrust for law enforcement or anybody affiliated with it aside, but I had more important things to be doing than having a chat with a fellow veteran.

"Rigby here lives outside of town," Ned said, picking up on my question. "On the way in this morning, he noticed something peculiar."

"Well, now, I didn't say that," Rigby replied, raising the spatula and pointing it at Ned, ignoring the line of pork grease dripping from the end of it.

"Just tell the man what you did see then," Ned replied, cutting him off.

The spatula stopped mid-air for a moment, Rigby not saying anything, before returning to the grill and shuffling a couple of eggs. As he worked, he glanced my way and said, "You ever, I don't know, pick up on something that just shouldn't be there?"

I did know the feeling, far better than either of these men could ever realize, more than I wanted to get into at the moment.

"What did you see, Rigby?"

"Well, that's just it," he said, dropping the spatula down and turning to face me full, his hands on his hips. "I didn't *see* anything, but I damn sure smelled it."

## Chapter Thirty-One

Everything happened quickly, one thing right after the other, Yvonne barely having time to process each before the next occurred.

The first was the sound of the truck engine starting, something enormous and rumbling, that drew her attention to the door. For a moment she thought maybe they were preparing to move the man beside her, that the requests she made hours before had fallen on deaf ears.

That thought brought a nauseating feeling to her stomach, coupling with the persistent throbbing in her head, making the world sway beneath her. Leaning forward, she pressed both hands down on the table, feeling it bow slightly beneath her weight, the omnipresent whir of the heater just a few inches away.

Next came the din of the outside door moving, the screech of frozen metal rolling in icy tracks. In her earlier state she hadn't even noticed the door and wondered if it was being opened or closed.

Just as fast as that sound began, a piercing howl filled the room, so loud she thought for sure it would wake the man beside her. Instead, the rush of cold air found every available crack in the makeshift structure, dropping the temperature 10 degrees almost instantly.

Goose pimples stood out on her skin as she nudged herself over to the heater, blocking its path from her charge, letting it hit her center mass.

For just a moment she considered him behind her, before dismissing the thought.

This was not a hospital, and he was not her patient. She would do what she could to help him, but her chief concern was her own survival, ensuring that should the opportunity arise, she would be strong enough to escape.

Already she was weak, her head continuing to ache, any quick movement causing the world to sway around her. More than 10 hours had passed since she'd had anything to eat or drink, dehydration amplifying the effects of her concussion.

As a physician she was bound by the Hippocratic Oath, but she certainly couldn't remember anything about helping someone who had knocked her cold and carried her away into a blizzard.

The wind persisted as the dominant sound in the room, filling Yvonne's ears, causing her to reach for another packet of Advil, before finally being replaced by the sound of the truck kicking into gear. The roar of the diesel engine picked up as it started to move.

Rising to full height, Yvonne turned and stared at the door, wondering if it would burst open at any moment, if she should be ready to move. Perhaps they would just take the man, leaving her to her own devices, cold and alone, but at least alive.

Or maybe the men were taking her advice, were going off to retrieve the medical supplies she needed.

Raising both hands to her face, Yvonne covered her eyes and sighed softly. It was possible. They were listening to what she was saying, if not seeing her as an actual person, then at least as a source of expertise to heal their friend.

His health and well-being depended on keeping her alive as well.

Just as fast as the noise of the engine grew, it began to recede, the banging of tire chains against the frozen ground diminishing as the truck pulled away, followed by the racket of the door closing.

Again, Yvonne took a deep breath, her eyes watering just slightly as her shoulders rose and fell by her side.

There was no way they would leave someone behind, especially someone they had spent so much effort trying to save. They were making a supply run, would soon return with the items she needed to help him.

The thought was so overwhelming that Yvonne lost focus of the world around her. She didn't hear as the door finished closing, didn't even notice the sound of heavy footsteps moving fast for the door.

Not until it burst open beside her was she even aware that only one of the men had departed, the leader still very much present, his face twisted up in anger. On his hands was a pair of heavy leather gloves, the ends of them stopping halfway up his forearms.

The rest of his arms were exposed to the shoulder, his outer layers of clothing having been stripped away, revealing sinewy muscles etched with heavy tattoos, the skin the consistency of leather.

Shoving the door as hard as he could, it swung back against the wall, a banging sound echoing through the room, causing Yvonne to jump. Any trace of the controlled menace he represented before was replaced now by a burning rage that threatened to lash out at her at any moment.

"How is he?" the man asked, striding across the room and staring down at the exposed torso of his friend. He remained there a moment before turning to face Yvonne. "I said, how is he?"

Again, she flinched just slightly, her hands, buried inside the front of her coat, beginning to tremble.

"He's the same," Yvonne whispered. "Until we can ease the pain he's in, his body won't let him wake up."

Chancing a look in his direction, Yvonne could see veins running down his forearms, his blood pressure high, causing them to stand out beneath the skin.

This was not good. It changed things, shifting her previous assessment and calculations tremendously. Before, she had believed that he was the leader because he was the strong one, focused on his job and able to direct others.

Now she could see that he was a proverbial powder keg, capable of going off at any moment.

Which meant the odds of her surviving dropped considerably.

Nudging herself back an inch or two, Yvonne kept her attention aimed at the ground, careful to avoid eye contact, to not even give the impression that she was aware of his presence. There she remained as he continued to assess his partner before turning to stare at her, his breathing loud, the chemical scent on his skin even more pronounced, mixed with the stench of old sweat.

"I told you to fix him."

Once, twice, Yvonne opened her mouth to respond, again feeling the tears come to her eyes.

There was no warning for what came next, no more words, nothing that would indicate she should brace herself. All there was was the quick flick of the man's arm, whipping by in a blur, the back of his glove connecting with her jaw.

So fierce, so unexpected, was the impact that it lifted her from her feet, the momentum carrying her backwards and depositing her in the rocking chair, where she remained as the man stomped from the room, slamming the door behind him.

## Chapter Thirty-Two

I didn't even bother going into the sheriff's station. I had no desire for another run-in with Baker, just another in an unfortunate string of local cops I'd encountered over the years, intent on proving their worth by standing up to the outsiders who were called in to help.

I also didn't care to waste the time discussing the news Rigby Myers had shared when the only person who needed to know was the sheriff.

Using the side entrance to the bar, I had cut through the alley, clutching a grease-splotched paper sack in my hand. Using the buildings on either side of me for cover, I was able to stay shielded from the wind and the whipping snow until just a block south of the station before turning and using the trench I'd carved a half hour earlier to get back.

Standing outside on the sidewalk I could see all three of them in almost exactly the same position as I'd left them, Ferris sitting perched on a desk, coffee mug in hand.

From the outside looking in it almost seemed like just another day at the office, with the exception of the strain on Ferris's face.

I raised my hand to catch his attention as he turned his head to the window.

It took just a moment for him to register who I was and what I wanted, before he lowered his mug and strode across the floor, grabbing his coat from the rack by the door as he went. I met him as he emerged, shrugging on the heavy garment, the wind twisting the hair on his head.

"You have something?" he asked.

"Yeah," I said, jutting with my chin toward his truck parked along the curb, a few inches of fresh snow covering the hood, a couple more shoved up along the tires by the wind. "You up for a drive?"

Ferris gave no response as he set off toward the driver's side, raising his knees up high to get over the snow bank and plunging his foot straight down into it. One leg at a time he made his way forward. I waited until he was halfway there before doing the same, heading for the passenger side.

I had spent so much time tromping through piled snow that feeling in my lower legs was only a distant memory. I could see the white slush clinging to my jeans, knew it was packing in around my ankles, but I paid no attention as I went for the truck, pulling the door open and climbing inside.

"What did you find, and what's in the sack?" he asked, shoving the keys in the ignition and cranking on the starter. Three long times it whined in protest before kicking over, a plume of icy air flying from the vents and hitting us square.

"Guy named Rigby Myers," I opened. "You know him?"

"Yeah, he's one of ours," Ferris said, making it clear that Myers was originally from Glasgow, a lifer, unlike many of the oil hands who had begun to trickle in. "Long-time Coastie, made his way back here a couple years ago."

I grunted slightly, matching it up exactly with what the men had told me a short time before.

There had been no reason for them to lie, both knowing I was working with Ferris and would easily be able to verify anything they said, though it still helped to know that they were above board on something so basic.

Made everything else they shared a little easier to believe.

"He see something?" Ferris asked.

"No, but he said he smelled something that had no reason to be there," I said. "Like wood smoke, but with a heavy chemical trace to it."

I glanced over to see Ferris's face scrunch slightly, computing what I'd told him.

"Okay, the wood smoke is straight forward enough, damn near every house in town having a fireplace. Chemical though?"

"That's what I thought," I said. "Might be worth checking out, at least give us a heading on the next place to take a look."

"Right," Ferris agreed. He nodded, putting the truck into drive and circling out away from the building, doing a lazy U-turn through the middle of the street and heading back in the opposite direction.

Not once did he ask me where Myers lived or where he had been coming from, apparently knowing his residence, and damn near every other one in town.

"You catch any hell walking in there?" Ferris asked.

"No, but he was quick to head me off the second I walked in. Even gave us these as a ruse," I said, holding up the paper bag and shaking it twice.

"Ha!" Ferris spat, the first crinkle of a smile I'd seen all night crossing his face. "Let me guess, hustled you off before any of the regulars even got a good look?"

"That he did," I said, realizing it was probably not the first time Ned had employed the trick.

Outside, the world was much lighter than our previous trip, the sun overhead buried somewhere behind a thick cover of clouds and frozen precipitation. It managed to push through just enough light to make everything glow, giving way to a world awash in white.

Overall, it looked like the weather was easing up a bit, what we were seeing now as much fallen snow being whipped around by the wind as fresh snow falling from the sky.

Not that it mattered much either way.

A whiteout was a whiteout.

Leaving Ferris to concentrate on driving, I opened the top of the sack and removed a breakfast sandwich, releasing the aroma of pork grease into the cab. I placed the first sandwich on the console between us for the sheriff before extracting the second one and tossing the sack to the floor.

Silence fell as Ferris worked us out past the edge of town, the snow a little deeper on the road as I gnawed on the food. After an entire night spent with nothing but station coffee it was a Godsend, the protein and grease passing straight into my stomach, soothing my body and lifting my spirits.

Six bites, and it was gone.

"You want that other one, have at it," Ferris said. "No way can I eat at a time like this."

If he was trying to make a backhanded statement about his surprise that I could, I let it go without a second thought as I took up the sandwich.

In my earlier days, my partners on the FAST team had joked that when working a case, I would forget everything else, often times failing to eat for an entire day. Only over time had I come to discover the necessities of fueling up when I could, both in terms of food and sleep, banking what would undoubtedly be needed later.

There was no way to know how much longer this investigation would run or when my next meal might be. If I was going to be of any help to Rake Ferris, or Yvonne Endicott, I needed to be at my best.

My guess was there would be a time in the not-too-distant future that the sheriff wished he had done the same, though I wasn't about to mention it.

I took the second sandwich a bit slower, dragging it out to 10 bites before discarding the wrapper, balling everything together and stowing it beneath the front seat. Reaching out beside me I depressed the button to lower the automatic window, the control making a clicking noise before stopping, the mechanism frozen solid.

I tried a second time, getting the same response, before tugging on the door handle and cracking the entire thing open, cold air pouring in around us.

Holding the door open a few inches, I waited nearly a full minute before slamming it shut, seeing Ferris look my direction, confusion on his face.

"Flushing the aroma out," I said. "Rigby Myers said he picked up on the scent. All we could smell was sausage."

Grunting in response, Ferris dipped his head toward the right side of the road and said, "Rigby lives about two miles on up ahead here. We should be coming up on it anytime now."

Leaning forward, I matched Ferris's pose, the vents piping air in from the outside just a few inches from my face. There I remained, my backside buried in the corner of the seat, my face turned to the side, waiting.

It took more than a mile for it to come to me, Rigby's words ringing in my ears the moment it did.

He was right. I was picking up on something that definitely shouldn't be there.

"You got it?" I asked, turning my head to the side, fighting to see past the blowing snow toward anything along the road that might be the source of the scent.

A moment passed before Ferris responded, presumably waiting until he too caught the smell before commenting.

"There it is," he finally muttered, a touch of disgust in his tone. "What the hell is that?"

The odor wasn't one I was especially familiar with, but fortunately for us it was one that was distinctive enough to be recognizable even after limited exposure.

"Wood smoke," I said, parroting Rigby's words from earlier, "and ether."

"Ether," Ferris repeated, saying it almost subconsciously, as if trying to place it in his mind. "As in..."

"Yep," I agreed, "meth."

The word hung between us for a moment, each of us fitting that in with what we had, not wanting to jump to any hasty conclusions, but certainly not wanting to ignore any obvious ones either.

"You think..." Ferris began, letting his voice trail off, reaching the same thought I had just a moment before.

"An explosion would explain why they needed a doctor in the middle of the night, why they couldn't just walk inside to get treatment."

Adjusting himself slightly behind the wheel, Ferris resumed his death grip on it, his mouth pulled back into a tight line.

I had no way of knowing what he was thinking, but to me the next thought was an obvious one.

"I don't suppose you have an extra weapon in here, do you?"

## Chapter Thirty-Three

Jasper Maxx wasn't concerned about the people inside the store. Dealing with the occasional stare was something he was used to, the kind of thing that had occurred his entire life. His mama had always said it was because he was special and people were attracted to things that were special, but his daddy had always just said it was because he was an idiot and people liked to gawk at idiots.

As a kid Jasper always tried to believe his mama, to think that she would never lie to him.

Now, 30 years later, he knew his daddy was right, just as he had been about most things, no matter how much twisted pleasure he got from pointing them out.

Each person in the store seemed to be glancing his way as he walked through the aisles, his shoulders rolled forward, holding the piece of paper in front of him. Every few seconds he glanced down at the blue ink scrawled in even lines, at the spots where water had smudged it just slightly.

The list, that small scrap of paper, was what he was most concerned with. Not because of anything written on it, even though it might be the key to helping Elias, but because Cuddy had trusted him with it.

In all their years together it was the first time Jasper could remember being allowed to drive, much less having such an important task put on his shoulders.

For as bad as the last 18 hours had been, this was a turning point in their group. No longer was Jasper the lowest of the three, the ne'er-do-well who could be given tasks of menial labor and nothing more. Now it was Elias's turn to be the screw-up, the one getting the dismissive look from Cuddy that cut to the core.

The mere thought of it, of a new world view in which he was important, in which he mattered, drew Jasper's head up a little higher as he scanned the aisles, in search of the things on his list.

Starting at the top, Jasper took up a red plastic basket from the floor beside a front register, rounding the aisles until he found Neosporin ointment, placing six tubes in the basket before moving on.

Second on his list were cotton swabs, starting over again on Aisle One, beginning his slow meander back through the store. He paid no attention to the young girl at the end of the second aisle pointing toward him, at the woman in the red apron looking his way and nodding slightly.

All he could think of was the next item on his list, of how proud Cuddy would be when he returned with everything, having braved the storm and saved the day.

Halfway down the third aisle he found the cotton swabs, two options presenting themselves, one box containing items just a few inches long, used for cleaning ears, the other, longer sticks with cotton on one end.

Glancing down at the list for help, Jasper stared at the words on the paper, scratching his head in thought.

"Excuse me, sir?"

The sound barely penetrated Jasper's consciousness as he examined the items before him, trying to decide which he needed.

He couldn't imagine that cleaning Elias's ears in his current state would do much good, but at the same time he didn't know what most of the items on the list were for.

"Sir?"

The second time, the question was asked a little louder with a bit more urgency to it, enough to grab Jasper's attention, ripping him from his thoughts.

"Hmm?" Jasper asked, his eyebrows rising as he turned to see the same woman in the red apron he'd noticed a few moments before standing in front of him.

"Is there something I can help you with?" she asked, a look on her face Jasper couldn't quite decipher, just knowing that it sent an uncomfortable feeling into his stomach.

"Oh...no," he managed, shaking his head, letting his hands fall by his side. "Just need to get the things on my list."

Rocking forward a few inches, the woman extended a hand toward him, her attention on the paper clutched in his hand. "Well, let me take a look here, maybe I can help."

A flash of anger, fear, agitation, roiled through Jasper as his hand shot back, his entire body recoiling out of her reach. There he remained as he stared at the woman, his head slowly shaking.

There was no way anyone, not this woman or anybody else, was going to keep him from doing what Cuddy told him to.

This was his chance to shine.

"No thanks, ma'am. I just need a few things, and I'll be on my way."

## Chapter Thirty-Four

I'd half expected Ferris to look at me like I was crazy, telling me there was a wrench or hammer or something equally archaic buried under snow in the bed of the truck if I needed a weapon. I still had the MK-3 tucked away in its usual position, but given the potential enemy and the elements, there wasn't much difference between that and carrying a blunt force tool.

To be fair, my status in the investigation was fuzzy, and despite my extensive background with the navy and DEA, having handled a weapon almost daily for a decade, I was now a civilian.

Albeit one living in Montana, where firearms were much more a common part of life than, say, anywhere else in the country.

The other half of me expected him to come out with an old revolver, the barrel rusted, a relic from another time that had been buried on the rear floorboards of his truck for years. It seemed most every person past the age of 40 I'd encountered since moving up north from southern California had at least one around, many displaying them on their mantles, others using them as paper weights.

No part of me expected what he handed me though.

The Kimber Ultra Carry was a newer model of something I had

used a bit with the DEA, a smaller piece that was easily concealed, designed for a holster that rode under the arm, hidden by a jacket. Matte black in finish, it held a mid-sized magazine and operated on a gas powered projection system, capable of emptying the entire clip in a couple of seconds.

Ferris passed it over to me without comment, extracting the weapon from the base of the driver's side door and handing it across as casually as if it were a soda.

The location and condition of it gave me the impression he had brought it along for this very purpose, though I said nothing as I slid it from the leather holster it was in and checked the slide, making sure a round was chambered, the safety on.

Unlike a majority of my brethren from both previous careers, I had never been an overt gun enthusiast. In my new job as a guide in Yellowstone I made sure to have at least one on hand at all times, never quite knowing when I or my party might unexpectedly come upon a bear and her cubs or a mountain lion crouched over a fresh kill.

Pacifists would say that a can of spray should be sufficient in such situations, but not once had I ever heard someone make that claim after standing in the forest, feeling their heart race as an animal stared at them, blood lust in its eyes.

In addition to a pair of handguns for use on the trail I had a Winchester 30.06 that was purchased a few months before, a weapon that oddly enough had a few human kills under its belt thanks to the incident at the cabin that everybody in town seemed to be intimately familiar with.

Of the three, none were with me, the Smith & Wesson still under my pillow at the hotel the only one even within 100 miles of me, all others safely locked away at my office in West Yellowstone. The trip to Glasgow was intended to be a quick one, the need for additional weaponry never once crossing my mind.

Placing the Kimber on the console beside me, I turned my attention back to the world outside, the smell of ether growing stronger, pulling us forward. Beside me Ferris alternated glances between the windshield and his side window, both of us scanning.

### Fire and Ice

I was the first to spot it, my visibility cut to less than 90 yards, the truck almost on top of the place before I noticed it.

"There," I said, raising my right hand and tapping it against the cold window, the contact making a dull thumping sound as I leaned forward.

Sitting back about 30 yards off the road was a small white clapboard farmhouse, standing two stories tall. The white of the exterior was matched in color by the blanket of snow covering the roof.

"You sure?" Ferris asked.

Standing behind the house were the remains of some sort of structure, either a large garage or a small barn.

By the time my gaze reached the opposite end there was nothing left at all, the back of the structure seeming to have been blown away, shards of charred debris sticking up out of the snow.

"Yeah," I said, leaning away from the vents as Ferris pulled past the top half of a mailbox along the road, the post it sat on buried in the snow. Hooking a hard right, he laid on the gas, the front of the truck bucking as we pushed forward.

Both of us remained silent as we drew closer, the house and the grounds looked deserted. Nowhere in any of the windows could a light, or any kind of activity, be seen as we made our noisy approach.

"Doesn't look like anybody's home," Ferris said, stating the obvious as he pulled to a stop and lowered his head a few inches to look up at the front of the house.

"No, but they have been," I said, motioning to a hollow spot just outside the garage, the snow clearly far less deep than everywhere else, large enough for at least one vehicle. Several sets of footprints, looking more like dents in the snow, dotted the area around it.

Ferris nodded, reaching up inside the flap of his jacket and tapping at the butt of his weapon. "I'll go try the front door, just to be sure. You want to go around and check out that building?"

I wrenched the front door open with only a nod in response, the same pervasive wind that had been on us for days gripping me in a swirl, managing to pull away any warmth from the truck in just seconds. It rode along the inside of my coat and up under my shirt, causing my teeth to clamp together as I pushed off for the side of the house.

There was no point in trying to raise my feet above the snow and take things one step at a time the way the sheriff did, the stuff too deep to bother. Instead, I locked my knees and pushed straight ahead, the fronts of my shins shoving snow to the side like a bulldozer, twisting my hips for leverage.

My first stop was the spot by the barn, the scene revealing what we already knew and not much else.

Just like at the hospital, there appeared to be two people present, one for each side of the truck. From what I could tell both had made multiple trips, the rear of the truck backed up just short of the garage.

What or who they were loading I could merely speculate at, the only clear evidence provided being that they had been gone for several hours at a minimum, probably most of the night.

The smell of ether and wood smoke, the same exact combination Rigby Myers had alluded to, hung thick in the air, the wind doing little to carry it away, the scent seeming to hover over the ground like a fog.

Each step closer to the remains of the structure seemed to bring me closer to the source, the odor causing my eyes to water, the wind pulling the moisture away just as fast.

It appeared to be a barn, or at least what used to be one. If I were to guess, I would estimate that at some point it had been nearly as large as the house, though less than one-third remained.

What from the road had looked to be a fire actually appeared to be more the result of an explosion, powerful enough to rip away most of the structure.

As I walked closer to the damage, I was forced to stop as bits of wood and metal smashed into my legs, shrapnel and debris having been tossed from the blast, buried in the snow.

Setting my jaw, I slowly worked my way over the last few yards before entering the remains, the stench almost overwhelming. Standing there I could see pieces of heavy wooden tables, most of them turned into matchsticks, some copper piping twisted and scorched, and in one place, a crater that had once been the floor.

Even with several inches of snow clinging to every surface, it was clear that this place had all the makings of a full-fledged meth lab, a large one.

"Jesus," Ferris said, stomping his way across the backyard toward me, a red handkerchief pressed to his face. "How the hell can you stand to be in there like that?"

Glancing in his direction, I scrunched my nose once at him before turning back to face the carnage before me.

"Busted my nose on a case in Panama years ago," I said, my delivery deadpan. "Lost some of my ability to smell stuff."

Ferris used my tracks to work his way forward, coming to a stop beside me, panting loudly.

"Son of a..." he said, the hanky dropping away to reveal his mouth hanging open as he gawked at the sight before us.

"Yep."

"Meth?" he asked, the question seeming to seek more confirmation than anything.

"Oh yeah," I said, "and this is high end stuff too. These guys weren't using lye and fertilizer in their bathtub here."

His jaw still hanging open, Ferris glanced in my direction, seemingly wanting to ask me how I knew all of that, before turning back to the tangle of piping before us.

"Best guess," he asked, "how much could a lab like this knock out?"

At the time I left the DEA, meth was still just beginning its ascent to prominence. It was seen as the younger, uglier stepsister of the major drugs on the market, a minor blip compared to cocaine or heroin, the kind of thing trailer trash brewed up one batch at a time, more often lighting themselves on fire than producing usable product.

The majority of my time was spent abroad, working our way through the South and Central American cartels, pissing off a lot of people in our attempts to control the drugs entering the States.

It was some of those people who eventually drove me away from the agency, taking away the two people I held most dear in the world as a parting gift.

"Based on what's left here," I said, "and assuming the rest of the place looked much the same? I'd say, maybe couple hundred pounds per batch."

"Jesus," Ferris repeated, his voice low. He just stood there, not saying anything, taking in everything before him.

It was not the first time I'd seen such a reaction, someone like him believing they were doing a good job, that their community was insulated from any of the major evils of the world.

Those were the things that went on elsewhere, plagued major cities, but surely not their little corner of Montana.

"I'm guessing nobody was home?" I asked, stopping him before he could get drawn too deep into thought, needing him to remain in the present.

There would be time for pity or loathing or whatever other self-imposed emotion he was feeling later.

"Uh," he replied, opening his mouth twice before saying, "no, nothing."

The news didn't surprise me in the least, the outside evidence already telling me they had packed up and left, most likely right after the explosion.

"Any idea who owns the place?"

"Used to," Ferris said, "but it sold a couple of years ago. I'll call in and have Mavis run it as soon as we get back to the truck."

"Hmm," I said, nodding once as I looked down at the wreckage, the scene already having told us everything it was going to for now.

As best I could tell, our working theory seemed to be looking the most likely. Whoever lived here had quite a lucrative lab going until they messed up, ripping the place apart. A hunch said that the head chef was inside when it happened, surviving the ordeal but getting torn up pretty good in the process.

That's where Yvonne Endicott entered the picture.

"The question still is," I said, thinking out loud, "where would they take an injured man and the doctor? They knew they couldn't stay here, knew they would have to have someplace to go so she could work on him."

Beside me Ferris started to answer, raising his eyebrows as he considered the information, his mouth opening slightly. Before a single sound crossed his lips, I cut him off, reaching out and grabbing his arm, my head twisted to the side.

"Shh," I hissed, eyes narrowed, listening intently. "You hear that?"

## Chapter Thirty-Five

Trick Reynolds's entire body was numb. Despite the fact that the snow coach had been purchased directly from Xanterra, the very company that conducted winter excursions throughout Yellowstone, and was equipped for covering long distances, four hours was still too long to spend seated in one position that didn't involve straddling a motorcycle.

The trek west had started just after 7:00 a.m., pulling away from the garage The Dogs kept all of their winter gear in, including the coaches and snowmobiles. At the time of their purchase both he and Wood had questioned the wisdom in spending so much on something so frivolous, but the decision was made far above their station, one of the last made by the old regime.

Upon assuming control, they had agreed it would be foolhardy to cast aside something potentially useful, especially given where the bulk of their business now resided.

This was the first time Trick had ever been forced to ride in one of the converted coaches, as far as he knew the first time either had ever been out of the barn for anything more than washing or tune-ups.

From a purely objective standpoint there was nothing wrong with the vehicle, the interior outfitted in leather and fine wood, plush carpeting on the floor. Two captain chairs up front, a padded bench seat behind it, a second one in the rear removed to make room for additional storage.

On this particular trip that meant a pair of extra fuel cans, some tools and copper piping to help nudge along the operation at Cuddyer's, and enough small arms to take out an army, should it come to that.

Even with all the trappings of a luxury ride, the combination of keeping the heat adjusted for their attire and the lack of shocks on the snow tracts gave Trick the sensation that he was riding in a World War I tank. Every small bump managed to lift him from his seat, each small shift in the landscape tossing him from side to side.

In the passenger seat Mac seemed to be having much the same experience, his mouth clamped shut as he worked the handheld GPS device.

Mac had a full name, but it had been so long since anybody used it, Trick couldn't remember what it was. He was pretty sure the Mac moniker was an abbreviation of his last name – MacMillan, perhaps – but he wasn't sure.

Not that it mattered much anyway.

The man had been with The Dogs for more than two years now, having joined up after Wood took over, another one claimed in the rapid member expansion that took place as the old guard was removed.

A glance into the rearview mirror showed no sign of Barnham, meaning he was still stretched out on the bench seat, his feet flat on the floor by the door.

At six and a half feet tall, Barnham was far and away the most distinguishable of the group, whether standing up or folded onto a chopper. In a previous life he had been a chemist for a small company somewhere down south, having moved north under personal invite of Wood, his expertise serving well in their newest financial undertaking.

"How we looking?" Trick asked, glancing over to Mac.

"Just stay on this road," Mac replied, his voice a deep baritone that always reminded Trick of Barry White, though he would never admit to a soul in The Dogs he knew who that was. "Clear sailing on in."

"ETA?" Trick asked, shifting his weight over onto his right haunch, attempting to give his left side a break from the continued pressure of sitting on it.

"No clue," Mac said, arching an eyebrow as he glanced to the speedometer and up to Trick. "But we've got about a mile and a half."

Three hours ago the attempt at levity would have drawn a smile from Trick, but at this point all he could do was grunt in response.

The reasoning behind the trip was sound. He and Wood had sat at that kitchen table sharing Cold Smoke beers and analyzing it from every angle, jointly deciding it needed to be done. At the time he had agreed with it, still felt that way now.

If he didn't, he would have told Wood, who would have listened.

It was what allowed their dynamic to work, had changed the culture of The Dogs for the better in the preceding year.

Still, it did nothing to lift Trick's mood as he pressed just a little harder on the gas, watching the RPM's rise by nearly 1,000, the speed barely increasing as they rumbled on ahead.

"Alright," Mac said, "we're getting close now."

He held the small device out in front of him, the tip of it just a few inches from the dash as he looked out his side window, Trick doing the same.

In the rear they could hear movement as Barnham rousted himself, taking up a post and peering into the snow swirling about the van.

"What are we looking for again?" Barnham asked, the van shifting slightly as he moved over behind Trick, pressing a shoulder against the outer wall and peering through the window, his head now visible in the rearview.

"Just the house right now," Trick said. "We need to find Cuddy and his guys, need to see how bad the lab is, then figure things out from there."

"Well, I can already tell you the lab is toast," Barnham said, letting out a small groan as Trick glanced to the back seat, seeing the large man press both palms into his eye sockets for a moment.

"Yeah, why's that?"

"Because I can smell it," Barnham said, "and trust me, that's not how any functioning lab is supposed to smell."

Despite his position, Trick had never really had much experience with meth. He had been around it a fair bit, never once taking even a sample, knowing his own personality well enough to know there was a weakness for indulgence.

He had moved it, he had brokered more than a couple deals involving it, but never had he gone near the production or consumption sides.

That was Barnham's department, and if the man said something was wrong, he would take him at his word.

"Quarter mile and closing, according to this," Mac said, all three falling silent as they stared out the windows, trying in vain to see past the blowing snow, the wind whipping the top layer up from the ground and enveloping the van.

For the first time all morning Trick let the misery he felt at being holed up in the coach fall away, his focus on the world outside, hoping for there to be at least something positive for him to work with when they arrived at their destination.

Little by little the house came into view, pulling away every bit of that hope. Dread, anxiousness, even a bit of rage, flooded in to take its place.

"That's not Cuddy, is it?" Mac asked from the passenger seat, registering what he was seeing at the same time as Trick.

"Get the sat phone up," Trick said, ignoring the question as he again leaned on the gas, moving straight past the driveway without slowing. "Prez isn't going to be happy about this."

## Chapter Thirty-Six

Standing in the open end of what remained of the barn, there was no way anybody inside the snow coach didn't see Ferris and me. Given the distance, and the snow continuing to swirl around us, it was impossible to get a clear look at the driver or any passengers, but it wasn't hard to notice the way the vehicle slowed upon approach, before hitting the gas and speeding past the house.

As much as a snow coach could anyway.

"What in the hell?" Ferris muttered, shifting just slightly to watch the vehicle, staring until it disappeared on the opposite side of the farmhouse, the sound of its engine revving the only sign of it passing.

"Snow coach," I said, not sure if his question was rhetorical, but answering it just the same. "Without a doubt the first time I have ever seen one outside the park, or pulling a trailer behind it."

"Any guesses as to what might be under the tarp in the back?"

Like Ferris, I stood staring at the back of the farmhouse, wishing I could see through to the other side, could get a better look at whoever had just driven past.

"Best guess? Either snowmobiles or supplies."

"Supplies?" Ferris asked. "As in, food and water?"

To that I shook my head slightly, already drifting away from the shattered barn, taking my first step back into the deep drifts surrounding us. "Food and water they could easily store in the van. Whatever was back there they weren't as concerned about the elements getting to."

I left the explanation at that, letting Ferris fill in the rest.

Before us were the remains of a large meth production facility, all of it constructed from wood, plastic and copper. Even the raw materials needed to feed it could be safely sealed and stored without concern for snow touching it, a simple tarp being more than sufficient to transport everything that was needed to get the place back up and going.

As my mind continued to piece together what we had just seen, my legs began to move, my pace picking up to a hurried walk before moving into a run, arms and legs pumping, fighting in vain against the deep snow piled around.

Thus far, in the 12 hours and counting that we had been on this case, we had seen at most a handful of vehicles out moving around. A couple of the regulars at Ned's, Baker and Azbell on their patrol, a person or two going to the hospital or Albertson's. None beyond the edge of town.

For somebody to have been this far out, driving that oversized contraption, was too far a stretch.

My quads and calves burned as I pushed on, a dull stabbing arising in my ribs. Ice crystals clung to the air, scratching my throat as I pulled in deep gulps, ignoring the bits of wood and metal passing against my legs, arms pumping, trying to develop some momentum.

I had no way of knowing if Ferris was behind me, no sounds reaching my ears beyond my own panting, the howling whistle of the wind as I made it to the indentation on the driveway. I plowed straight through the shallow snow before delving into the deeper stuff again, using the trough Ferris and I had cut on the way in, moving directly for the truck.

This time I didn't bother waiting for him to take the wheel, going straight for the driver's side, wrenching the door open and starting the engine. Just minutes removed from the trip out, the machine roared to

## Fire and Ice

life on the first turn, warm air blasting through the vents, hitting me square in the face.

My pulse raced as I drew in heavy breaths, the shelter of the truck allowing bits of sweat to form on my brow, streaking south on either side of my face.

It took more than a minute for Ferris to arrive, jumping into the passenger seat, throwing a spray of snow across the front of the truck before slamming the door. Leaning forward, he braced his right forearm against the dash, his left hand pointing out through the windshield.

No words crossed his lips as he signaled for me to move, his breath so short it resembled angry wheezing, his face void of color as his mouth gaped.

Under different circumstances I might have had concern for his state, even paused to make sure he was okay, wasn't having a heart attack.

As it were, I focused on his directive, pulling a K-turn in the driveway, the snow crunching beneath our tires as I followed our trail back out onto the road, the rear end fishtailing slightly behind us.

It took less than 100 yards behind the wheel for two things to become immediately apparent. The first was that I now understood why Ferris was so tense the entire time he was driving, the elements giving the truck a mind of its own.

Every part of me wanted to jam the gas to the floor, to speed forward, find out who had just happened to show up in a snow coach and find us on a desolate country road, a load of mystery supplies on a trailer behind them.

Once or twice I even indulged myself, pressing my foot down hard, only to hear the engine whine, to see the RPM's spike, but notice no effect at all on our speed.

The second thing that stood out were the tracks of the snow coach, the tank-like treads leaving a clear path through the middle of the road. More than a foot wide with thick rubber slats every few inches, they cut an obvious trench through the drifts, a second set of tracks resting comfortably within them from the trailer they pulled.

Even with the swirling snow outside, it was some of the easiest tracking I had ever done.

"You see anything up ahead?" Ferris managed, the words coming out one at a time, placed between breaths. My previous assumption about his graveled voice seemed to confirm a lifetime of cigars, his breathing sounding pained, punctuated by a cough thick with phlegm.

"Trail is clear as day," I said, realizing I was maintaining the same stance he had before, my chin just a few inches above the wheel as I stared out at the road.

"I mean the coach," Ferris pressed, "you see it?"

Angling my gaze upward a few degrees, I squinted into the sea of white moving about us.

"No," I said, giving a quick shake of my head.

I had never been behind the wheel of a snow coach, but I'd encountered more than my share of them in the preceding five years. No less than three different companies used them for winter tours to popular attractions, allowing people to travel in warmth and comfort.

My own shop was closed from Halloween to the first of May, having done a few experimental runs using snowmobiles before deciding that it just wasn't worth the effort of trying to keep business going in the winter, the elements and the liability too much to bother with.

What I knew was that the coach was far better equipped for these conditions than any truck ever would be, even with the heavy chains wrapped around the tires. The treads on the coach allowed it to sit much higher, riding along the top of the snow rather than trying to plow through it.

As such, it had a top speed of at least 10 miles an hour faster than us. Coupled with the extensive lead they had, the outcome of our chase was already clear.

"There's no way we're going to catch them," I said, stating the realization out loud, letting Ferris hear the disgust in my voice as I delivered the news. "They're too far out, have a top speed much higher than ours. All we can do is keep tracking them, see what we find when we get there."

Even as I said the words, I knew it was an eventuality that wasn't

## Fire and Ice

particularly attractive. They would arrive wherever they were headed long before us, no doubt have more men, probably all with heavy firepower.

The reality of our situation was that there wasn't anybody we could call on for help, no SWAT teams or air support that could give us a hand. With only two people, arguably four if counting the deputies back at the station, we had to be careful what we did.

"Of course," I said, "the noise of the truck will alert them long before we get there. Someone could probably hear this big engine more than a mile out, even with the wind."

I glanced over to see Ferris raise his hands to his face, the skin loose and moving beneath his fingers as he rubbed twice before dropping them to his lap.

"Yeah," he finally said, resignation in his voice.

I knew the feeling. The very last thing I wanted to do was stop our pursuit. This was the first clear lead we'd had on Yvonne Endicott since she was kidnapped.

Still, we had to do things intelligently. Showing up and getting ourselves killed wouldn't do anybody any good.

"So what are you thinking?" Ferris asked.

Again, I noticed his deference to me, though whether he was just showing professional courtesy or legitimately seeking my counsel I didn't know. Didn't much care either.

"We stop at the station," I said. "Find out who owns that house we just came from, maybe figure out where they're headed from that, start working our way out from there."

I paused, lowering my gaze to look up through the window, and said, "Even with the snow coming down like it is, I figure we've got hours before this trail is filled in.

"Let's try to be smart about this while we still have that luxury."

## Chapter Thirty-Seven

Sam Cuddyer turned and whipped the welded copper pipe he held toward the back wall of the barn. His momentum spun him in a complete revolution across the smooth concrete floor, the overhead lights reflecting off the polished metal, the entire sequence resembling a bizarre discus throw.

Once it was released, Cuddyer didn't bother watching, not giving it a second thought as it slammed into the metal wall and clattered to the floor, two distinct sounds indicating that it had come apart on impact.

Reaching out and cutting the gas feed to his torch, Cuddyer pulled off his welder's gloves and threw them at the ground. For a moment he stood over them, fuming, before lashing out with his foot, sending them across the floor.

This was not how things were supposed to be. He was supposed to be home, in the farmhouse, his feet propped up. Every so often he and Elias would take a walk out back, make sure things were coming along as expected, sending Jasper to lug in more supplies whenever they needed something.

It didn't matter that it was a damn blizzard outside, his occasional walk out back a little colder than usual, but nothing more.

All he had to do was tell Jasper to clear a path and the man would, his eagerness to please so ingrained it was difficult not to exploit it from time to time.

In a couple days, when the run was finished, they would load it all up and drive it over, collecting a nice duffel bag full of cash for their efforts, getting instructions on how much to prepare the next time.

It wasn't millions, but it was damn sure more than Cuddyer or his crew had ever seen before.

That's not how any of it was playing out though. Somewhere along the line Elias had gotten lazy, had given himself over to his long dormant addiction, had begun dabbling in his own product again.

Raising both fists to his temples, Cuddyer ground his knuckles into the soft flesh, pushing until pops of light burst behind his eyelids.

In a way, this was his fault too. He had also gotten lazy, had not kept a close enough eye on Elias, had maybe even chosen to ignore the obvious for the sake of keeping things going.

And now here they were, down to their last few precious hours, their enterprise, their very lives, hanging in the balance.

Standing at the end of the unfinished production line, Cuddyer couldn't help but feel bitterness rising like bile in the back of his throat. Right now his cook was in a bad way, unconscious for 12 hours with no signs of emerging from it. He had been forced to farm out a job to Jasper that the man was ill-equipped to handle, trusting someone who could barely navigate under the best of conditions to make it into town and get what was needed without arousing suspicion.

Adding to the mess was the girl locked up inside, someone whose abduction was foolish, an act of desperation, the kind of thing Cuddyer usually tried so hard to avoid.

Making it even worse was the fact that she had managed to do basically nothing for Elias, her only accomplishment being pushing Cuddyer someplace he didn't want to go, making him raise his hand to a woman.

Things were unraveling. The situation was getting beyond his control, was threatening to come apart completely at any moment.

Making the conscious effort to unclench his fists, to let his fingers extend themselves to full length, Cuddyer pushed out a long breath. Drew in another and held it, tried to force his pulse to slow down.

This was the moment, that point where he could either get things back on track or watch them go careening off the road. He just needed to tackle one item at a time, to make progress, to show they were moving in the right direction.

Moving through the middle of the two rows of tables, Cuddyer left his gloves and torch where they lay. He went straight for the far corner table, taking up the satellite phone and extending the antenna.

It took more than 30 seconds for it to come to life, the phone an old one that Cuddyer had gotten years before to use when going out into the back country. Dialing the number from memory, he pressed it to his ear and leaned against the closest table, the corner of the wood digging into his backside.

The first call went unanswered, every possible reason of what could have gone wrong running through Cuddyer's mind. Again, he had to force himself to breath, to push back the anger he knew was just beneath the surface, as he dialed the number again, this time pressing speaker phone.

The shrill sound of the ringing echoed through the room. It rang twice before being picked up, nothing more than deep panting audible.

"Jasper?" Cuddyer asked, again feeling his apprehension and anger rising.

Three more deep breaths could be heard before Jasper's voice sounded, his tone confused. "Cuddy?"

"Jasper, where are you? What's going on?" Cuddyer asked, pushing himself away from the table with his hips and raising the phone just shy of his mouth.

"Cuddy," Jasper whispered again. "What happened? Where am I?"

His eyes sliding closed, Cuddyer raised his face toward the ceiling. He remained fixed in that position, forcing his voice to remain even.

"Jasper, look around. Where are you?"

Another grunt could be heard, followed by some movement, the familiar sound of a parka rustling.

"I'm in the truck," Jasper managed. "It's cold in here, starting to get dark."

Completely ignoring the last line, Cuddyer said, "Okay, you're in the truck. Are you parked?"

He knew even as he asked the question there was no way that Jasper had just stumbled into a parking lot and fallen asleep, envisioning the rig overturned in a ditch or lying upside down in the center of the road as a deer traipsed off into the distance.

"I...I don't know," Jasper said. Another grunt from exertion, followed by, "I don't think so. For some reason the truck is tilted."

The veins in Cuddyer's forearm bulged as he squeezed the phone, his initial fears confirmed. He shouldn't have sent Jasper. He should have just risked the time it would have taken to go himself.

Or better yet, just made the woman do her damn job with what she was given.

"The truck is tilted," Cuddyer said, pushing the words out through gritted teeth. "Are you hurt?"

There was no response for a long moment, Cuddyer continuing to grip the phone, his entire body straining, waiting for any type of response.

"Cuddy? I'm going to have to call you back. Somebody just pulled up."

## Chapter Thirty-Eight

Our sudden arrival seemed to surprise Baker and Azbell, both jerking around from their computers to stare at us. True to form Baker wore a scowl on his face, continuing to glare in my direction, while his counterpart seemed startled from the unexpected entrance.

"Need one of you to run an address," Ferris said, bypassing any sort of greeting. It was far and away the most tense I'd heard him since meeting the man 14 hours earlier, the pressure of the situation having been ratcheted up by the emergence of some suspects.

Both of the deputies seemed surprised by the directive, neither moving, simply sitting and staring back at him.

"Now!" Ferris said, slapping his hands together, the crack of his palms causing Azbell to jerk again. In unison both turned to face forward, putting their backs to us.

"854 Mountain View Lane," Ferris said, leaving his coat on as he strode across the floor and took up his coffee mug still perched on the edge of his desk from more than an hour before.

He glanced down at it once, checking that it was empty, before wagging it toward me. "You want any?" he asked while drifting toward the hall.

I waved him off, content to wait where I was. After the low-speed chase and the prospect of a new heading, I had enough adrenaline surging through me to keep going for days. Adding caffeine to the mix would only make me jittery, something I could ill afford at the moment.

It took just over a minute for Ferris to fill his mug and return, Azbell having the information he requested upon return.

"Original owner was—"

"Art and Bea Buchanan," Ferris said. "I know. Who did they sell it to?"

"Henry Lott," Azbell said, reading it off of the screen.

"Hank?" Ferris said, his eyebrows rising.

"That's what it says," Azbell answered. "I thought he lived..."

"Over on Highland," Ferris said, completing her sentence for the second time.

"So you know him?" I asked, sensing from his responses, from his tone, the information was news to him as well.

"Hell, everybody does," Ferris said. "Hank's been around here forever, owns the hardware store in town."

The fact that the man was so well known, coupled with his owning a second property in town, told me that the farmhouse we had just been to was most likely a rental, something he had picked up for some residual income.

"Any idea where we can find him?" I asked.

"Oh, yeah," Ferris replied, raising his wrist and using his mug to push back the cuff of his jacket. "Unless this storm has forced him inside, he's at the same place he's been every day for lunch the last 10 years."

Without further explanation I turned for the door, already knowing where our next stop was.

"Hold on," Baker said, "you should also know, *Sheriff*, that we got a call while you were out."

My hand froze a few inches from the doorknob, my head turning, waiting for him to continue.

A moment passed, no sound coming as he glanced in my direction.

"About?" Ferris said, his posture and tone letting Baker know this was no time for pettiness.

In the short time since Ferris had come to my room, I hadn't spent much time considering a ransom call. It just seemed that the nabbing of Yvonne Endicott had been part of something bigger.

Given the weather, there were too many variables for a simple money grab to seem plausible.

"The kidnappers?" I asked, ignoring whatever prick tendencies Baker had.

Flicking his gaze to me, Ferris drew a bit closer to Baker.

Making a point of scowling at me again, Baker focused on the sheriff and said, "No, from Albertson's, actually."

At once the previous tension bled from both Ferris and me, a glance between us showing neither one appreciated the false lead or its delivery.

"Yeah?" Ferris asked. "And what did they want?"

"It seems they had a, quote-unquote, *vagabond* show up there a while ago," Baker said, lifting his hands to make air quotes.

"Vagabond?" Ferris said, his face scrunching in confusion.

"That's what the woman said," Baker replied. "Said some guy wandered in, looked like hell, smelled like death, wandered the aisles for the better part of an hour."

Ferris and I exchanged another look.

"What did he smell like, exactly?" Ferris asked.

"I don't know," Baker said, "that's all she told me."

"What did he buy?" I asked.

"I don't know that either," Baker said, refusing to look my direction. "All she said was that he kept to himself, but he was bothering some of the other customers, looking and smelling like he did."

The same perplexed look remained on Ferris's face as he glanced up at me, trying to make sense of what we were being told.

"So then, why did she bother calling it in?"

Both shoulders rose as Baker shrugged. "Just wanted us to be aware, maybe keep an eye out for him around town."

I could see my own thoughts play out across the sheriff's face, going the full range from questioning how we would just spot this man in a snowstorm to why Baker had held us up to mention it.

"Come on Hawk, let's go."

## Chapter Thirty-Nine

Wood Arrasco stood in front of the picture window in his office, his arms clasped behind his back, and stared out at the world. Already completely buried in white, more continued to fall, piling higher on every available surface.

At best he thought it might be slowing, but only slightly.

On most occasions, Wood had no real problem with the snow. It was a marked difference from what he'd grown up with in the south, something he had hated for years before finally accepting it as a reality of his new home.

Today was not such an occasion.

To someone who loved nothing more in the world - with the possible exception of Maria – than being out on the road, opening the throttle on his Harley Fat Boy, hearing nothing but the roar of his engine, feeling nothing but the wind on his face, seeing snow brought with it the harsh reality that he was stuck inside. The freedom that he so craved was completely cut off, always bringing with it the feeling that some small part of him was missing as well.

It wasn't that he needed to ride every day, but just knowing it was there as a possibility helped immensely. Every time the business of the club became overwhelming, each moment that he didn't quite feel like being inside, listening to Maria yammer away, he liked knowing precious release was within his grasp.

At the moment, the feelings of muted rage were even more pronounced, the snow bringing with it the harsh reality that he could not be where he was needed, could not see to things as he should. Instead of being out on the road, assessing whatever Sam Cuddyer and his crew had gotten themselves into, he was stuck inside, waiting.

It was not a skill anybody would ever say he was especially adept at.

The sound of the phone ringing erupted from his desk, the tone turned up to full volume, seeming to reverberate off the wall. Wood gave no outward reaction at all to the sudden intrusion, remaining planted in front of the window until the third ring before turning and taking two steps to his desk, snatching up the phone.

The sat phone was a big and blocky model, an older design that was used only in circumstances such as this, when cell signals were down or they were someplace too remote. To his knowledge only a handful of people even had the number, Wood not bothering to check the screen for the ID, just keying the phone to life and pressing it to his face.

"Arrasco."

"Prez, Trick," the voice replied on the other end.

It was the same basic opening that always preceded club business, each side keeping it short, giving the other the chance to alert them if anybody was nearby, if anything could be overheard.

This time Wood pushed right past it, his growing impatience getting the best of him. "How bad?"

If there was any surprise at all by him getting right to it, Trick did not show it, responding in the same even tone he always used. "Bad. From what we could see, the lab was pretty well destroyed. Most of the barn was completely gone."

Wood paused a moment, processing what he'd been told, trying to envision things in his mind.

"From what you could see?"

"Yeah," Trick said, the whine of his snow coach engine just barely audible in the background. "We had to abort getting any closer than the road."

Wood paused, his mouth dropping open in surprise. It wasn't like Trick to leave something unfinished, especially after going so far to see it through.

"Feds?" he asked, closing his mouth, setting his jaw.

"I don't think so, but the law for sure," Trick said. "Only one truck, two guys, but enough for us to keep right on going."

At that Wood nodded, the information fitting much closer with what he expected from Trick.

Taking down a pair of locals would have been no problem, not with Mac and Barnham riding along, certainly not with the amount of firepower stowed in the back. Still, it would have brought along more attention that could be ill afforded at the moment.

Blizzard or not, two dead officers would pull every able-bodied person in town out.

Right now the weather was keeping people away, was probably the reason the law had just discovered the damaged lab instead of 12 hours before. No need to make it a bigger problem when they didn't have to.

"Okay," Wood said, "did they spot you? Follow you?"

"Not that we could see," Trick said, "but visibility is so poor, it's hard to tell. Either way it's been a good half hour, and we still haven't spotted them."

Raising his eyes out to the winter scene outside, Wood nodded.

"Good. En route now to the fallback location?"

"We are," Trick said, pausing for a moment.

Just a hint of something in his voice caught Wood's attention, his eyes tightening just slightly. "What is it?"

"Well, we've had a complication," Trick said "You're never going to believe what we just stumbled on out here along the road."

Raising his free hand to his brow, Wood kneaded his thumb and index finger over his forehead. The bottom of his stomach dropped, the familiar feeling of dread seeping in.

"Let me guess, Cuddyer stuck in the snow, frozen solid," Wood said, the thought bringing with it a flash of anger.

If anything was going to happen to that bearded bastard or his team, he wanted to be the one to do it, not letting them get off so easy by freezing along the side of the road.

"Close," Trick said. "It's Jasper, and he's alive, but the way he's stumbling around out there looks like he's banged up pretty good."

"Jasper?" Wood said, pulling his hand away from his face, his features twisted. "Alone?"

"That's what it looks like," Trick said. "Mac and Barnham are out there now trying to lend a hand. I stayed behind to call you, then I'll go take a closer look."

"Holy shit," Wood muttered, shaking his head at the inanity of the entire situation, at how fast things had devolved.

"You don't know the half of it," Trick said. "Looks like the dumbass went right off the side of the road. Truck is sitting at a 40 degree angle right now. We'll be lucky to ever get it out."

"Don't even bother trying," Wood said, the anger continuing to build. "Just get him in the van and get on to the site. We need to know how bad this is, and fast."

A moment of silence passed, Wood continuing to try in vain to swallow down the venom within him, wishing nothing more than to be able to cut off Cuddyer and every person connected to him, moving on without ever having to bother with any of them again.

"The meeting didn't go well this morning," Trick said, piecing together what Wood was telling him, the words very much a statement, not a question.

"It went fine," Wood replied, knowing that the acrimony he felt toward Cuddyer was seeping into the words but making no effort to mask it. "Chance and his crew make okay product, and they're happy to push out as much as they can for us, but they're about out of materials."

"Oh, shit," Trick muttered. "The storm."

"Exactly," Wood said. "Without raw goods, they can't make any more product. The trucks aren't running, so they can't get what they need."

"And by the time they do, we're already too far behind schedule..."

"And the buyer goes someplace else," Wood said.

"Shit," Trick whispered again, the same thing Wood felt creeping into his voice.

The reality of their situation was not lost on either one of them, their success having created a market that was now threatening to overtake them, move on without them.

"Once this is over, we'll bring in some new suppliers, make sure this never happens again," Wood said. "Until then, get them up and running, make enough to get us through the next couple of weeks."

"You got it, Prez."

## Chapter Forty

A few more people had wandered into Ned's since my original pass through two hours before. Both of the televisions above the bar were now up and running, the volume muted, *Sportscenter* playing on one, Fox News on the other.

Neither surprised me in the slightest, tracking perfectly with every outward indication the place had given on my two previous visits.

True to form, every person in the room turned to stare as we entered, their expressions tightening, their hands clamping down on whatever they were holding.

There was no way to know if such a reaction was caused by something Ferris had done in the past, or maybe even an auto response to me after everything they'd heard about six weeks prior. More likely, though, it was just an ingrained response to anything resembling law enforcement.

Behind the bar Ned was perched with a towel over his shoulder, both hands pressed against the back edge, a smile on his face as he stood in conversation with a guy seated before him. At the sight of us the grin faded away, his head dropping a few inches, his previous hope of not seeing either one of us again dashed.

I gave Ferris the lead as we entered, staying behind him as he walked forward, his thumbs hooked into the front pockets of his jeans. He swept his gaze across the room, finally finding what he was looking for along the back wall.

He walked straight to the table, four men grouped around it, playing cards and beer glasses scattered over the tabletop.

Apparently, Ferris had taken some liberty with what he earlier referred to as a *daily lunch*.

All four of the men seemed to be Ferris's age or older, all dressed in jeans and flannel, coats hanging off the back of their chairs.

"Gentlemen," Ferris said, approaching the table slowly, making sure his hands were visible at all times. "Sorry to interrupt, but I was hoping we might borrow Hank for a few minutes."

On cue, three of the men turned their attention back to their cards, the fourth – I presumed to be Hank Lott – sitting with his arms folded over a thick midsection, a frown on his face.

"What's this about, Sheriff?" he asked without moving, making it quite clear from his stance and his tone that he had no interest in being borrowed for any length of time.

"There's been an accident at your house," Ferris replied, choosing to sidestep the question a bit and come in from the side.

"My house?" Lott replied, his eyes opening wide. "When? What happened?"

Turning and casting a quick glance over his shoulder to me, Ferris looked back to the table. "It looked to be some sort of explosion, most likely sometime during the night."

Lott sat perfectly still, processing the information, before a disdainful smile spread across his face, his head shaking just a bit to either side.

"Well, Sheriff, I appreciate your concern, but I am afraid you are mistaken. I just left my house a half hour ago. Everything was still standing, thank you."

Every word seemed to drip with derision as he delivered it, glancing to his friends on either side, eliciting small chuckles of support from the group.

"Your *other* house," I called out, aware that every person in the room watching the exchange was now turned to look at me, not especially caring.

This was about Yvonne Endicott. It was about the men making meth grabbing her, and whoever was in that snow coach coming to clean up the situation.

We did not have time for these clowns to sit around and have a laugh at the expense of the town sheriff.

The smile that had been on Lott's face melted away as he looked past Ferris to me, replaced by a scowl that told me he did not appreciate me entering the conversation or divulging such information in front of the room.

I matched it, having to stop myself from taking a step or two forward, knowing that any sign of aggression would only escalate the situation further. I knew there was no way one older man would be foolish enough to make a move, no matter how thick he might have been in the midsection, but a room with more than a dozen men was a different matter altogether.

The Kimber Ultra Carry was still tucked into the small of my back, but that would only lead to something bad.

A moment passed, both of us peering at one another, before Lott unfolded his arms and stood.

"Boys, will you excuse us for a minute?" he said, his attention never leaving me as he stepped around the table and came toward the door, Ferris bringing up the rear behind him.

It was clear from his posture and the continued stares of every person in the room that this was not a conversation that was going to take place inside Ned's, Lott not wanting to speak before an audience and the group not willing to give us the privacy needed.

I waited until he was just a few steps away before turning and exiting through the front door, moving just a couple steps down the sidewalk, my feet in the middle of the narrow trench dug through the heavy snow outside. A moment later Lott and Ferris both stepped out behind me.

With our backs to the building, most of the wind and whipping snow was blocked, the full wrath of the storm continuing to play out before us. Overhead the lone pair of stoplights in town swung back and forth, pushed by the wind as one swirl after another of ice was lifted from the ground and twirled through the air.

"You have two minutes," Lott said, his arms folded over his chest. He had not bothered to bring his coat, a thermal undershirt and a plaid flannel his only protection from the cold.

Up close he didn't look quite as old as I had previously thought, the impression coming from the thatch of silver hair atop his head. Beneath it he had gray eyes and a face shaved clean, bearing just a few lines around the mouth and eyes.

"Who lives in the farmhouse?" I asked, taking the lead.

Already, it had been apparent that Lott had no interest in being cooperative, Ferris's evenhanded approach falling short.

If my playing the role of Bad Cop was what was needed to move this along, I was more than happy to do it.

"Why?" Lott shot back.

"Because they've got one hell of a meth lab going out there," I said. "Or at least, they *had* one, before it blew up and took most of your barn with it."

The scowl receded just a bit with the information, surprise flooding in momentarily, before Lott collected himself.

"Bullshit."

Buried in the front pockets of my coat, I felt my hands curl into fists, my fingernails grinding into my palms.

"We just left there," I said. "You've been harboring an operation putting out hundreds of pounds of crank a month for who knows how long."

"Yeah? And you're some kind of expert?" Lott said. "I'm just supposed to believe you?"

"Yes," Ferris said, jerking both our attention toward him. "I'd say 10 years with the DEA makes him an expert. And I was there too, saw the whole damn thing. He's telling you the truth."

The awkward arrangement of us against the building, hemmed in by the knee-deep snow piled in front of us, forced Lott to rotate his head between the two of us, making sure we both saw the look of disdain on his face. It was clear he was debating something, his long held disgust with the law fighting with the reality of what we were telling him.

"Let me put it this way," I said, intent to help along that internal battle, "we don't think you have anything to do with this. If you did, we wouldn't be having this conversation out here.

"But if you don't give us the names of whoever rents off you right now so we can go save a woman's life, we're hauling your ass to the station and leaving you there for obstruction of justice. Got it?"

## Chapter Forty-One

The second blow wasn't enough to knock Yvonne unconscious. Instead, it merely amplified the effects of the first, making it feel as if her head might explode. Bit by bit the pressure grew, shoving outward against the sides of her skull, bringing pain in undulating waves.

Still sitting in the chair that Cuddyer's backhand had deposited her in, Yvonne lowered her head between her knees in an effort to stop the nausea she was feeling, drawing in deep breaths of air.

Every few seconds she opened her eyes, attempting to see just how much damage had been done, the floor beneath her distorted through the sheen of tears covering her eyes.

Already, she had taken three packages of Advil, having nearly wiped out the small supply. With nothing to eat or drink since leaving the hospital, she could feel herself getting queasy, the NSAID's wreaking havoc on her stomach. Any more would cause her to vomit, hastening dehydration, exacerbating the effects of her head injuries even further.

Lowering her hands to the legs of the chair on either side of her, Yvonne squeezed, seeing her knuckles shine white beneath the surface of her skin, her teeth clamped to keep from screaming out.

Despite her every inclination being to do just that, she knew she couldn't. Doing so would only draw attention to herself, would bring her captor back.

She had been wrong, something that seemed so foolish now through the lens of hindsight. She had mistakenly believed that the leader was in control, that he would see the value of her being there, would do her no harm.

In making such a mistake, she had overplayed her position, leaning on him for more supplies.

There was no way to know if that was what had caused his recent outburst. She had heard the truck start and the door open, had heard the vehicle drive away, not yet having returned. It was possible that the other man had been unable to get what she needed, had ended up in trouble.

Any of a number of things could have been the cause for his rage.

Yvonne remained folded in half, letting the position calm her. Little by little the nausea settled, the intrusive throbbing receding into the same steady agony she felt since she came to hours before.

With her condition somewhat stabilized, her resolve became clear, bringing with it a new realization.

The time of simply waiting – of doing what was asked of her, of trusting that they would keep her alive and well, maybe even release her afterward – was gone. With just one blow, one outburst, the man had completely obliterated any hope she had for surviving once the man beside her was healed, if he could be.

In the time she had been held captive he had not moved, had made nary a sound. It was now past the point of Yvonne believing his condition was entirely based on his body trying to protect him from the trauma of the burns, moving into a state that suggested whatever had caused his coma was most likely ingested.

Knowing that the operation out there was a fledgling meth lab, it was not much of a stretch to imagine him having imbibed in his own concoctions. Without the ability to perform blood work and do a full and proper physical, lacking the supplies she needed to treat the wounds topically, she had been reduced to nothing more than a babysitter.

Raising her head a few inches, Yvonne turned to stare at the man, everything just as it had been a moment before, just as it had been an hour before that.

Sitting up to her full height, she stood, pausing, her hands outstretched to either side, waiting for the inevitable bout of spinning that gripped her.

Once it had passed, she took a half-step forward to make sure her balance was okay, followed with a second and then a third, reaching the table and leaning against it. One palm she left pressed flat, supporting her weight, while the other she used to pick through the meager supplies before her, taking up a roll of gauze.

Holding her middle and index fingers together, Yvonne wound the gauze around them, watching as her mocha color skin disappeared, replaced by a single mummified object.

She turned back to the man, her hand extended. Feeling anxiety, uncertainty, roil within her, she leaned over him.

Using those two fingers she slowly parted his lips, inserted the fingers and pulled his jaw down.

It was so much worse than she thought.

The number of teeth in the man's head could be counted on both hands. Of those, at least a few showed signs of rot and decay, a telltale sign of heavy methamphetamine use. Given the state of his mouth, it was not a stretch to imagine his entire body was affected in ways she couldn't treat.

He was not the first drug addict Yvonne had ever encountered, her feelings not particularly sympathetic. Nobody had made this man take drugs, had forced him to ingest well past the point of doing physical harm.

Even under the best of conditions, the odds of her being able to treat someone with just the exterior wounds, given their extent and what she had to work with, were minimal. It was clear that she had been handed a losing proposition, this man in his condition never being strong enough to survive whatever had happened.

Again, Yvonne's mind came back to the incident a few moments before, to the bearded man walking through, backhanding her for no clear reason, using her as a release for his frustration. If that was his reaction to whatever had happened outside, there was no doubt about how he would take to the news that the man could not be fixed, or worse yet had died on her watch.

Feeling as if her insides were being squeezed, Yvonne felt the air grow short in her lungs. Her vision began to blur as she stumbled back to the chair, sitting down, staring at the floor.

One breath at a time she drew in deep gasps of oxygen, knowing if ever she were going to survive, she could not simply wait for help to arrive.

She had to do something.

She just had no idea what.

## Chapter Forty-Two

Ferris was back at the wheel, navigating the streets while I scanned the paperwork we had just printed out in the office, committing as much of it as I could to memory.

Hank Lott had tried his best to be obstructive, letting a deep-held disdain for enforcement of any kind cloud his judgment, just south of the point where it would land him in jail. Ferris had explained to me on the way back to the station that it was nothing personal, a feeling stemming from a run-in with a state trooper years before that Lott had seized on and never quite let go.

At the time, my adrenaline was so spiked from the interaction, from forcing myself not to fly into the man, that I only half-listened as I powerwalked back, ignoring the deep snow as it curled away on either side of me.

Even now, the better part of an hour later, I still didn't feel much sympathy.

The man was an ass. I didn't care when or how he'd gotten his feelings bruised. If he hadn't started playing ball when he did, I would have done a hell of a lot worse to him in order to help Yvonne Endicott.

What he had eventually handed over were the names, Sam

Cuddyer and Jasper Maxx, a pair of men that he said weren't gay but had been living together since he bought the place. Both were somewhere in their 40s, but beyond that he had no idea what they did for a living, didn't much need to know, so long as the money arrived on time and in full every month.

Arriving back at the office, Ferris gave the names to Azbell, having her run them through the system while he again made a coffee run and I went to visit the lavatory. Three minutes later we both emerged to find her waiting on us, Baker still sitting on his condescending perch a few feet away.

As with Lott before him, I almost dared the man to do so much as give me a funny glance, my growing agitation desperately needing to find an outlet.

Rather than wait for the full report from Azbell, Ferris told her to print whatever she found, handing the stack to me as we again headed out.

After hours trekking around outside, my body barely even noticed the temperature difference as I plowed straight for the passenger side, the wind whipping at the pages in my hand. It passed over my exposed scalp, turning my ears red, as I reached my destination and climbed in, long past bothering to brush the snow away from my jeans.

Seeming to be of the same mind, Ferris had climbed in and set off just as fast.

"Alright," I said, separating the top sheet from the stack and holding it up a few inches, letting the others rest in my lap, "Samuel Jones Cuddyer, born 1969 in Fort Benton. String of small stuff through his youth – MIP, driving with a suspended license, petty theft. Wasn't until his 20s that he hit the big time, doing two years for possession with intent."

"Drug offense," Ferris said, the words little more than a stream of consciousness as he processed what I read off.

"Right," I said. "That was in Butte. Doesn't say when or how he ended up here, no mention of anything since."

"Hmm," Ferris said. "Seems unusual for someone to have a steady flow of stuff and then suddenly go clean."

"Right," I agreed, moving Cuddyer's sheet to the bottom of the pile, pulling up the next in order. On it was his mug shot from booking, the image nearly 20 years old, showing a man in his late-20s with the beginnings of a beard and a sneer.

"I would say maybe jail scared him straight, but somehow I doubt it had that effect on this guy," I said, holding the picture up for Ferris to see.

Shifting his attention away from the road, Ferris nodded. "I've seen this guy a couple times. He's obviously older now, but I'll recognize him if we cross paths again."

"Noticed, as in..." I began, letting the implication hang, not finishing the thought.

"Not in relation to anything in particular," Ferris said. "Just another guy that kind of rolled in one day. I assumed he was an oil hand, but who knows."

I grunted softly and moved the picture down, unable to argue with the simple logic. There had been a lot of unfamiliar faces push through town recently, mine as well. It was easy to attribute them all to the new economic boon in the area, a fallacy Ferris was no doubt regretting at the moment.

"Up next is Jasper No-Middle-Name Maxx," I said. "Forty-two-years-old, a sheet that reads a lot like Cuddyer's, only in each instance the charges are a little less severe. Culminated with a possession charge that got him probation, didn't rise to the level of jail time."

"Sounds like a textbook crony," Ferris said.

"Looks the part too," I said, moving to the fourth page in the stack and holding it up for him to see. On it was an image of a rat-faced man with short cropped hair, the markings on the wall behind him stating he stood just 5'6".

In the image his shoulders were rolled forward and his mouth drawn tight, his expression looking like he might cry at any moment.

An indistinguishable sound slid from Ferris as he maneuvered us into the Albertson's parking lot, the enormous space holding only a pair of vehicles, one a truck, the other an SUV. Eschewing any manner of parking lot decorum both had parked straddling the front door, Ferris pulling up alongside the SUV, both of us climbing out.

The snow beneath us was no more than three or four inches deep, steep embankments around the edge of the lot indicating that someone with a snow blade had been through within the last six hours or so.

Folding the pages into quarters, I pushed them down into the front pocket of my coat and followed Ferris through the front door. We both paused just inside, letting the fans overhead blow heated air down on us, stomping our feet a few times before stepping on through.

The interior lights had been cut in half, the supermarket a bit dimmer than I expected. Along the front of the store nearly all of the registers stood empty and silent, only a single person manning one, an older man in a white dress shirt and apron, the remains of his hair white and wispy atop his head.

"Afternoon, Sheriff," he said, raising a gnarled hand to us as we stood and surveyed the place.

"Hey there," Ferris said, bypassing any use of a first name, taking a few steps forward. "We got a call a little while ago about someone loitering in here."

The man's brow came together before he shook his head, extending a finger toward the back of the store.

"Wasn't me, must have been Grace. She's in the pharmacy aisle, can't miss her."

Ferris gave a wave of thanks as a man and his daughter emerged from the opposite side of the store, both bundled up against the outside cold, each carrying red plastic baskets in their hand. As they approached, the old man behind the register turned his attention to them, leaving us to find Grace, to determine if one of the people we were looking for and the one she had called about were the same person.

Discovering they were wouldn't give us a clear direction on where they might be, but it would tell us if they were still in the area.

Knowing what they were after might also give us some indication if Yvonne was still alive.

"This way," Ferris said, turning right, leading us past two more rows before coming to a stop, a woman in a red apron standing at the

## Fire and Ice

corner. The open box at her feet indicated she had been stocking shelves.

"Hi there," she said, offering a smile that came off a bit forced. Beneath the red apron she wore jeans and a plain turtleneck, dark hair framing a round face wearing thick glasses.

"Grace?" Ferris asked.

"Yes," she said, clearly not recognizing him as her counterpart had a moment before.

"I'm Sheriff Ferris, this is Deputy Hawk. We understand you made a call a little while ago about an interloper here in the store?"

The plastic smile fell away as she looked between us, running her hands down the front of her apron, smoothing it flat against her thighs.

"Yes, that's correct. I didn't expect anybody to come by though, certainly not in this. I just wanted to make you guys aware that somebody was out there looking and smelling like he did."

"What did he smell like, exactly?" I asked, drawing her attention to me. I almost made the mistake of asking if it was something chemical, cutting myself off short, ensuring I didn't sway her decision in any way.

Pausing for a moment, Grace pulled in a deep breath, her mouth twisting up just slightly.

"I don't know," she said. "It kind of smelled like rubbing alcohol, only not quite. Which didn't make sense, considering he was very dirty."

In my periphery I could see Ferris cast a glance my way, his eyebrows rising just slightly. Without acknowledging him, I extracted the stack of pages from my pocket and unfolded them, rifling through to the image of Cuddyer and holding it out.

"Could this be the man you saw?"

Behind the lenses of her glasses, her eyes grew a bit larger as she looked from the paper to me. It was clear she wanted to ask what all this was about, why a simple call about vagrancy had turned into showing her mug shots, but to her credit she did not.

"No," she said, shaking her head slightly. "I'm sorry."

Placing the photo at the bottom of the stack, I moved on to Maxx.

"How about this man?"

Frowning slightly, the woman looked from me to the image, her lips parting just slightly.

"Yes," she said, pulling her gaze away from the image almost instantly. "He's older now, looks a little different, but that's the guy, for sure."

Again I could see Ferris glance over at me. This time I met his gaze, nodding just slightly.

"Tell me," I said, "you wouldn't happen to remember what it was he was buying, would you?"

## Chapter Forty-Three

"Rubbing alcohol, cotton swabs, Vaseline, Advil," I said, rattling off the first few things Grace had told us. There was a lot more on the list, more than a dozen items, though the rest of it had eluded her, not being able to linger close enough to see everything.

She was unequivocal though in stating that aside from a can of Pringles and a Mountain Dew, not one thing in his basket was for consumption.

"Looks like the makings of a first aid kit, don't know you think?" I said.

"Right," Ferris agreed, walking away from the store. As soon as we were in the truck, he jammed the gear shift into drive and punched the gas, the chains biting into the shallow snow of the parking lot.

Unimpeded by the thick covering of white on the ground, we tore through the lot, making the best time we had all day, before moving out onto the road, the going again slowing to a crawl.

Fortunately for us, Grace's busybody tendencies caused her to watch as Jasper left the store, standing at the front window as he pulled away. She had apologized for not being able to get a license plate number, making sure to jot down what she could about his truck though, even watching which way he went.

As we already knew who he was, and who the truck likely belonged to, there was no need for the plate number. Seeing which way he headed though helped us immensely, giving us a direction to go, a set of tracks to follow.

"So how do you see it?" Ferris asked. "Cuddyer was the guy doing the cooking, Jasper his gopher?"

I nodded once, thinking through where he was going. "Possible, maybe even likely. From what we know about Jasper Maxx, he definitely wouldn't be the guy in charge of anything. Just like this here, his role was as an errand boy, nothing more."

A few feet away Ferris looked over at me, doing a double take before turning his attention back to the road. "But you don't like Cuddyer for the cook?"

For some reason, between seeing the operation first hand, the video at the hospital, and now both men's sheet, something wasn't sitting right with me. There was still a hole there, my mind struggling to process everything just yet.

"Again, possibly," I conceded, "but it doesn't seem to fit. Remember, we saw two men on the video pull Yvonne Endicott into the truck. Neither one looked to have any trouble moving, certainly not bad enough to indicate they'd been in a blast."

Ferris let out a long breath, the sound clear over the heater. "Dammit," he muttered, smacking the top of the steering wheel with his palm. "Forgot about the video. So now we're looking at three guys."

Three fit better with the size of the lab at the house, though I remained silent. I didn't want to agree with him, to make him believe there were only three when there could easily be more.

Leaning forward, I extended a finger, tapping it against the windshield. "More than that if you count them."

It took Ferris a moment to pick up on what I was alluding to, his eyes squinted tight. There he remained before running a hand over his face.

"Treads, from the snow coach."

"Yep," I said. "So we know Grace was right. Jasper came in for supplies, took off in this direction, the cavalry moved in right behind him."

Ferris shifted the front of the truck just a bit, aligning our tires with the treads. There we remained for several minutes, neither saying anything, both deep in thought.

Whatever operation Cuddyer had been running was big. The ruined barn proved that, but even more so was the fact that reinforcements had arrived, in a snowstorm, just over 12 hours later.

Who they were or where they were coming from was anybody's guess, but their having a snow coach showed it was an eventuality they were prepared for.

"Lookit here," Ferris said, extending a finger over the steering wheel, drawing my attention in the direction he was pointing.

Looming ahead, just barely visible through the snow, was a dark shape, a vehicle of some sort, most likely a truck. Tilted on a side, it sat just off the side of the road, a thin layer of white almost obscuring it from view.

"You don't think?" I asked, raising my hands and cupping them on either side of my eyes, creating tunnel vision to get a better view.

"It would have to be, wouldn't it?" Ferris asked, the truck a short distance in front of us. "Who else would be out in this?"

I reached into the console beside me and took up the Kimber. Again, I checked to make sure a round was chambered and flicked the safety off, waiting as Ferris pulled to within just a few feet of the rear bumper and came to a stop.

"We have to assume this is him, right?" he asked, leaving the engine running, his voice low.

"Yes," I said, not a bit of hesitation, watching as he reached into his jacket and drew his weapon as well.

Like most older law enforcements types, he opted for the Beretta M9, a model with a larger grip and a magazine holding 15 rounds.

"I'll follow your lead," I said, shoving my door open, the frozen metal squawking in protest. Stepping outside, I wrapped my hand around the base of the gun, my finger lying just outside the trigger guard.

My left hand I cupped beneath it, ready to use as support if needed.

Moving around to the front of the truck as fast as the snow would allow me, I fell in behind Ferris. Adrenaline pulsated through my system, the warmth it provided offset by the cold enveloping my lower body.

Wind whipped over the exposed surface of my cheeks, the skin already raw, beginning to burn from the sensation. Cold gnawed at my fingers as I squeezed the metal base of the gun, my focus singular, ignoring every warning sign my body was giving me.

Walking up to the side of the truck, Ferris balled his right hand into a fist and banged it against the metal, a dull thump echoing out on contact. He hammered at it twice in succession before stepping forward another couple of feet and pounding again.

"Jasper Maxx! This is Valley County Sheriff Rake Ferris! Open the door and keep your hands where I can see them!"

Moving out a couple more feet from the truck, I had Ferris and the driver's door both in a direct line of sight. I was close enough not to have my view obstructed by snow, feeling my pulse pass through my temples, my right index finger tapping at the side of the gun.

The angle of the truck was too severe to allow him to do anything from the passenger side. If an attack was going to come, if Maxx was lying in wait, it would have to be from this side.

I appreciated the fact that Ferris announced himself as the sheriff, told Maxx to open the door and keep his hands up. There was no consideration for the truck belonging to somebody else, no concern for the driver being injured.

Given what we knew, what had transpired in the preceding day, it was the only way to play it.

The ground around the truck was chewed up by the tracks of at least two people, maybe as many as four or five, the treads of the snow coach just 10 feet away, the steps connecting the two.

Best guess was that somebody had come along in the wake of Maxx going off the road and picked him up, helped him transfer over whatever supplies he had.

Still, we had to be certain before moving on.

Ferris made it as far as the back edge of the cab before looking over his shoulder to me. He held his left hand up and pointed to the door, letting me know that he was going in.

Without responding I plowed three steps forward, snow spraying up around me as I moved to within just five feet of him, the loaned gun at the ready.

Without lifting his feet from the snow, Ferris slid sideways, burrowing his way through, stopping just back from the door. Leaning forward, he grasped the handle, easing it open a few inches, the dome light inside coming on as he did.

It was only then that I saw it, the piece of thin black string connecting the door to the frame, the material silhouetted by the interior light. My voice caught in my throat as I took just one half step forward before diving at Ferris's back, dropping the Kimber and reaching out with both hands for his canvas coat.

Barely clearing the top of the snow, I pulled him backward, falling flat to the ground, him landing on top of me, his head smacking me in the nose.

We had no more than hit the ground when a blinding flash of light spread across us, followed by a thunderous roar and the sound of glass shattering, a shower of debris falling down around us.

## Chapter Forty-Four

A circle a little over 18 inches in diameter was the best Yvonne could manage. After what she guessed to be 16 hours with no fluids, she was fortunate to have even that much urine in her system.

Squatting over nothing, trying to balance herself just inside the door, was not an easy task. Doing it in front of a man she now knew to be a drug addict made it even less so.

Despite the fact that he was unconscious, she still couldn't ignore him as she did what she had to, blood flushing her cheeks.

Afterward, she retreated to her chair, trying to make her head was as clear as possible, knowing she would need it in the coming minutes.

Just the sight of the small puddle, no matter how pathetic the act of creating it might have been, brought her renewed purpose. Pressing her mouth into a tight line, she drew in a deep breath and stood, the pain in her head having receded, making way for the task she was about to undertake.

She crossed the room and took up the small ceramic heater. The exterior surface felt hot between her hands as she carried it to the far end of the table and placed it on the corner.

Grabbing the table under the top edge, she pulled it over until it was just a couple of feet away from the entrance. The corner of it was positioned close enough to catch the door as it swung open, the heater directly above the puddle on the floor.

Once more Yvonne looked everything over, running the figures in her mind, working up the nerve she needed to see it through.

It would work. It had to.

Tucking herself away in the corner, hidden behind the door, protected by the edge of the table, Yvonne closed her fists and raised them over her head. One at a time she pounded them against the top of the door, swinging her arms like a Polynesian drummer, the entire door shaking against its frame.

One loud hollow thud after another rang out as she continued to beat, hot tears coming to her eyes as her anger, her frustration, her desperation, grew.

She was a doctor, a good one at that. She was young and healthy and was in Montana for the right reasons.

She would be damned if her story ended because a couple of drug runners almost blew themselves up in a blizzard.

"Help! Come quick!" she yelled, raising her voice toward the opening above the door. "It's bad! Something's happening!"

Four more times, twice with each hand, Yvonne hammered at the door, making sure she was heard, before retreating off to the side. She stood with both hands gripping the heater, the implement still whirring away, the hot metal beginning to burn her fingers.

Ignoring it, knowing there was no way she would release her grip, Yvonne stood and waited, her heart pounding. Her breath came in shallow bursts as she stood poised, straining to hear the sound of the lock being removed. She wished with everything she had that she could turn the heater off, could listen closely for the man coming for her, but that wasn't a possibility.

The heater had to be on. She was only going to get one shot at this.

Seconds ticked by, each one bringing renewed anxiety – fear that summoning him before might have used her only chance at getting his attention, that his previous outburst showed a shift in temperament that meant he no longer cared about her or the man on the bed.

The better part of two minutes passed before the telltale sound that Yvonne was waiting for found her ears, the lock scraping against the mechanism on the door. Holding her breath, feeling like her heart had stopped in her chest, Yvonne waited, listening as the lock was pulled free and the doorknob turned.

With her hip pressed tight against the side of the table, Yvonne watched as the door swung toward her, slamming into the corner, stopping just inches from her face.

"What the..." the man muttered, Yvonne waiting just one more second before shoving the heater off the side of the table and stepping back, pressing her body against the wall.

A single spark flashed, bringing with it a blinding blaze of light. On contact there was a loud bang as the circuit in the heater blew, the whining of the fan she'd been listening to for hours mercifully coming to an end.

Overhead the lights dimmed for a moment before regaining full strength, starting a dull humming sound Yvonne hadn't noticed before over the whirring of the heater.

Keeping her place against the wall, Yvonne waited a full minute for any sound at all from the other side of the door. She hadn't heard the man hit the floor, had not picked up on any cursing that would denote the shock hadn't worked.

Instead, she heard nothing beyond the buzz of the lights.

Waiting as long as her frayed nerves could take it, she used her hip to shove the table away from the door and moved out to the side, craning her neck to see if her plan had worked.

## Chapter Forty-Five

Just as fast as the explosion came, it was gone. There was no secondary mechanism, nothing tied to the engine or the gas tank to send the truck up in fiery blaze.

Whoever had rigged the door had done so with a simple explosive device, most likely a grenade, just enough to take out a first responder without drawing anybody else to the scene.

A delaying tactic, nothing more.

"Ferris?" I asked, fully aware of his weight still piled on me, his body limp.

"Ferris?" I asked again, drawing my knees and elbows up under me, feeling him topple over.

The snow softened his landing, the sheriff making no attempt to catch himself as he fell to the side, his hip and shoulder burying themselves in the drift.

Around us bits of the interior of the truck dotted the grounds, blacks spots against a white backdrop. Most appeared to be from the front seat, singed pieces of cloth and plastic, charred chunks of yellow foam cushioning, twisted metal mixed in as well.

"Sheriff?" I called again, my voice rising as I pushed myself up onto my knees, flakes of snow clinging to my front side. On the snow around me were puddles of blood, at least one stemming from my nose, a result of his skull connecting solidly as we fell.

Remaining on my knees, I grabbed hold of Ferris's hip, rolling him over onto his back. Just as before, his body gave no recognition of what was happening as he flopped over flat, his arm swinging free.

The lower half of his body looked the worst, his legs taking the brunt of the explosion after I had jerked him backward. Pieces of metal were sticking out of his calves and feet at odd angles, the wounds still steaming in the cold air. Blood soaked everything from the knees down, the top half of him spotted with soot and debris, but appearing mostly unscathed.

"Ferris," I asked, sliding up the length of him and slapping the side of his face. "Ferris!"

There was no response from the old man as I pressed my index and middle finger up under his jaw, feeling just the slightest tremor of a pulse, his face ashen.

"Shit," I muttered, rising to my feet and moving over to the truck door, the force of the blast blowing it away from the cab. I peered around the rear edge of the frame and stared inside, dark smoke obscuring my view.

From what I could see, most of the driver's seat was gone, nothing more than a metal frame, pieces of cushion continuing to smolder. The scent of singed fabric and my own blood filled my senses as I made a quick assessment of everything, not one thing to indicate a person, or a body, had been inside.

Shoving myself away, I slid in on my knees alongside Ferris, stopping just short of his boots. Tugging the MK-3 combat knife from the rear of my waistband, I made two long cuts along the outside seams of each leg, the charred material slicing easily beneath my blade.

I gently lifted the fabric, and leaving the shards of metal in place to prevent further bleeding, I scooped up snow, one handful after another, and packed it tight around his legs.

By the time I was finished the lower portion of Ferris's body resembled the Michelin man. Once the jeans could take no more, I pulled the fabric back into place to try to keep as much of the snow packed tight as possible.

Improvised and rough as hell, but if anything major was hit, it would help keep him from bleeding out, at least for a while, until I could get him to the hospital.

As much as every part of me wanted to jump back in the truck, to put the headlights on the snow coach treads and follow them to Yvonne, there was no way I could do that. Not now.

Ferris was unconscious, the lower half of his legs were mangled. There was no telling when he might come to, what state he would be in when he did.

The man had come to me in good faith, had put himself out there to seek my aid, even when it was an unpopular decision.

I owed him enough to make sure he got help before anything worse happened, like losing the use of both legs or even more worrisome, slipping into hypothermia while I pushed on.

I could only hope the tracks I needed to find Yvonne Endicott would still be visible when I made it back.

Rising to my feet, the wind continued to pull at my body, getting inside my jacket, touching the sweat that had formed in the small of my back. I could feel it pushing over the blood covering the bottom half of my face, crusting it to my skin, but paid it no mind.

Instead, I hooked my fingers through Ferris's armpits and dropped my backside toward the ground, using my bodyweight to leverage him backward. I pulled until his shoulders were flush with my ankles before backing away a few feet and repeating the process, not a sound or reaction coming from the man.

Along the way I spotted the Kimber lying right where I had dropped it. Pausing just long enough to stow it next to the knife, I went straight back to tugging on the sheriff, my lungs beginning to burn.

One foot at a time I pulled him, wishing we had parked closer, that the damn snow wasn't so deep and unwieldy, making the smaller man feel like he weighed three times his normal weight.

Using the rumbling sound of the diesel engine as a guide, I kept pulling backward, finally reaching my goal. Walking around by his feet, I took one arm and jerked his limp body up at the waist. Grabbing his coat with both hands, I hefted him up onto a shoulder, his legs still packed with snow.

There was no way to know exactly how long it took me to get him back to the truck and wrestled inside. I just knew that by the time I did, I felt the way he looked, every part of my body aching, burning, wishing nothing more than to climb behind the wheel and turn the heater on high, go somewhere and sleep until this was all far behind me.

## Chapter Forty-Six

Finding the man flat on the floor, his arms and legs sprawled out away from him, felt like a bad dream to Yvonne Endicott, wishing nothing more than to be able to wake up from this terrible nightmare in her bed back in Atlanta, where it was warm, where things made sense.

Where she belonged.

After discovering that her plan had worked, that the crude electrocution device had rendered her captor unconscious, it had taken several minutes for her mind to compute what had happened. The whole time she had been planning, it always ended with her shoving the heater off the table. Not once had she considered how to handle things after.

Seeing him lying on the ground, Yvonne's first reaction had been to cry, feeling the emotions of the last day finally releasing. There was no sorrow from what she had done, no pity for the man lying prone on the ground, only the sobering realization of what she had been forced to do.

Once the initial shock passed, her mind finally was able to force her body into action, piecing together the next steps, making a plan.

There was no way she could stay in the barn. It was only a matter of time until the third one returned in the truck, no doubt armed, looking for the man now lying on the floor. She would not be able to hide what she had done, probably not even able to move the man if she tried, not wanting to for fear of waking him up.

It would be plainly obvious what had transpired, no way to predict how things would play out without the clear leader of the group awake and calling the shots.

Hiding wouldn't work for the simple reason there was no place they wouldn't find her in what was more or less an open room.

The only option left was leaving this building, taking her chances against the storm outside. There was no way of knowing where she was, how far from anyone who could help her, but if given the choice between freezing in the snow and waiting to be executed inside, she had to take that risk.

She had come too far not to.

Going outside meant facing the cold, a prospect she was ill prepared for. Dressed for the floor of the emergency room, already she could notice a chill in the room without the ceramic heater, her scrubs and white coat doing nothing to keep her warm. For just the slightest moment she even wished she had been less faithful to her running regimen, allowing a layer of natural insulation to have built up, to protect her in moments such as this.

Assessing first the man on the floor, she saw him wearing nothing more than a sleeveless shirt and jeans, both heavily soiled. She dismissed that thought, knowing neither was worth the risk they presented in getting them free.

Turning her attention to the bed, she was careful to avoid the mess on the floor, picking her way over the remains of the heater as she crossed the room. Grabbing the blankets bunched at the man's waist, she pulled them back, jerking the bottoms out from beneath his feet.

Yet again, there was no response, his drug addled state rendering his system mute as she wadded the blankets into a ball, moving gingerly through the room and out into the barn.

The smell of chemicals and moth balls met her nostrils as Yvonne dropped the clump to the floor and began peeling them apart, assessing what she had. Twice she glanced back into the room, checking to make sure both men were down, a thought occurring on the second glance, giving her pause.

The man on the floor had been wearing a coat earlier.

Dropping the blankets, Yvonne strode away from the room toward the tables stretched out before her, finding what she was looking for sprawled on the ground at the far end. Snatching it up from the floor, she pulled the heavy garment on around her, the nasty scent of old sweat clinging to the canvas material.

At least two sizes too large, Yvonne tugged at the sleeves as she made her way back, stopping halfway, her second bit of good luck laying right out in the open. Never before had she seen such gloves, the material originally brown leather that had been stained black.

Without thought, Yvonne grabbed them and shoved her hands inside, pushing them up under the cuffs of the coat, the gloves reaching almost to her elbows. Like the coat, the interior was slightly damp with sweat, both reeking badly of body odor.

One last peek into the room showed neither man had moved. Her heart rate increasing, the clock in her head making her hyperaware of how long it had been since her captor went down, how much time she might have left, Yvonne snatched up the closest blanket and shoved it up under the bulky front of the coat.

The wool material pressed tight against her as she bent over and took up a second blanket, forcing as much of it as she could under the back of the coat, leaving the tail of it hanging down over her legs.

The third she draped over her head as she turned for the door, her pace increasing to a jog as she crossed the floor of the barn.

She was warm for the moment, but there was no way of knowing how fierce the storm was, the sound of the wind outside the only indicator she'd had for the better part of a day. Finding the coat and gloves had been a boon for sure, but her legs were woefully unprotected for trekking through snow, the thin cotton pants and running shoes not going to offer much help at all to whatever she might find outside.

Her jog took her just short of the far wall, her attention sweeping over the length of it, searching for an exit that did not exist. The place had been built as a barn, only a single access point breaking up the solid metal exterior, that being the very same door she had heard opening and closing earlier.

Feeling her stomach constrict, Yvonne paused before going to the single button mounted on the wall beside the door.

Her pulse rising, Yvonne pressed it, the overhead motor rumbling to life with the same loud grinding of gears she remembered, a fierce plume of icy air hitting her in the face, threatening to lift the blanket away from her head.

Taking two steps back away from the door, Yvonne waited, careful not to create a silhouette against the backlight of the barn. Counting off seconds in her head, she waited until the door was past the top of her head, every bit of her wanting no part of the world outside, at the same time knowing she had no choice.

Gritting her teeth, clutching the blanket tight in front of her, Yvonne pushed out of the barn, setting her course at an angle.

With the very first step she sank to her knee in the dense snow, cold enveloping her leg, pulling the air from her lungs. On the second, feeling fled from her bottom half, both legs growing numb, walking merely an exercise in muscle memory.

Tears formed at the corners of her eyes as she made her way forward, bending at the waist, the wind whipping at her back, the tail of the blanket flapping behind her.

Keep going.

She just had to keep going.

## Chapter Forty-Seven

Every few seconds Trick Reynolds glanced into the rearview mirror, seeing the scowl on Barnham's face, the big man forced to sit upright, sharing his bench seat with Jasper.

The smaller man seemed oblivious to the glares he was receiving, his focus aimed out the side window. Occasionally he would raise a hand to his mouth and gnaw on a fingernail, completely silent since they had all loaded into the coach and set off again.

If he was in pain, or even noticed the gash above his left eye, he didn't let on.

Bringing him along wasn't something Trick was especially keen on, though he conceded to the logic in doing it. At the moment they still had an arrangement with Cuddyer, and killing one of his men, especially his lackey, would not do much to preserve it.

"Turn here," Mac said from the passenger seat, extending a hand to the right, pointing out the top half of a sign just off the side of the road.

While barely lifting his foot from the gas, Trick maneuvered the machine onto the side road, his body desperate to get out of the coach. What he might find or have to do in the coming hours he wasn't excited about, but at the moment the simple thought of extricating himself from the vehicle, letting his aching body stretch, was most appealing.

"Just another quarter mile," Mac said, checking the GPS in his hand one more time before glancing up, his head tilting back slightly in surprise. "Right there, as a matter of fact."

Leaning forward, Trick glanced up ahead, seeing exactly what Mac had referenced, having the same reaction.

There, shining like a beacon in the snow, was a bright light.

Feeling a sense of dread, Trick propped his left hand over the steering wheel and turned in his seat, looking at Jasper still staring out at nothing.

"Hey, you, is that the place?"

There was no response at all, the man catatonic, his eyes glassy, as if he might burst into tears at any moment.

"Hey! Jasper!" Trick snapped, letting everyone hear the growing frustration he felt. "That the place?"

The raised tone, the angry tenor, together managed to penetrate Jasper's mind. Snapping his hand down from his mouth, he looked to the rearview mirror, matching Trick's gaze, before leaning forward between the front seats.

The smell of chemicals and intense body odor followed him, Trick and Mac both leaning toward their respective windows as Jasper stood frozen between them, a hand on the back of either seat.

"Why's Cuddy got the door open?" Jasper asked, his voice relaying the surprise that was plastered across his face.

Who he was posing the question to, or who he thought would answer, Trick had no idea, his agitation only growing more pronounced.

"It's not supposed to be up?"

"It wasn't when I left," Jasper said. "And the truck is back there, so I don't know why he'd have it open."

Agitation gave way to anger as Trick leaned forward, using his elbow to leverage Jasper back into his seat. Lifting himself up a few inches, he adjusted the front of his snow suit, watching the light grow closer.

For as annoying as Jasper's presence had been, in this particular case he wasn't wrong. There weren't many reasons why anybody would leave a door that large standing open, especially in a snowstorm, the temperatures below freezing.

Even worse, the storm was bringing an early evening to the area, the light from within the barn standing out, easily visible to anybody approaching.

Not exactly the type of thing somebody running an illicit operation wanted to be doing.

Glancing to the sat phone on the dash, Trick considered calling Wood to tell him things were not good, to prep him for the bad news that surely lay ahead, before thinking better of it.

He would assess things completely before making the call, the only question in his mind being how much damage control he was going to have to do before returning home.

The faintest outline of tracks could be seen cutting through the snow along the right side of the road, Trick easing back just slightly on the gas and veering the coach to follow them toward the barn. The heavy van jostled hard twice as they left the road, each man getting lifted from his seat before settling back in, the metal frame groaning a few times in protest as it continued to move forward.

The world seemed to darken even further as thick trees crowded in on either side, lodge pole pines with their boughs heavily weighted by snow. Together they managed to blot out any rays of light that were making it through the gray sky, the headlights of the van and the open door the only illumination.

Aiming the van right at the opening, Trick kept the gas steady as the front end of the tracks rolled up onto asphalt. On contact the ride became easier as the machine leveled out, the whine of the engine receding.

Pushing them far enough inside so that the van and the trailer were both on the concrete, Trick cut the engine, sitting behind the wheel, surveying the scene before them.

It was the first time he'd been inside since construction had taken place six months prior, the place a near replica of the holding facility used by The Dogs for their winter gear. Large and open, the ceiling was almost 20 feet high, the walls metal, strips of insulation filling the gaps between studs.

Given what had taken place at the previous lab, with all the supplies stored inside it was a fire hazard to say the least, but not something Trick was overly keen on analyzing at the moment.

Twin rows of workbenches lined most of the middle of the room, a makeshift lab coming together. Along the back wall appeared to be enough raw material to keep them running for quite some time, certainly enough to take back to Chance should they need to look elsewhere for their product.

Along the left side of the room was a small room that had been built out from the side of the barn, a door standing open in the center of it.

As far as Trick could tell, there wasn't a soul moving anywhere about.

"Did they open the door to go outside and take a piss?" Mac asked, noticing the desolation of the room and being the first to comment on it.

"No," Jasper whispered, his voice surprising both men in the front seat. "The can is back in the corner behind us."

"Then where the hell are they?" Trick asked, turning over his shoulder, directing the statement at Jasper.

"I don't know," Jasper replied, the word said low and fast, coming out as one long jumble, just barely decipherable.

Again, feeling a pang of irritation, Trick pushed open his door and stepped out, the interior temperature of the barn almost identical to what it had been outside.

For whatever reason the door was open, it had been that way for a while.

On the opposite side of the van the other three climbed out, the sound of their boots echoing through the building, disturbing the almost spooky stillness.

The thought of asking Jasper if there was any way for Cuddyer to have made a run for it, to have had another vehicle and just vanish into the night, passed through Trick's mind, replaced only by his strong desire not to engage Jasper in any further conversation. Instead, he walked straight for the room ahead, stopping just outside the door and peering in.

"You have got to be shitting me," he said aloud, turning to glance at the others, Mac and Barnham walking toward him, Jasper staying back a few steps.

Remaining rooted in place, he leaned a shoulder against the doorframe, allowing the others to see past him into the room.

Along the back wall was a rusted bed with a thin mattress, Elias lying on top, his shirt raised to his chin, his body chewed up by what Trick figured could be anything from burns to Ebola.

Five feet away, lying splayed out on the floor, was Cuddyer. Face down, head turned to the side, his body was spread out like a starfish, a small ceramic heater on the ground between his feet, the smell of piss in the air.

In his time, Trick thought he had seen it all. Riding with a crew like The Dogs, he had witnessed some horrific things, seen fights that spiraled well out of control, seen things done to bodies that should never be done.

Still, he could never remember seeing a scene like this.

"What the hell?" Barnham asked.

Trick shook his head, at a loss for words as he stared into the room, taking it all in.

"What?" Jasper asked, his voice still low, drawing their attention to him. Standing back at least 10 feet from the group, he kept his hands clasped before him, his gaze aimed at the floor. "Is it the girl? Did he do something to her?"

Feeling his teeth clench tight, Trick closed his eyes, raising his face toward the ceiling. "What girl?" he practically shouted.

Jasper pulled back, retreating further into himself, trying to find the strength to speak.

"Cuddy said we couldn't take Elias to the hospital, so we'd bring the doc to him."

Trick felt his eyes pop open, threatening to bulge from his skull.

"You're telling me you dumb shits kidnapped a doctor?"

## Chapter Forty-Eight

Meredith Shek was the first person to emerge from the operating suite. More than 12 hours had passed since our first encounter, the bags under her eyes and the wrinkles in her scrubs seeming to indicate that she was still on the same shift, having slept exactly as much as I had. She walked slowly and deliberately, exhaustion clear.

Azbell, Baker, and I all stood.

On the ride back I had used the radio mounted on Ferris's dash to call into the station, telling them that their man was injured and to meet me at the hospital. First Azbell and then Baker had tried to get me to divulge exactly what happened over the radio, the former simply asking, the latter trying to pull rank to force me to.

Ignoring them both, I turned off the radio, driving through town as fast as the elements would allow. My thoughts were in a dozen different places, my mind trying to make sense of everything that was occurring around me, prioritizing what lay ahead.

The first step was clearly to get Ferris some medical help. I had laid down the passenger seat as far as it would go, placing his feet at the front of the floor well, the bottoms of his jeans still holding at least some of the packed snow.

He had made the trip without waking up or making a sound, but his color seemed to improve, even if just a little.

Whether that was real or wishful thinking I didn't much know, not that it especially mattered.

Either way, he was clearly out of the game, and I still had work to do.

There was no way I was going to leave Yvonne to herself, one woman against at least three men, who knew how many more on the way. Ferris knew the area better than anyone, he trusted me, plus he had a vested interest in finding her.

At one point he had even mentioned deputizing me, though how much all that held sway should he slip into a coma, there was no way of knowing.

If the previous day had taught me anything, it was that there was no way Baker would want me anywhere near the investigation.

Both of the deputies had been waiting when I arrived, swinging up within just a couple feet of the front door. They had called ahead and prepped the doctors that Ferris was on his way in, enabling them to have him out of the truck and inside within minutes, disappearing behind the swinging doors into the operating suite.

That had been 45 minutes earlier.

Twice in the ensuing time I had recounted the story, once for Azbell, a second time for Baker as he tried to pick it apart, more than once insinuating that somehow I had had something to do with what happened.

Each time he did I wanted to snap back that if I had, I would have left the old man in the snow to die instead of spending time to get him help, would have pointed out that it was my blood crusted to my chin from when I pulled him away from the blast.

Still I managed to swallow the words, knowing it would only agitate the situation. He was trying to take over a case that he knew nothing about.

That wasn't going to happen. If I was to have any chance at slipping away, I needed his guard down.

By the time Shek arrived, all conversation had died away, and most of the hostility.

"Well," she said, "the sheriff was extremely lucky. Most of the wounds he sustained in the blast were superficial, tearing up the skin and some of the muscle, but not hitting anything vital."

A strained smile crossed her face as she added, "With a little time, and if we can keep him pinned down long enough, he should make a full recovery."

An audible sigh passed from Azbell as she raised both hands to her chest and looked at Baker, whose only response was to again glare at me.

"Mr. Hawk," Shek said, addressing me directly, "that was some good work with the snow. Kept bleeding down, prevented too much burn damage from the metal."

Every bit of me wanted to turn and match Baker's glare, even more to ball my hand into a fist and drive it like a piston through his nose, but I merely nodded in acceptance of the praise, saying nothing.

"He's also awake," Shek said, "and is asking to see you."

In unison Azbell and Baker both took a step forward, only to be stopped by Shek, a hand outstretched in their direction.

"Actually, just him," she said, pausing long enough to ensure her message was received before motioning for me to follow her on back.

Again, I wanted to smart off to Baker, to flip him the bird at the very least, but I forced myself to stay even, to swallow my animosity for the man, to focus on what was important.

If Ferris was asking to see me, it meant he was still in the game, even if he was confined to bed for a while.

Hopefully it also meant he was yielding control of the investigation to me.

Shek led me through the deserted halls, as still as they had been on my previous trip. The only difference I could see was that all the overhead lights had been flipped on, making it almost too bright as we walked on.

"He's still very weak," Shek said, her voice low as she slowed before stopping just outside a small recovery room, "so try to keep it brief, don't let him get too worked up."

Now that I knew he was okay, brief was the most important thing running through my mind.

As for his getting worked up or not, I could promise nothing.

Nodding in understanding, I passed through the doorway to find Ferris propped up in a patient bed, his frontier lawman attire having been cast aside for a hospital gown. Several heavy blankets covered his body from his knees to his chest, the bottom half of his legs resting atop the sheets, encased in a thick swath of gauze. An IV line was attached to his arm, a bag of some indeterminate solution hanging from a silver pole beside him.

Otherwise, there was only a single chair alongside the bed, the rest of the room barren.

The idea of sitting didn't even cross my mind as I took up a post beside the bed, my hands in the front pockets of my jeans.

"Nurse said you're going to be alright," I opened. "That's good news."

"Bah," Ferris said, raising his hand just slightly, attempting to wave me off but stopping short, the effort too much. "They tell me you saved my bacon."

While it was true I had, there was no need to belabor the point at the moment. We both had something far more important that needed finishing before we got together around the campfire to swap *remember when's*.

His expression hardened, the flinty veneer I had seen for the previous 18 hours pushing past the pain and his current situation.

"Why do they call you Hawk?"

I had expected a great many things when Shek told me he wanted to speak to me, none of them concerning the etymology of my name. I made no effort to hide my surprise as my eyebrows rose, very much aware of the dwindling timeframe we were on.

"My pop was a big *Jeremiah Johnson* fan," I said. "My full name is Jeremiah Hawkens Tate."

Lifting his head an inch from the bed, Ferris rolled his face to stare at me. "No shit?"

"No shit," I said, having no idea why we were having this conversation, anxious to get back to work.

"First movie I ever saw in a theater," he said. "Played right down the street. Everybody in town liked it so much, they kept it here for more than three months."

Forcing a half smile, I nodded, bouncing on the balls of my feet, letting him see I was aching to be moving again.

"I was hoping you'd tell me it came from some badass story about your time with the DEA," Ferris said, letting his head fall back into place, "but I reckon that will do."

I had just saved his life, was still wearing my own blood, and knew he was fully aware of what had taken place at my cabin six weeks before.

For the time being, that would have to be badass enough.

"You know I'm going after her."

"Why?" Ferris asked, his head still reclined, only his eyes shifting to look at me. "When I came to see you, I wasn't actually expecting you to come along for the ride. I just knew if you were half as good as the story I'd heard, I needed you to make sure Yvonne got home."

Again he attempted to raise his hand, giving up and simply flicking his fingers toward the door.

"Hell, you've seen what I've got to work with out there. Mavis is a follower and Coop's so worried about gunning for my job this fall that so far all they've done is make one lap around town and sit in the station house."

More than once I had had that same exact thought, repeating it each time Baker glowered in my direction, but had said nothing.

At least it now made sense why he hated me so much. Ferris working with an outsider to solve the biggest case to hit town probably ever would not only solidify his job for life, it would display a distinct lack of faith in his deputy's abilities.

"But you did come," Ferris said. "Less than an hour, there you were, haven't left since."

He paused, his face trembling just slightly, before the last thing on earth I expected to happen, did.

A single tear rolled out from the corner of his eye, streaking down over his face.

In that moment, it all became clear to me. How Yvonne Endicott had discovered her father was ill. Why she had decided to leave a promising post in Georgia to come to Glasgow. The pained expression Ferris had been wearing most of the day.

"You called her," I said.

Pressing his eyes shut tight, another tear leaked down as Ferris nodded.

"I tried to help Mike as much as I could, but I'm no doctor. He never married, never even dated after the thing with Yvonne's mother. There was nobody else, so I called and asked for her help.

"Being the young woman that she is, she came right up, no questions asked."

"And now you feel responsible," I said.

"I *am* responsible," Ferris said, opening his eyes, fixing his gaze on me. "And now I'm about to hand that responsibility to you, so I need to know why.

"Why were you so compelled to help when you had no good Goddamn reason to do so?"

# Part Four

## Chapter Forty-Nine

All organizational activities had been called off under the guise of letting everybody stay inside through the storm. Under normal circumstances it wouldn't have mattered, everybody gathering at the traditional watering hole anyway, riding it out while shooting pool and drinking copious amounts of beer.

As much as the men enjoyed riding, they were also aware that the Dakotas and Montana just weren't suitable for it a good chunk of the year. To get around that, The Dogs had built the infrastructure to keep them occupied, the recent influx of cash from their arrangement with the Bakken giving most of the men even more time to hang out, watch ballgames, wager on anything they could think of, and wait for the weather to break so they could get outside again.

The amount of apathy that was beginning to set in six months into the winter was something Wood Arrasco was growing concerned with, something he would have to address before winter came around again. Most years the majority of the men held down jobs through the winter months, taking whatever they made to subsidize the remainder of the year spent out on the road.

Now that a major source of income had materialized most had foregone working, spending more and more time huddled around the bar, their growing waistlines and increasing lethargy becoming noticeable.

As much as it bothered Wood, for the time being it would have to wait.

Avoiding returning home just yet, having to explain to Maria what was going on, trying in vain to hide his concern, he remained at his office. For a group the size of The Dogs there was always something that needed to be done, a series of menial tasks that kept his mind just busy enough to place the situation in Glasgow on the back burner, always there, lurking beneath the surface, without dominating his every thought.

When the phone rang at half past 5:00 in the afternoon, Wood shoved aside the paperwork he was completing without a second thought, leaving it stacked in the middle of his desk and rising to his feet. His heart rate spiked, a tremor passing through his stomach as he took up the phone and returned to his post by the window.

Despite the early hour, nightfall was already well under way, the sky dark. What light did exist was cast through the window by the desk lamp behind him, his own shadow stretched out on the ground.

"Yeah?"

"Prez," Trick said. Wood knew in his gut that things were just as bad as he had feared.

"I'm listening."

A moment passed before a sigh was heard over the line, bringing with it a realization

Trick was trying to figure out how to best word what he had to say.

Feeling his grip tighten on the phone, Wood fought the urge to demand that Trick get on with it, knowing his lieutenant would proceed when he was ready.

"It's bad," Trick finally said, a touch of resignation in his voice.

"Worse than last time?" Wood asked, remembering their previous conversation, right after Trick had found Jasper alongside the road.

"Much," Trick said, not a moment of hesitation. "We just got to the secondary location, arrived to find the damn door standing wide open, all the lights on."

Making his free hand into a fist, Wood held it directly out in front of him, wishing he had something, anything, to bury it into.

"Fools," he said, the word passing through his gritted teeth. "Are they trying to be spotted?"

"That's just the start of it," Trick said. "We pulled in to find Elias circling the drain and Cuddyer flat on the floor, damn near dead himself."

Releasing the fist, Wood let his hand fall to his side.

"Cuddyer was sampling the product, too?"

"No," Trick said, "not an overdose, he was electrocuted."

There was no stopping Wood's jaw as it dropped, his chest tightening.

Trick paused to let that sink in before he continued, "That's not all. The idiots also kidnapped a doctor to try and treat Elias. *That's* who electrocuted Cuddyer."

Wood had no response, the words eluding him, his mind unable to fully comprehend what he'd just been told.

"And now she's gone?" he eventually asked, already knowing the answer.

A moment of silence passed before Trick said, "I'll send Mac out on a snowmobile to find her. In this weather, it shouldn't take long."

Wood shook his head. Already this situation was pushing itself past the limit, no amount of product being worth what Cuddyer and his crew were putting them through, regardless of quality.

"And the lab?" Wood asked.

"Getting there," Trick said. "Barnham is on it, has Jasper helping wherever he can, but let's be honest, the man is basically worthless."

Wood nodded in agreement, his jaw set.

"I'm going to go back and try to revive Cuddyer, see if I can't get him up, get this thing running shortly."

"How long until it's ready to go?" Wood asked.

"I don't know," Trick replied. "They were coming along pretty well before Cuddyer got his ass lit up. Barnham seems to think an hour or two."

"And how much we talking in raw materials?"

"Enough," Trick said, leaving his explanation to just a single word, both sides knowing exactly what he meant.

Standing there, staring out at the snow, Wood raised a hand to his brow. He kneaded it with his thumb and forefinger, pressing down hard, trying to massage away the pain that had settled just behind his eyes.

His first inclination, damned near every inclination in fact, was to tell Trick to just pack up the raw materials, dispense with Cuddyer's crew and head back. Once they returned, he would deliver it all to Chance, have him take over the lion's share of the production.

It would be a downtick in quality for sure, but he highly doubted demand would suffer in the slightest. They had a captive economy with the oil fields, a huge consumer base of low-class individuals with plenty of cash and nothing resembling a major city within hundreds of miles.

If the difference between the two products was even noticed, he doubted it would do much to affect sales, offering the added benefit of being close to his customers.

Still, for whatever reason, he couldn't quite pull the plug on things in Glasgow just yet. They had invested in creating a lab and a backup, were just an hour away from being able to knock out what was needed to keep their supply chain moving for the time being.

As much as he despised Cuddyer for the situation he was in, he couldn't do anything rash, not just yet anyway.

"Do what you can," Wood said, "make as much as you can carry, and then get the hell out of there."

"You got it," Trick replied. "And the crew?"

"Make an example of them."

## Chapter Fifty

Rake Ferris was only 50 percent right.
    He was correct that the responsibility for Yvonne Endicott now fell to me. The fact that I had never met the girl, likely never would have if not for this situation, was irrelevant.

She was a young woman, a physician, who had done nothing wrong. In fact, she had found herself in this position because she had done things right. She had picked up the phone when her estranged uncle called, had listened as he explained the situation with her father.

Had come running without a moment's pause to help in any way she could.

When she arrived, she had accepted a position below her worth, was attempting to make the best of it, was even working an exceptionally long shift when she was nabbed.

Put simply, she was better than Sam Cuddyer or Jasper Maxx or anybody like them who might be out there. If there was any way I could help make sure that they were not the last people she ever encountered in this life, then it was my responsibility to try.

Ferris was absolutely wrong, though, when he claimed that I had no earthly reason to offer assistance.

I couldn't fault him for being wrong, his experiences with me being secondhand stories he had heard about the incident at my cabin six weeks earlier. And while they did illustrate the lengths I would be willing to go to, they said nothing about the reasons why.

Not a soul in Montana had any idea why I called the state home. They could not fathom that the place was chosen not as a refuge, but as a hideout, a spot I sought more than five years before to evade the world.

There was no reason for him to be aware that I had come here just weeks after offering my resignation from the DEA, that event coming just months after returning home early from a case to find my wife and daughter burned alive in the front yard, our home reduced to rubble behind them.

There was no way he would ever grasp the guilt I still carried with me, the fire burning in me to help every person I could, to honor every promise I had made, to atone for the fact that I had not been able to protect those who meant the most to me.

At just 35-years-old, I knew my soul was charred beyond repair, my body just an empty husk of who I once was. No amount of doing what was right, of putting myself in harm's way for others, would ever make up for that.

It didn't matter that Rake Ferris, or really anybody else, didn't know any of that.

I knew it.

And it was the reason I answered when he knocked on my door, the very reason I would do the same the next time somebody came seeking my help.

The thoughts played through my mind as I pulled Ferris's truck to a stop outside his brother's house. Under the heavy blanket of white I couldn't be sure where the driveway ended and the front yard began, not particularly caring as I hopped out. In two quick steps I was through the heavy drift, immune to the wet snow clinging to my clothes, and made my way across the porch, the floorboards echoing beneath my feet.

I went straight in without knocking, stopping on the rug inside the door. Everything appeared to be exactly as it was the last time I was there, the only difference being a noticeable lack of light, a single lamp burning in the living room.

Seated beside it was Mike Ferris, a hardback book in his lap, a pair of glasses perched on the end of his nose. He remained perfectly still as I entered, finishing the page he was on, before closing the book and looking up, pulling the glasses away and letting them hang from a chain around his neck.

If he was surprised in the slightest to see me standing there, he gave no indication whatsoever.

"Is Rake okay?" he asked, raising a gnarled hand and motioning me forward.

My wet shoes squeaked as I walked, water tracing my path across the floor.

"He will be," I said. "His legs got chewed up pretty good, but nothing vital was damaged."

How he had known his brother was hurt, I couldn't be certain, though he most likely reasoned I wouldn't be here alone unless something had happened to Rake.

"So you found her?" Mike asked.

"Not yet, but getting closer. We found their truck abandoned along the side of the road. They had rigged a grenade to the door..."

I left it at that, already having let enough time slip past, the afternoon fast giving way to evening.

"He told me you would have some things I could use," I said.

I didn't have any real idea what he had meant when he said it, knowing only that I couldn't roll up on whoever was out there in Ferris's truck carrying only the Kimber and the MK-3. I now knew of at least three men, possibly many more, waiting for me, and I knew that if they had grenades, they could have any number of other weapons.

What Mike, a withered old man, could have that would help, I couldn't imagine, but it was worth 20 minutes for me to stop and find out.

After that, there would be no more stops.

Not until I found Yvonne.

"Did you know, I was the one who convinced Rake to find you?"

Mike said, fixing his gaze on me, waiting for a response I did not give. "He was already toying with it, trying to balance it against his guilt, feeling like me and Yvonne were both his responsibility."

Turning his head to the side he coughed twice, a wet, guttural sound that echoed in the room before falling away.

"I told him he was being an idiot. Someone out there had our Yvonne, and he needed someone like you on his side."

"Someone like me?" I asked, narrowing my eyes.

His gaze met mine for a moment.

"There's no need to play it off or be ashamed. This is a small town, we all know what happened. We also know that the only reason you are breathing free air is that you were in the right."

I remained fixed in my spot, standing halfway across the room from him, saying nothing.

"And that's the guy we needed to find Yvonne. Someone who doesn't mind kicking a whole lot of ass, so long as he's in the right."

Just like his brother, Mike Ferris was only partially right. I had never thought to put anything I had done into those terms, but I could see how from his perspective, it could be construed that way.

"So," Mike said, not bothering to wait for my response, "how can I help you go do that?"

## Chapter Fifty-One

The first part of the journey had been easy. Yvonne's legs had gone numb within seconds, helping her to move past the searing pinpricks of the cold as it passed through her scrubs and running shoes, gnawing at her toes. Her progress was slow, but fairly steady.

The coat and gloves, the three blankets, had kept her upper body warm, her blood pumping, reaching her lower extremities even if she couldn't feel them.

She knew it wouldn't be enough to keep frostbite at bay for long, praying with each step that town wasn't too far beyond the scope of her vision, that it was just the swirling snow that kept her from seeing the lights of the hospital in the distance.

Time became irrelevant, she was making progress, the light of the barn and the men inside it, fading from view behind her.

Moisture continued to leak from the corners of her eyes as she pressed on, a natural reaction to the bitter cold, the wind freezing it to her cheeks. Her throat felt raw as she drew in ragged breaths of the icy air, the blanket pressed over her face, covering everything but her eyes.

The only way Yvonne could think to describe it was like a frigid

Hell, a complete inversion of the traditional stereotype of the fiery afterlife.

Not until she spotted the light emerging in the distance did she have any idea how much worse things could get.

When she first saw it, her initial thought was that she had made it, that the edge of town was just up ahead, a beacon to guide her in. Her mouth turned up in a smile as relief flooded through, her progress stopping for a moment, her gaze raised to the sky, giving silent thanks.

It wasn't until she lowered her face and opened her eyes again that she heard the sound accompanying it, the persistent rumble of an engine, unmistakable as it cut through the howling wind around her.

With every part of her clenching tight, Yvonne felt her jaw drop open, seeing the light grow from a tiny speck to a small orb, each moment bringing it closer.

The third man was returning.

The thought of help arriving, of someone having found her, never entered Yvonne's mind as she stood and watched the light grow closer, frozen in place, unable to react. Gripped by cold, her feet entrenched in the snow, she waited, her psyche forcing its way past the elements, tapping into the most primal of all human instincts.

Self-preservation.

Without thought or reason, without even looking where she was going, Yvonne turned hard to the left, flinging herself over the edge of the elevated surface she assumed to be the road. Turning on her side, she rolled three times, the snow and the blankets padding her body, a spray of ice flying up around her, whipping at her face, entering her mouth.

With each revolution her momentum grew, the pitch of the ground sharper than she realized, her body gaining speed before stopping abruptly.

Pain erupted in Yvonne's ribs, stars appearing in her vision as she slammed into the base of a lodge pole pine, the trunk almost the width of her midsection, bending her in half around it. Her eyes bulging, she released her grip on the blanket, the wind ripping it away, pinning it to the tree behind her.

She forgot her frozen extremities, her raw lungs, as she lay wrapped around the base of the tree. Only vaguely did she notice the light as it passed her by, the enormous outline of the truck as it rumbled past never once slowing, giving no indication that anyone had seen her.

In that moment, for the first time, the thought of quitting entered Yvonne's mind. Lying face down in the snow, all she had to do was wrestle her way out of the coat and gloves, let the blankets blow away. There she could remain, the bed of snow beneath her sapping all warmth from her body, forcing her into an eternal sleep within minutes.

Nobody would find her for days or even weeks, let alone disturb her as she slipped into the afterlife.

Just as fast the thought passed, ripped away by the wind as if it were the blanket that had enveloped her head.

She had come too far, had endured too much. Already, she had bested her captor, would find a way to make it back, to best the elements as well.

The last face she ever saw would damn sure not be that bearded bastard lying back there in the barn.

Forcing her legs up under her, Yvonne rose to a kneeling position. Her head ached, the world spinning just slightly, the last of the Advil beginning to fade from her system. Every breath was pained, a knife jabbing into her side, the instant diagnosis seeming to indicate at least one broken rib, potentially more.

Yvonne had seen enough such injuries through her training to know she had to be careful, the possibility of a piece of fractured bone piercing her lungs or heart very real.

Still, she was out of options. She had to chance it, to make her way back up the slope and keep moving toward town, to hope her body would hold up long enough for her to make it back.

Scooping a handful of snow from the ground beneath her, Yvonne pressed it into her mouth, holding it on her tongue a moment in hopes that it would melt before giving up and chewing slowly, the crystals forming a slush that she swallowed straight down. Twice more she took up massive scoops, fighting a losing battle to ignore the aching in her side, hoping the hydration would help, before rising to full height.

No matter how hard it was, no matter how long it took, she had to keep going.

## Chapter Fifty-Two

I had made the mistake of letting my eyes tell me that I knew everything there was to know about Mike Ferris. I saw the breathing tube, the gapping bathrobe, the withering frame, and assumed that he was just another old man, the kind prone to sitting around and embellishing the past, the very kind I would probably be if there was any chance of me actually making it to his age.

What I had discounted was how much of what I saw was attributed to the sickness, sapping the vitality from the man long before his time. I had forgotten his life in the army, the fact that he was a Montana man through and through, with all the trappings that came with it.

When I was growing up, my father had a gun safe. It held one .30-06 for deer hunting, one Wingmaster for the occasional trip out for birds, and two antique handguns that had been passed down to him by my grandfather.

Back when I had an actual home of my own, beyond the hermit's cabin outside of Glasgow, I had a gun cabinet, a handsome wood and glass job with a heavy lock on it to make sure that even if my daughter ever did ignore my repeated admonishments, she couldn't open it.

Inside were two shotguns and a deer rifle, along with the same two antiques my father eventually gave me.

When not on the job, my service piece was stowed there as well.

Mike Ferris had a gun *room*.

The old man couldn't get up from his chair, but directed me to the basement stairs, telling me where the light switch was on the wall, and instructing me to take whatever I wanted.

The hinges on the door screeched in protest, indicating it hadn't been opened in some time, Mike probably unable to make the trek down, Yvonne having no need to.

The pale glow of yellow light illuminated everything as I flipped the switch. I descended the old creaking stairs into an unfinished basement cluttered with boxes, yard tools for summer, an ancient freezer that was unplugged, and the usual assortment of junk.

All of that I processed and pushed aside in a matter of moments, my attention drawn to the right, to the spread that was laid out on the opposite half of the space.

"Be all you can be," I muttered, as I stared at what he had put together, an arsenal with everything needed should an invasion come sweeping over the Canadian border.

Three metal racks were affixed to the wall, large bolts countersunk into the concrete block. On them hung more than a dozen rifles, ranging from a .30-06 Winchester matching my own, to what looked like an Israeli assault weapon.

There was an M-16 and an AK-47, enough firepower to take out a small army, or make a certified gun nut swoon.

A glass case was positioned in front of the racks with least as many handguns, big revolvers on down to a Derringer that would fit in the palm of my hand. Each one had been cleaned and polished, all resting on oil cloths, ready to go.

Beneath the case were scores of ammo boxes matching each of the weapons.

The opposite wall had racks with army camouflage uniforms for all seasons, even heavy coats and other accessories for winter.

In the corner more boxes were stacked almost to the ceiling, the letters MRE – Meals Ready to Eat – stenciled on the side along with a description of whatever army delicacies were packed inside.

There was no stopping my mouth as it dropped open, staring at the display before me. For five years I had lived in Montana, had heard the stories about anti-governments types and militias hiding in the mountains, but had never put much stock in them.

Never would I have imagined...

Just as fast I pushed the notion aside, unbuttoning my canvas coat and letting it drop to the floor. I placed the Kimber on top of it, not knowing what was about to take place, but reasonably certain the sheriff would appreciate me not using a weapon registered to him in a gunfight.

Starting on the far wall, I snatched a white blizzard parka off the rack and shrugged it on. The shoulders were a bit snug, the sleeves just a touch too short, but the front zipped fine, the garment much warmer than the one I had just stripped off.

It would do.

I also grabbed a watch cap and heavy gloves, both made from thick wool knit, and a pair of goggles. Despite the cold outside, that would be enough to keep me warm without inhibiting my movements.

I moved to my left and took up a matching pair of Walther PPK's, both with full magazines inserted, a round chambered. I stowed them in my front pockets, my gaze lingering on the ammunition piled on the floor, before shoving aside the notion.

The Walther's alone held 30 rounds, the odds of firing even a fraction of that low, any more than that nonexistent.

My last acquisition before heading up out of the bunker was an M-16 with a full banana clip, the same weapon I had cut my teeth on in the navy years before.

The Israeli weapon was bigger, offered a larger magazine, and the AK had a bit more stopping power, but there was something to be said for familiarity. I had trained with the M-16, could switch from single shot to three round bursts without glancing down at it, knew it wouldn't seize up in the cold.

My old coat and the Kimber I left where they lay, ascending the steps, my body temperature rising in the army winter gear, the new weapons filling me with renewed resolve.

I now had a heading for Yvonne Endicott, or at least some clear tracks cut through the snow. I also had the firepower I needed to meet whatever challenge may await when I arrived.

Together, those two facts combined to put me in a state I had once been intimately familiar with, had spent most of the last five years hiding from. The guesswork was over. Now all that was left was the matter of riding out to meet the enemy, of seeing which side was the better prepared.

One of the guys on my FAST team liked to say the person who wins a fight is the one willing to take it the furthest.

I didn't know the men who had Yvonne Endicott, but I knew for certain that they were not willing to take things as far as I was.

As I emerged from the basement, Mike Ferris had managed to work his way into the kitchen, the canister of oxygen by his side as he leaned against the counter taking in deep breaths of the precious air.

He looked me up and down, apparently approving of what I had chosen, a small nod his only response. He reached out to the side and pointed at a single silver key lying on the countertop beside him, a rabbit foot's keychain attached to the end.

"Take this out to the garage," he said. "I think you'll find something better than Rake's big truck."

I offered my own nod before taking up the key and moving through the side door into the garage. A single overhead light was already on as I entered, an older Dodge Ram sitting beside the door.

Glancing to the key in my hand, seeing it would clearly not fit the truck, I moved around it.

I couldn't help but smile again as I saw what Mike had been directing me to, a polished black Polaris Switchback snowmobile tucked away on the opposite side. It was backed in, facing outward, ready to shoot out into the storm.

As if reading my thoughts, the garage door began to rise, a quick glance over my shoulder showing Mike leaning against the kitchen door, his hand pressed to the opener.

Over the noise of the door I heard him mutter something about "those sonsabitches" before the force of the wind took over, blocking all sound, slamming into me broadside.

Just 10 minutes later I was outside of town, Jasper Maxx's truck in my wake, the tracks of the coach stretched out like a map before me in the snow.

## Chapter Fifty-Three

In my other life, the one where I carried a weapon solely for use against the occasional rogue animal and wore a smile for my customers, I had spent more than my fair share of time on snowmobiles. Between the months of November and May it was really the best way to get around the park, trading some of the warmth and comfort of a snow coach for an extreme upgrade in speed and accessibility.

I didn't own any snowmobiles for my guide business, the liability insurance exorbitant to cover guests, many from warm climates who had never even seen, let alone been on one. I did have a standing agreement, though, with a rental company in West Yellowstone for the rare occasion I did take a group in during the winter months.

It had been a while since I'd been on a Switchback, the model a few years old, the kind a private citizen like Mike Ferris would buy secondhand once an outfitter decided to upgrade.

Even at that, the machine was more than capable for what I needed, the gas gauge indicating the tank was full, the treaded belt running along the undercarriage, propelling me along.

Some of the newer models were reported to be capable of speeds topping 90 miles an hour. The model I sat on was doing 20, a decision springing from my unfamiliarity with the terrain, and the visibility still essentially non-existent.

Even with a pair of orange-tinted goggles protecting much of my face and eyes, I could see nothing more than 30 or 40 feet ahead. The wind continued to whip the top layer of snow, a steady spray rising in the wake of the machine.

Hunkered low behind the small windshield, ice crystals still lashed at my cheeks, a burning sensation settling over the skin as I worked the throttle with my right hand, my gaze aimed at the twin tracks in front of me.

Adrenaline and my newly acquired clothes kept my body from succumbing to numbness, my heart pounding, my breathing short and shallow. Beneath the weight of the coat I could feel moisture forming in the small of my back, the weight of the M-16 thumping against my spine with each small knoll we crested.

I kept the speed up a full five minutes after passing Maxx's truck before throttling down as I extinguished the front lamp on the machine, having to raise my body up over the shield and stare straight at the ground to continue picking out the partially covered tracks of the snow coach.

At such a low speed I wasn't concerned about anybody hearing the whine of engine, trusting that the storm would carry it away, or at the least mask it enough that nobody would think twice about it.

The light wouldn't be ignored though, making myself an easy target.

Acutely aware of how much time had passed, of how much time Yvonne Endicott may not have left, I nudged the gas just a little, praying that I was closer to the end of the trail than the beginning.

## Chapter Fifty-Four

The blanket was gone, the wind pulling it away from Yvonne's head, turning it into a sail as it hurtled off into the night, disappearing as if it had never been there at all. Her fingers were too cold, too numb, to even try holding onto it. Leaning the only angle that didn't seem to set her ribs to blazing, she kept her gaze on the ground, every step looking exactly like the previous.

The pain in her head swelled as she moved on, the only sound her own breathing echoing through her ears.

She had to keep going, one step at a time, past the burn in her quads, through the agony waiting to erupt in her ribs.

Over and over again she reminded herself of what she had once heard called the 40% Rule, a maxim adopted by the Navy SEALS, the idea being that every person's physical will outpaced their mental fortitude by 40 percent.

Her body could make it, would make it, she just couldn't let her mind tell her otherwise.

So intense was her focus on just moving that she didn't notice the light, didn't even pick up on the whine of the engine. She didn't realize she was no longer alone until the snowmobile pulled up alongside her.

With one pulse of gas he sped by, sending a plume of snow over her, coming to a stop in her path. There he sat staring back at her, his entire body mummified in black, no way of knowing who he was.

Given that he had come from behind her, seemed intent on keeping her from going any further, it wasn't difficult to figure out that he wasn't a friendly.

The only question was how hostile he was.

The last of her strength waning, Yvonne felt more tears leak from the corners of her eyes. A single sob wracked her entire body, setting her ribs afire, the pain rippling through her, pulling the air from her lungs.

Again, a single burst of the engine could be heard, Yvonne remaining where she was, staring straight down at the damnable snow that was everywhere.

If the man had seen her reaction, had any inkling of the injury to her ribs, of the pain she was in, he gave it no mind as he clamped both hands around her stomach, lifting her from the snow.

Unable to fight back as the pain ripped through her, Yvonne offered no resistance as he carried her two steps and deposited her onto the front of the snowmobile seat. Unceremoniously, he forced her tired, aching, frozen body into position and took a seat behind her, his arms reaching past her to the handlebars and kicking the machine to life.

Gulping in oxygen, feeling the wind rushing into her face, Yvonne's body rocked back against the man, her system beginning to shut down, unable to react to anything that was going on around her.

Ahead in the distance a single light showed itself, much larger than a headlamp from a truck or snowmobile, strong enough to be seen at a distance. For a moment Yvonne thought it was the edge of town, the hospital offering refuge, calling her to safety.

Just as fast that thought faded away, replaced by the realization that it was the barn, that all her efforts meant nothing, erased in a matter of minutes.

Leaning forward, her forehead just inches from the handlebars, she drew in a deep breath.

She could not let them get back to that barn. In it was certain death, if not for what she'd done to the bearded man then surely for what she was unable to do for the other.

Her body was broken, her spirit just seconds behind it. Never again would she go home to Atlanta, never get married or have children. Those things were now beyond her control.

But this, this she could do.

Raising her gaze above the handlebars, Yvonne watched as the light grew steadily larger, the snowmobile veering to the right, descending from the road toward the structure. Drawing her hands up slowly before her, she flexed her fingers twice, willing them to have just enough life left in them for what must be done.

One more breath.

Summoning the last remnants of everything she had left, Yvonne smashed her palms into the handlebars, using the sudden movement to jerk them hard to the right.

In her ear she heard the man let out a grunt of surprise, heard the front end of the snowmobile moan as it pulled to the side, a spray of snow washing over them.

The last thing she remembered was the sensation of flight, of hanging suspended in the air, before everything cut to black.

## Chapter Fifty-Five

It was by pure blind luck that I even saw the light, nothing more than a quick flash from left to right across the road ahead, like the pass of a lighthouse beacon in the distance. Just as fast it was gone, not to be repeated.

Had my attention not been raised for an instant, looking ahead to see if the trail veered off as the woods grew thicker on either side of the road, I would have missed it.

Icy snow whipped past me as I raised my head above the shield. Cold air blasted me in the face, forced its way down my throat, as I leaned harder on the gas, pushing forward.

There was no way the light was an illusion, a mirage ahead in the distance. Not in this storm, and not in the darkness of night.

It was too bright to be a flashlight.

Most likely a snowmobile, just like the one I now sat on.

Feeling my adrenaline spike, a tense feeling arose in my stomach, the familiar signs of impending danger. Just as it had untold times before, my body reacted the way I knew it would, calling on instincts that until recently had been dormant for more than half a decade.

A person can have all the training in the world, have been through a million simulations, but until they had actually gone through battle, had experienced the psychosomatic response to actual violence, they had no idea what to expect.

Just the same, once they had been through it, they would never forget.

A warm feeling spread through my limbs, blocking the cold, blotting out the pain of the snow whipping me in the face, the aching of my nose from the crash. It spurred me on, my right wrist twisting slightly, the throttle on the snowmobile moving it along at a low rumble.

On the ground in front of me new tracks appeared, slicing over the previous trail of the snow coach, clean lines cleaved through the recent snowfall. It was definitely a snowmobile heading in the same direction I was, the destination becoming clear, a second light emerging in the distance.

Once more I ratcheted up the gas, knowing the noise of my machine couldn't be heard over that of the one I was following.

The light ahead grew steadily larger, clearly a doorway into some sort of structure, the outline of the building coming into view.

Giving the handlebars a quarter turn, I nosed the snowmobile off the road, continuing to follow the new tracks. The back end of my machine bucked as I hit the uneven ground, launching my backside up off the seat, my hands the only point of contact before dropping back onto the seat again, sending a jolt up through my hips and spine.

The pain barely registered through my heightened senses, the adrenaline serving to put my nerve endings on high alert as ahead of me, for the first time, I caught a glimpse of what had caused the light I saw before.

Silhouetted against the bright light of the building, it was clear that I was chasing another snowmobile. Based on the size and shape there appeared to be two riders, though there was no way for me to determine who they might be.

Twisting the throttle back again, the engine whined, giving me a burst of speed to close the gap between us.

I had to reach them, whoever they were, before they got to the door. Once inside they would have support, untold numbers lying in wait, no doubt heavily armed.

Even worse, they would lower the door, making my job that much more difficult.

Leaning forward, trying to exert my will on my machine, I kept heading straight at the rear of the snowmobile, watching, praying for it not to make that door.

At no point did I expect what happened next, the machine ahead bucking wildly to the side, the headlamp streaking across the side of barn. Twisted at an angle for just an instant, I could see both riders seated on the machine before centrifugal force took over.

Traveling at such a high speed, the machine tilted, lifting it from the ground, sending it hurtling, launching both riders into the air.

My muscles seized tight as I saw them both fully for the first time, the figure on the back end clearly a man, tall and thick, the one that had been riding up front smaller with a slight build.

I pegged the big guy as Sam Cuddyer, or someone from his crew, and the other as Yvonne Endicott.

Seeing the bottoms of hospital scrubs and the wild hair on her head gave me no doubt, my eyes widening as I watched.

End over end their machine toppled, stopping with a thunderous crash of steel hitting steel as it smacked broadside into the side of the barn.

The light grew brighter as I continued, closing the gap between us, knowing I had a decision to make.

There was no way anybody inside had not heard that collision, would not immediately come running.

I had to do everything I could to sway the odds in my favor before they did.

## Chapter Fifty-Six

I backed the throttle down just enough to ensure I could throw myself clear without sustaining too much injury, the speed dropping by more than half as I aimed the nose of the snowmobile at the man struggling to his feet before me. With legs spread wide, arms swinging, fighting for purchase, it was obvious he was still dazed from the fall. Standing with his back to me, he gave no indication of even knowing I was there, never once turning as I goosed the gas one final time, aiming at him before flinging my body off to the right.

Landing on a shoulder, the snow did little to brace the jarring impact, the M-16 causing the vertebrae in my spine to pop as I rolled once, digging my hands and feet into the ground, forcing myself to a stop flat on my stomach.

Lying face down on the ground, I could see what I presumed to be Yvonne sprawled in the snow nearby, making no movement of any kind. Beyond her was the crumpled pile of the man I had rammed with the snowmobile, his head and shoulders buried in the snow, his legs twisted at an unnatural angle beside him.

Past that I could see the remains of the Switchback, the front end having collided with the corner of the doorway, the fiberglass body impaled on the metal support beam, steam rising from the engine.

I could feel fresh warmth dripping over my lips, taste the blood in my mouth as I shoved myself to my knees, clawing for the nylon strap across my chest. Hooking a thumb beneath it, I pulled the M-16 over my head and rushed forward, using a foot to kick the man over flat on his back.

His entire face was covered with goggles, not even his eyes visible, giving no indication if he was alive or dead.

Gripping the M-16 around the barrel with both hands, I smashed the butt end of it down into the man's throat before adding a second and a third blow, feeling his larynx disintegrate.

The odds of his having survived the crash were minimal at best, but there was no way I would now have to worry about him rising just long enough, like a villain from a bad movie, to shoot me in the back.

Leaving the man where he lay, I switched the gun into my left hand and shuffled two quick steps to the side. Voices drifted out of the barn as I grabbed Yvonne by the ankle with my right hand, jerking her backward, getting us both back as far away from the opening as possible.

Whoever was coming to inspect the noise would see the crumpled remains of their compatriot. My only hope was it would be enough to draw them into the open long enough to get a shot off.

Yvonne Endicott was taller than I expected, though by no means a large woman. My hand easily passed around her ankle, nothing more than bone and tendon as I pulled. Still surging on adrenaline, her weight was almost non-existent as I slid her over the snowpack, the ground littered with remnants of the first snowmobile, black specks of fiberglass dotting the area.

The two of us made it several yards before the first shadow appeared through the doorway, spilling out onto the ground. A moment later a second appeared, this one moving in a sideways gait, the unmistakable posture of a shooter's stance.

I had to get us, or at least Yvonne, to cover.

Pausing for just a moment, I swung my gaze to look for anything to serve as a blockade.

With the exception of a couple narrow pine trees, there was decidedly little around, most of the area having been cleared to make room for the structure.

Bit by bit the shadows came closer, growing bigger as they approached, bound to pop out at any time, weapons ready.

As poor as it was, I had only one option.

Dropping the M-16 into the snow, I reached down and grabbed Yvonne by the hips and hefted her from the ground, tossing her toward the base of the building, the remains of the first snowmobile the best cover I could manage.

Bending over, I snapped up the M-16 and flung myself down alongside her, our shoulders pressed against each other, her unconscious features aimed toward the sky, mine focused on the doorway.

The first man through was small, awkward, his sole focus on his colleague. He shot out of the doorway, fighting his way through the snow, before coming to a stop beside him.

Keeping the sight along the top barrel aimed for his center mass, I flipped off the safety, switching to a three shot burst, waiting, hoping for the other to show himself.

The second man clearly had more experience than the first, remaining hidden behind the doorway. After a moment I saw an arm and the top of his head extend outward followed by a double muzzle flash, two orange blossoms of light.

The rounds were nothing more than exploratory, both hitting the trees out away from the building.

Right now, he had no way of knowing where we were, but that would not last for long. It was only a matter of time before he or his colleague looked over at the rubble of the crash, saw it for the only cover around, knowing we couldn't have gotten much further pushing through such thick snow.

At that point they would begin leveling every bit of firepower they had over here, maybe even tossing another of those grenades that had gotten Ferris.

On my side, I had the momentary advantage of a clear sightline, and the extreme concern for an unconscious Yvonne. Already, I could feel the snow starting to draw heat from my body, despite the winter gear Mike loaned me.

If the frigid ground was having that effect on me, I could only imagine what it was doing to her.

It was clear that any hope I might have had of extracting Yvonne and retreating without a fight was gone. I had killed one man and destroyed my mode of transportation, meaning that at one point or another we had to get inside.

Doing that meant going through every last person.

There was no pause, no delay at all as I stared at the base of the barn, firing one three round burst, seeing a trio of sparks ignite from the metal. I paused, adjusting my aim just a fraction of an inch, before firing a second cluster, the result the same as the first.

Shifting my focus out to the left, I zoned in on the man standing over his cohort, the gunshots seeming to have paralyzed him, and squeezed the trigger, his body rising, tensing, before falling prone atop his friend.

That was two.

Pushing the muzzle of my gun back toward the front corner, I paused, waiting for a sign of movement that never came. Whoever was there had retreated back inside, fortifying his position, waiting for me to make a mistake.

I'd be damned if I was going to make it that easy for him.

## Chapter Fifty-Seven

Steam continued to rise from the front end of Mike's Switchback, the engine just starting to cool. Wedged against the far corner of the doorway, it looked like an enormous bug, the elongated black body bunched into a wad.

Once more I laid a burst of suppression fire at the front edge of the door, this time not bothering to wait for a response, not even letting the sparks clear the air before turning my focus on the shattered snowmobile.

I didn't bother with just a single burst, keeping my finger tight on the trigger, sending a steady hail of bullets at the machine.

As such, it was impossible for me to tell which one finally struck the gas tank, igniting the liquid accelerant.

What was clear was that it worked, the machine turning into a fiery pyre, the body rising more than four feet off the ground. When it reached the apex of its ascent, it seemed to hang suspended before a second explosion occurred, this one taking the entire engine with it, shrapnel shooting out over 20 feet in every direction.

As soon as the initial shock wave of the blast passed, I was on my feet and moving as fast as I could, snow clumped to the front of my clothes, falling away as I moved. With my right hand along the trigger guard, my left around the underside of the stock, I churned through the deep snow, ignoring the protests of my legs, my focus on the front corner of the door.

Heat emanated off the charred skeleton of the snowmobile as I approached. I slid to a knee along the front corner, taking up a position just inches away from where the second gunman had been a few moments before.

Dropping flat to my stomach, I held the M-16 in firing position before me, twisting my body around the edge, peering inside the cavernous space.

As best as I could tell, it was a single room, the snow coach Ferris and I had seen earlier parked ahead of me, the trailer still hitched to the back of it. Beyond that a second lab was already well underway, most of the chemical reservoir and piping in place, a few odds and ends still missing.

To my left a small room jutted out, a makeshift structure thrown together for sleeping or storage.

A blur of movement drew my attention back to the lab, a black flash that was gone as fast as it appeared.

Otherwise, I could see nobody.

I knew that two men were already dead, and I knew that both Sam Cuddyer and Jasper Maxx had been at the original house. I also knew that somebody had driven that snow coach over to this new site, and he hadn't showed up alone.

That meant a minimum of two people were still left inside, possibly as many as four or five.

Keeping my weapon set to a three-shot burst, I raised myself up onto my knees. I didn't know exactly how many I had fired to ignite the snowmobile, only that I had just under half the clip remaining before it would be time to switch to the Walthers. At that point my range would diminish greatly, as would my ability to spray, but my aim would improve.

Ideally, things wouldn't get that far.

Releasing the grip of my left hand from the stock, I peeled the goggles off the top of my head, hefting them twice before tossing them several feet into the room. On cue, as if summoned, a trio of gunshots erupted, someone getting anxious, shooting at the first sign of movement.

I could still hear the sound of the shots pinging against the wall as I dropped flat onto my left shoulder, the M-16 extended before me, and squeezed off a quick burst.

All three were aimed too close to the wall, the shooter out a little wider, moving in a sideways motion toward the cover of the lab tables. With one arm stretched in my direction, he began to fire a steady stream of bullets, not even looking as he snapped off shots, the rounds slamming into the wall or passing through the open door, all of them well above my head.

Slowing my breathing just slightly, I sighted in on him as he continued to make his way forward, cutting him down halfway across the floor, his arms jerking back by his sides, his weapon flung in the air.

He was dead before he hit the floor, his head smacking against the concrete, blood puddling around him.

That was three.

Rolling onto my chest, for the first time I was exposed, my body extending out into the room, an easy target if somebody saw me.

Clawing with my hands and boots, all wet with snow, I fought for purchase on the sealed concrete. My gaze was fixed on the back end of the snow coach as I scrambled to my feet, keeping myself bent at the waist, duck-walking across the open expanse for cover.

Halfway across I raised the M-16 and fired off another round of suppression fire, not even looking where I was shooting, hoping the sound was enough to keep whoever might be out there at bay.

Three more steps and I completely gave up on the hunched movement, rising to full height and running as hard as I could, unable to feel my legs, only knowing that they were working because the van continued to grow closer.

Everything - from my lungs to my quads and hamstrings - craved oxygen as I dove between the trailer and the rear of the van, the side window shattering just ahead, return fire coming from the far end of the room.

Once the first round found a target it seemed to embolden my opponent, the shots coming faster. A moment later, a second shooter joined in – one offering the rat-a-tat of an AK, the other, the smaller crack of a handgun.

Wedged in tight along the rear bumper, the thick rubber tread of the tank track offering me protection, I drew the M-16 up in front of me.

I was down to my last couple of rounds before having to switch to the handguns, and I knew I had two shooters on the opposite end of the room, perhaps more hidden about the space.

Rounds continued to slam into the van, the sound of glass breaking audible above me, punctuated by metal slamming into the body of the vehicle. After a few moments the sound of the handgun faded away just long enough to reload before beginning again, a few rounds striking the concrete nearby, sending up the occasional spark as it skipped across the ground before pinging into the wall behind me.

Waiting, concentrating, I continued to listen for the sound of a third weapon, for any indication of someone else inside.

Happy to oblige, rounds continued slamming into the van, never once changing their sound or direction, coming in a steady pattern. They continued for more than two full minutes before slowing, finally dropping off entirely.

The inside of the barn fell silent, the persistent wind outside the only sound.

Still, I waited, straining, listening for what I knew would soon be coming, the indication that it was my turn again.

When at last it finally found my ears, it was all I could do to keep from smiling.

# Chapter Fifty-Eight

The sound of voices drifted through the room, just as I hoped they would. Masked as whispers, they were loud enough for me to hear over the sound of the wind outside, confirming what the gunfire had already told me.

There were only two of them.

They were squirreled away at the end of the lab tables, too far to hear what they were saying, but close enough for me to tell that the two were not in agreement.

If I were to guess, based on the tone, I would say that they were from opposing factions, one from the original Cuddyer clan, the other from the crew sent in as cleanup. Who they were and what they were saying, I couldn't care less, my entire focus on killing them both and getting Yvonne out of the cold and away to safety.

After the better part of a minute, they stopped pretending to whisper, the words exchanged growing more hostile. It was apparent they must have thought they finished me off, my lack of return fire and the state of the van both giving them the false assumption that I was done.

Most likely the argument was over who would be the one to walk up and make sure, neither one wanting to step away from the safety of the heavy wooden tables.

I had to assume that if they had any grenades on them, or anything heavier than small arms, they would have already used it, the van an easy target that would have taken me out when it exploded.

Which left me with a choice to make.

I could stay where I was, wait for their bickering to end, for one of them to emerge and walk directly toward me. At that point I would have a clean line of fire, after which the remaining combatant and I would be stuck firing at one another, making it a war of attrition.

Conversely, I had a second option, which was to hurry things along. I had to remember that Yvonne was still outside, lying unconscious in the snow.

That single thought, the mental image of her tucked against the side of the building, her curly hair billowed out around her head, pushed the first choice completely from mind.

Over the course of the last day there was no telling what that girl had been subjected to. I would be damned if she had fought so hard only to freeze to death while I traded shots with a bad guy.

As quietly as I could, I unfastened the banana clip from the bottom of the M-16, hefting it twice in my hand, feeling the weight of no more than a handful of rounds left inside. A bit of the familiar dread settled into my stomach as I snapped it back into place, flipping the select down to single shot.

Rising onto a knee, I turned to face the rear of the van, bringing the rifle to my shoulder.

I was only going to get a few cracks at this.

I had to make them count.

Driving up off my back foot, I rose to full height, stepping away from the vehicle. No return fire came my way as I emerged, the two men still arguing, their voices audible right up until the moment I pulled the trigger, letting the first bullet fly.

Tailing high and right from my target, the round caromed off a copper pipe running the length of the tables, sparks rising in its wake. A moment later it could be heard smashing into the far wall as I adjusted my aim and pulled the trigger a second time, the round going just a bit left of my goal.

Coming to a complete stop, ignoring the first crack of a handgun as return fire came my way, I sighted in on what I wanted, letting out a slow breath before squeezing back on the trigger.

A split second after letting the bullet fly it found its mark, smashing into the closest chemical vat. On contact the container went up in a twisted inferno, setting off a chain reaction that engulfed the table. Shards of plastic and wood were sent high into the air, hanging suspended for a moment, all of them smoldering or burning bright, before falling to the floor.

One by one, more than a half dozen tubs went up in quick order, each seeming to be a bit larger than the one before it, obliterating that side of the building as I shifted my attention to the other side and opened fire again.

This time I didn't have to be quite so careful, unloading everything I had left in the clip, the end unit going ablaze just as the firing pin began to click empty, the weapon in my hand reduced to one hellacious club and nothing more.

Whatever little return fire there had been was gone, replaced by the sound of the shrapnel from the twin units being annihilated hitting the concrete, nothing more remaining than the charred bases of the tables and assorted debris. Black smoke hung thick in the air, coupled with the smell of chemicals, my eyes beginning to water as I drew the Walthers and stepped forward, holding them both at arm's length before me.

Moving out wide to the left of the wreckage, I increased my pace to a jog, keeping my knees bent, watching for any shadows, any sign of movement through the thick haze hanging in the room.

After the weight of the M-16 the Walthers felt light in my hands, my index fingers looped through the trigger guards, ready to squeeze off a round at anything left standing. As I moved, a familiar scent found my nose, mixed with the acrid smell of chemicals and smoldering wood.

The odor was undoubtedly charred flesh, though if it was one or both men, I had no way of knowing.

I could feel beads of sweat along my scalp as I inched forward, the heavy watch cap and the fire burning nearby raising my body temperature. It was time to end this and get outside, perspiration something I could ill afford once I stepped back outside.

Dropping a few more inches, I increased my speed, swinging around the end of the table.

There, on the floor, lay the source of the smell.

Dressed in solid black, just like the snowmobiler and the man I had shot upon entering, he looked to be extremely tall, having at least several inches on me. His winter clothes were still smoldering, his face charred and blistered, unrecognizable as human.

There was no need to waste a bullet or to give away my position by firing into a corpse.

I had one more yet to find.

In the closed end of the barn there was nowhere for the smoke to go, rising to the ceiling and swirling like a cyclone. From where I stood I couldn't get much of a read on anything nearby, the fifth man either hiding or dead.

I had to assume he was hurt, but I also knew he was armed.

Backing out the way I had come, I returned to my crouch, moving past the front end of the tables, the smoke thinning around me.

Once I was out in the open, I turned and sprinted for the coach, coming up along the driver's side. Pressed tight against the exterior, I inched my way toward the shattered window beside the steering wheel and stuck my hand in, flipping on the headlights.

The beams cut a wide path through the thin smoke hovering close to the floor, illuminating everything for more than 50 feet ahead.

The charred remains of the lab. The makeshift room built off to the side.

The outline of a man trying in vain to crawl across the floor.

Standing there, looking at everything before me, I couldn't help but feel that the scene was like something scripted. It was the moment in an old movie where the protagonist saw his enemy struggling, knowing he had won, turning to the camera to deliver a witty one-liner, something to make the folks at home clap their hands and cheer.

I had no interest in doing anything of the sort. He was the last remaining bad guy, likely one of Yvonne Endicott's kidnappers and who knew what else.

He didn't deserve the dignity of any final words.

Keeping my left arm outstretched, I grabbed the second weapon from my pocket, raised it alongside the other, and took careful aim. I fired five rounds from each gun, seeing his body twitch on impact, at least half of them finding their mark.

Only then did I step away from the cover of the vehicle, moving straight ahead, watching for any sign of movement, my guns still held at the ready. I maintained that exact same position as I closed the distance between us before firing again, seeing the rounds strike flesh, his body giving no response.

The tension inside me eased a tiny bit as I covered the last few steps, walking close enough to see my final victim lying prone, his unseeing eyes staring straight up.

He was older than the mug shot, his beard had grown in, had some gray, but there was no mistaking him.

Sam Cuddyer was dead.

## Chapter Fifty-Nine

In my haste to clear the barn, I had overlooked one detail. There were five able bodied men who lay dead. One by one I had stacked them into the snow coach, filling every available space.

What I had forgotten was the reason Yvonne Endicott had been abducted in the first place.

The answer to that I found inside the little plywood room, the man lying flat on a decrepit mattress, his shirt lifted to his chin. Nearly every bit of his exposed flesh was covered in severe burns, the need for medical attention obvious.

The fact that he had slept through two snowmobiles crashes, a lengthy firefight, and the demolition of the entire lab told me the odds of him ever waking weren't good, though I took no chances as I put two rounds into his chest before jerking his shirt down and adding him to the pile in the van.

Before beginning the cleanup, I had carried Yvonne inside, positioning her as close to the warmth of the burning benches as I could, dropping my coat onto the floor to keep her off the cold concrete.

Twice she had stirred while I relocated her, each time her eyes fluttering without fully opening, a string of mumbles passing over her lips, but nothing intelligible.

Just seeing the state she was in brought renewed anger, justifying everything I had done, confirming that I would do it again without hesitation. As pale as she was, it was plain to see that she had been beaten, her cheeks swollen and lopsided, heavy bruising on the left side.

What other abuse she had suffered I could only guess, moving her as gently as possible, hoping she would be able to endure the ride back to the hospital, the exact place her ordeal had started almost 20 hours before.

When I had left Mike's, I hadn't given much thought to cleanup, not until after the fact did my mind slow down enough to consider it.

People like Sam Cuddyer could not afford labs the likes of which Ferris and I had found earlier. They certainly didn't have backup locations that were even larger, with teams dispatched to assist them in emergencies.

That meant that whoever he was cooking for had some clout, and needed enough product to warrant putting in the time and expense for everything we had witnessed.

It also meant that Cuddyer feared him enough to risk going after Yvonne and nabbing her to begin with.

That left only two possibilities for the source of funding, one being Billings, the other being the oil fields. Given the geographic location and the amount of time it took reinforcements to arrive, it wasn't hard to put together where the product was meant to go, many of the new people Ferris mentioned the likely consumers of Cuddyer's product.

My time in Montana had kept me away from situations like this, but it was pretty clear that anybody with a meth business of this scale would not take kindly to a half dozen associates being killed.

That meant I needed to make things as difficult for them to piece together as I could before leaving.

Lashed to the trailer behind the van was a second Arctic Cat. Easing it down the ramp, I moved it past the door, well away from the building.

In the back of the snow coach I found more handguns and automatic rifles like the men inside had been using, and, more important,

## Fire and Ice

a handful of grenades matching the one that could have killed the sheriff.

Leaving two in the back of the van, I placed one on the front console, another in the backseat. The remaining two I carried with me toward the door, leaving them on the floor beside it.

Once everything was in position, I went back for Yvonne, nudging her slightly, again getting nothing more than a muted response. Bypassing any attempt at revival, I lifted her from the floor, her body already feeling warmer as I carried her to the snowmobile and placed her on the front of the seat.

My last trip back inside was to collect my coat and Mike's guns, leaving nothing behind that could be traced to us. The Walthers I stowed into the front pockets of the jacket, the M-16 I looped over Yvonne's shoulders, cinching the nylon strap tight, pinning her arms by her side to ensure if she did wake up she didn't become disoriented, repeating what she had done on her previous snowmobile ride.

It took me just over 20 minutes to get everything in order, the last of the fires still burning, smoke hanging in a thick cloud in the room. My eyes burned and my throat ached, no part of me wanting to go back into the storm, but it was the last task I had to perform to get Yvonne to safety.

Lifting the pair of grenades from the floor, I balanced them in my left palm and pressed the single button on the wall, stepping just outside the garage door.

There I stood, buried to mid-calf in the snow, waiting for the metal door to lower, the macabre scene inside one I would never see again.

When the door passed my head, I jerked the pins on the grenades, flipping them both inside, aiming for the floor under the van.

From there it was just a matter of letting the chain reaction I had put in place do its job.

The last I heard as the door closed was the percussive sound of the explosives finding their target, igniting its gas tank and the extra cans stowed in the back, eventually setting off the other grenades one by one, finishing the job I started.

I did not envy the next person to step inside that place, but I couldn't honestly say I much cared as I positioned myself behind Yvonne and leaned on the throttle, hurtling us away into the night.

# Part Five

## Chapter Sixty

Despite more than a dozen men crammed into the room, the space was completely silent as Wood Arrasco entered. His mouth was drawn into a tight line, his expression sullen as he walked to his desk, ignoring the chair behind it to lean against the front edge.

He folded his arms across his chest, his natural stance when addressing the club, before dropping them to his side, letting everyone see the black stripe that slashed through the middle of The Dogs emblem on his vest.

To anybody who had ever ridden with The Dogs, nothing was more sacred than the emblem they wore, announcing their allegiance to the club.

Only something as momentous as a fallen brother would allow one to alter it any way, a fact that every person in the room picked up on immediately.

Ranging from just shy of 30 to just north of 50, the men represented a cross-section of the members, from the older crowd about to hang it up for good, to the hungry newcomers, still trying to make a name for themselves.

Each one wore signs of the lives they led, their skin aged beyond their years, the occasional scar carried with pride. Dressed in various denims and flannels, all sported leather vests matching Wood's.

There were some differences in the emblems, depending on years of service and their position in the club, but without question the biggest was the diagonal stripe on Wood's.

"It's been three days now since Trick, Mac, and Barnham were sent out to check on one of our suppliers," Wood said, his eyes burning, having not slept in that time.

"Since *I* sent them."

He paused, feeling the words cut into him, hearing them aloud for the first time.

As the President, it was true that all decisions ultimately came down to him, but this was different. This was not a leader taking blame for something the club had agreed to do, not a leader taking the fall for something that was only nominally his fault.

This one was on him. He and Trick had sat up late at night and discussed the notion, but his mind was already made up before his lieutenant even arrived.

He had allowed his greed, his determination to maintain the empire he had built, to cloud his judgment.

And as a result, three good men, including his best friend, were gone.

"This morning I got a call from Harris and Wheat," he said, his voice even. "From jail."

An audible murmur swept through the room at the last two words as the men exchanged glances.

"When Trick and his crew failed to check in for the second straight day, we sent them over to see what was going on. We had suspicions of the worst, but we needed confirmation."

Every part of him wanted to look away from the men he had failed, but Wood forced himself to stare directly at them, meeting the faces of those brave enough to look his way.

"They arrived at Cuddyer's backup lab this morning to find the place swarming with law enforcement personnel. The local authorities had called in the DEA from Billings, who had come in on a chopper once the storm passed."

Once more Wood paused, trying to determine how to best relay the news he had received earlier.

It had been clear from Harris's tone that the scene they found was disturbing, the details something he could not share over an unsecured line.

The mere thought of whatever that could mean for his friends, for his brothers, caused Wood's stomach to twist itself into a knot that threatened to never release.

"There were no survivors," Wood said quietly, leaving the details at that.

As much as he hated not having more to give them, as much as he knew the men who had perished deserved better, he simply didn't have the information.

Several heads dipped toward the floor at the news, others going in the opposite direction and clenching their fists. Regardless of their reaction, Wood knew exactly how they felt, having been through the spectrum of emotions himself in the preceding hours.

Still, right now they could not afford to be emotional.

That time would come, but it wasn't there yet.

"I know this comes as a blow," he said, "and believe me, nobody is hurting more than I am right now. Trick Reynolds and I..."

Pressing his lips together tight, not trusting the next words that might come out of his mouth, or the tone with which they would be delivered, Wood stopped there. He made no attempt to hide the reaction, letting each of the men see it, wanting, needing, them to understand how deeply personal he took his role as President, and how much the men in the organization meant to him.

"They will be properly mourned," Wood whispered, "and I promise – *promise you* – they will be avenged."

Just like many of the men around him, he felt his hands ball into fists, his fingernails digging into his palms, every muscle in his upper body clenched tight.

"But right now, we need to go underground. Harris and Wheat weren't wearing the colors and they both know to keep their mouths shut."

Even the phone he had taken their call on, a disposable bought for cash at a Wal-Mart in South Dakota, was gone, destroyed the minute they were done speaking.

"But this could be a big score for some agency, and there's no way they're going to let it rest. Grabbing Harris and Wheat was just the start of things."

Along the back of the room a single hand rose, most of the arm exposed, revealing tattoos that had long since faded and blurred, resembling nothing more than ink blotches on his skin.

"When you say underground...?" he asked, his voice graveled from decades of smoking.

"I mean for the time being, all business activities have been suspended," Wood said. Just days before he had been willing to send three of his best men out into a blizzard to protect their interests, but now he knew there was no choice but to let the business go.

The demand for product would still exist, their competitors all too eager to fill the void.

When law enforcement eventually made their way to the oil fields – and there was no way they wouldn't – they would find somebody else providing the meth.

Wood knew this was not how The Dogs operated. They were not a club that tucked tail. It wouldn't be the first time the law had been sniffing around them, wouldn't be the last.

But this time was different.

"Rest assured," Wood said, "we're not going anywhere, and that has nothing to do with the snow piled up outside. The Dogs have survived before, we'll survive this."

Several of the faces that had turned down at the news of Trick and the others rose back up to look at him, the same expression of determination on their features as his own.

"And whoever is responsible for this?" Wood said. "They won't be so lucky."

## Chapter Sixty-One

For the third time in as many days, I walked through the front door of Mike Ferris's house without knocking. I paused just briefly on the front mat to stomp away the snow clinging to the sides of my boots before heading on in, the rubber soles squeaking beneath me.

Unlike on my last visit, the crowd awaiting me in the living room had tripled in size, all three individuals sitting and staring back at me.

In the chair directly in front of me was Mike Ferris, still dressed in the same velour robe with a pair of flannel pants and a thermal under it.

Despite his weakened condition and his self-imposed mandate to appear curmudgeonly, I could see just a hint of pleasure underscoring his features.

The first stop I made after leaving the barn three nights before was to Valley Memorial Hospital, performing an exact opposite of what had taken place just 24 hours earlier. Starting on the south end of the parking lot, I used the combined trenches cut by Sam Cuddyer and myself earlier in the day, whipping up to within feet of the front door.

As I had no way of alerting anybody that I was on my way or that

Yvonne was with me, nobody was awaiting our arrival as I pulled up, forcing me to pry my frozen fingers from the handlebars and lift Yvonne from the seat. In my arms she felt rigid, any previous warmth from the fire in the barn long since sapped away despite my best efforts to protect her from the cold.

The hospital was just as deserted as it had been on my previous visits as I entered, my voice echoing through the cavernous space.

The first person to appear was Myles Breckman, this time very much awake, an extendable nightstick in his hand. Where he had gotten it or what he thought he was about to do with it I had no idea, a look of genuine relief flooding his features as he saw us standing there.

If that was from seeing Yvonne was alive, or just absolving him of any associated guilt, there was no way to know.

Probably a hefty dollop of both, if I were to speculate.

The next two people to arrive from the back were women, one wearing blue scrubs and the other a white doctor's coat. At the sight of us they both fell to tears, clutching each other, completely forgetting that there was a woman in dire need of care nearby.

Not until Meredith Shek appeared, seeming to have endured the very same day-long stretch that I had, did anybody make a move to help, the nurse nabbing a wheelchair and rushing forward. Seeing her movement seemed to snap the others from their trance, using their sleeves to wipe away tears, sniffling slightly as they took Yvonne straight back.

Left alone in the front lobby, I located a night receptionist and asked her to direct me to Ferris's room, finding him very awake and staring at the wall, his nerves wired.

Not a single word was said as he took me in, seeing the soot and smudges covering my clothes, the blood still crusted to my face. His mouth parted just slightly, his back leaning forward off the angled bed, a look somewhere between hopeful and terrified on his features.

"She's here," I said, leaning against the door frame. "Banged up, but alive."

His shoulders dropped at the news, his face crinkling slightly, as his body released the tension that had flooded it.

### Fire and Ice

"Nobody else is," I said, leaving my explanation at that.

In the days ahead I would explain everything to him in painstaking detail three different times, doing so at his office, where he could make phone calls to Billings, to direct needed resources into the area, to turn the case over from a kidnapping to an investigation into a drug ring.

This was not the moment though. I could tell by the look on his face what was coming next, knowing the guilt he felt, imagining what a sweet relief a happy ending must be.

Pulling the door shut behind me, I left the man to cry in peace, saving him the indignity of me standing there watching.

Two hours later Shek found me pacing an empty waiting room, the last of the adrenaline coupled with my concern for Yvonne keeping me too wired to even consider dozing. Back and forth across the tiles, I felt like I was wearing a trench in the floor, Breckman twice popping his head out of his office to watch before disappearing back inside, never once summoning the courage to come over and say anything.

Where Azbell and Baker had gotten off to since I left, I hadn't a clue, feeling no responsibility to track them down or fill them in.

I had been at the far end of the room when Shek entered, her reflection in the outside window flashing in my periphery. She had taken no more than three steps before breaking into a sprint, practically leaping at me, and throwing her arms around my neck.

Unsure how to respond, I remained rooted in place, my hands by my side, listening as she pressed her face into my chest and cried, gentle sobs shaking her body.

"Are those happy tears or sad tears?" I whispered.

"Happy," she responded, never once pulling her face away from me. "She's sleeping, going to be just fine."

Hearing the news said aloud, feeling the tension I had been carrying ease, I raised my hands to Shek's back, one across her shoulder blades, the other behind her head.

The faint smell of apples, far and away the most pleasant fragrance I'd encountered in days, hit my nostrils as we stood that way for a long time.

Ten minutes later I left, back on the snowmobile, en route to the very house I now stood in.

Mike's response had been much the same as his brother's, the man fighting his weakened condition as he struggled to his feet to shake my hand. Twice I offered to return the weapons to the basement, clean them and stow them away, reasoning with him that it would give me something to do, but he wouldn't hear of it.

Even tried to go to the basement to fetch my coat and the Kimber for me.

A half hour after arriving, I backed the stolen Arctic Cat into place in his garage, hoping it would be a suitable replacement for his Switchback once it was repainted to hide its original owner. I departed well after midnight, taking Ferris's truck back to my motel and falling into bed, praying that nobody would come knocking again.

Given that I dropped straight down into bed and slept for 12 hours immediately thereafter, I'm not sure I would have known even if they did.

In the time since I had rotated among the three, checking on the health of Yvonne, aiding Rake with his budding investigation, and acting as conduit to both for Mike.

Somehow, I had even attained the status of family friend as the days passed.

"I know that look," Mike said, rocking his head back slightly to peer at me. "That's a man about to take off."

Walking forward, I paused just inside the open doorway that connected the hall to the living room. Lying flat on the sofa to my right was Rake, his heavily bandaged legs propped up. Opposite him was Yvonne in an armchair, her legs curled up beneath her, a woven blanket wrapped around her body, cocooning her tight.

"Yeah," I said, leaning a shoulder against the wall, my hands in the front pockets of my jeans. "Need to get back down to West Yellowstone. They've got most of the roads cleared by now, have to start getting ready for the new season."

Pushing his hands down into the soft sofa cushion, Rake attempted to wrestle himself around to face forward, his heavily bandaged legs making the movement difficult.

"You don't have to leave already," he managed. "Here, have a seat."

"No, no, no," I said, raising a hand to him. "Thank you for the offer, but I'm good. Like to get back before dark, with the roads being what they are and all."

"We be seeing you this way again anytime soon?" Mike asked, his eyebrows rising just a bit.

I glanced down to my shoes, lifting my right foot and using the toe to poke at the edge of the rug covering the floor.

"Oh yeah," I said, "eventually. During the summer I stay down there pretty much all the time, but once the season ends, I'm sure I'll be back up.

"This is where my home is, after all."

"You damn right it is," Mike said, Ferris and Yvonne both nodding in agreement.

Feeling a flush of blood come to my cheeks, I tapped at the rug twice more before lowering my foot, shifting my gaze over to Ferris.

"You need anything else, you be sure to let me know, alright?"

I didn't bother to elaborate further, knowing full well that he had already shared with his brother what had happened at the barn and the investigation that was underway.

More than once we had discussed the possibility of somebody turning this back on the town, on the need to get Yvonne and whoever else out if it came to that, but for the time being he seemed content to let the DEA do their job and see where things went.

I had told him I didn't know if that was necessarily the safest way to approach things, but that if there was anything else I could do to help him or Yvonne, to call me.

I'd be there.

"You do the same," Ferris replied, having made the argument that I too could now be in somebody's crosshairs and needed to keep an eye out.

My reply to him was that the only way they'd even know I existed was if somebody told them.

Besides, I felt reasonably certain that I could handle myself, especially in the vast wilderness of Yellowstone.

We left it at that, speaking in code so that Yvonne wouldn't be privy to our concerns, wanting her to focus on healing.

As if sensing what was going on, she stood, dropping the blanket into the chair.

"Come on, I'll walk you out."

Nodding at her invitation, I raised two fingers to my brow in farewell. "Gentlemen."

Both replied in kind, neither saying anything, their expressions telling me everything.

I've heard women complain before that men seem to have their own language, but that's not entirely correct.

Oftentimes, the best way for us to communicate is not by speaking at all.

Yvonne's stocking feet moved silently across the floor as she stepped to the side of the door and shoved them into a pair of snow boots, grabbing a parka off the coatrack by the door as she did. Without pause she turned the knob and stepped to the side, allowing me to go through before following me out to the porch.

Closing the door softly behind her, she stood with her hands thrust into the front pockets of the coat, using them to hold it shut in front of her.

Her face still displayed what she had gone through, the bruises just beginning to fade, the swelling receded.

"How you feeling?" I asked.

She smiled just slightly as she looked at me before glancing out at the yard.

Still shrouded in white, it would be some time before all the snow was gone, despite rumors of spring making a long overdue appearance by week's end.

"It only hurts when I breathe," she said, again offering the same contained smile.

Having once sustained a broken rib myself, I recognized the sentiment, a conscious effort on her part to avoid any laughter, anything that might cause that searing pain in her side.

"And you?" she asked. "Everything working?"

"As much as it ever was," I replied.

## Fire and Ice

The faintest hint of midday sunshine was poking through the thick cloud cover, reflecting off of the snow, giving everything an ethereal glow.

Just one of the many things I had come to appreciate about Montana.

"So what next?" I asked. "Back to Georgia?"

Glancing my way, Yvonne shook her head, her curls swinging from side to side. "No. Not yet, anyway."

She paused there, her voice dropping, and added, "I made a promise when I came up here."

A moment passed as she continued to stare out, the expression on her face telling me she was trying to corral a dozen different thoughts, ranging from the situation with her father to how to best address everything that had happened in the last few days.

"Some people would say I'm crazy for staying on," she said, turning to face me. She removed her left hand from her coat and placed it on my arm, squeezing just slightly, the same half smile appearing on her face. "But I don't need to explain honoring a commitment to you, do I?"

Of everything she could have said in that moment, I don't know that anything would have been more fitting.

"No. You don't."

⸻

**Continue reading in *Hell Fire*, Hawk Tate book 4: dustinstevens.com/HFwb**

## Thank You

Thank you so much for taking the time to read my work. I know you have literally millions of options available when it comes to making Kindle purchases, and I truly appreciate you taking the time to select this novel. I hope you enjoyed it.

If you would be so inclined, I would greatly appreciate a review letting me know your thoughts on the work.

In addition, as a token of my appreciation, please enjoy a free download of my first best-selling novel, and still one of my favorites, *21 Hours*, available **HERE.**

Best,

## Free Book

Join my newsletter list, and receive a copy of 21 Hours—my original bestseller and still one of my personal favorites—as a welcome gift!

dustinstevens.com/free-book

# Bookshelf

**Works Written by Dustin Stevens:**

### Reed & Billie Novels:
*The Boat Man*
*The Good Son*
*The Kid*
*The Partnership*
*Justice*
*The Scorekeeper*
*The Bear*
*The Driver*

### Hawk Tate Novels:
*Cold Fire*
*Cover Fire*
*Fire and Ice*
*Hellfire*
*Home Fire*
*Wild Fire*

## Bookshelf

**Zoo Crew Novels:**
*The Zoo Crew*
*Dead Peasants*
*Tracer*
*The Glue Guy*
*Moonblink*
*The Shuffle*
*Smoked*
*(Coming 2021)*

**Ham Novels:**
*HAM*
*EVEN*
*RULES*
*(Coming 2021)*

**My Mira Saga**
*Spare Change*
*Office Visit*
*Fair Trade*
*Ships Passing*
*Warning Shot*
*Battle Cry*
*Steel Trap*
*(Coming 2021)*
*Iron Men*
*(Coming 2021)*
*Until Death*
*(Coming 2021)*

**Standalone Thrillers:**
*Four*
*Ohana*
*Liberation Day*
*Twelve*
*21 Hours*

Bookshelf

*Catastrophic*
*Scars and Stars*
*Motive*
*Going Viral*
*The Debt*
*One Last Day*
*The Subway*
*The Exchange*
*Shoot to Wound*
*Peeping Thoms*
*The Ring*
*Decisions*

**Standalone Dramas:**
*Just A Game*
*Be My Eyes*
*Quarterback*

**Children's Books w/ Maddie Stevens:**
*Danny the Daydreamer…Goes to the Grammy's*
*Danny the Daydreamer…Visits the Old West*
*Danny the Daydreamer…Goes to the Moon*
*(Coming Soon)*

**Works Written by T.R. Kohler:**
*The Hunter*

## About the Author

Dustin Stevens is the author of more than 40 novels, the vast majority having become #1 Amazon bestsellers, including the Reed & Billie and Hawk Tate series. *The Boat Man*, the first release in the best-selling Reed & Billie series, was named the 2016 Indie Award winner for E-Book fiction. The freestanding work *The Debt* was named an Independent Author Network action/adventure novel of the year for 2017 and *The Exchange* was dubbed a fiction novel of the year for 2018.

He also writes thrillers and assorted other stories under the pseudonym T.R. Kohler, including the *My Mira Saga, The Hunter, The Ring, Shoot to Wound,* and *Peeping Thoms.*
A member of the Mystery Writers of America and Thriller Writers International, he resides in Honolulu, Hawaii.

**Let's Keep in Touch:**
Website: dustinstevens.com
Facebook: dustinstevens.com/fcbk
Twitter: dustinstevens.com/tw
Instagram: dustinstevens.com/DSinsta

Made in the USA
Coppell, TX
25 July 2021